TALES
FROM THE DARK SIDE

By the same author

Tales, Weird And Whimsical   ISBN 0 9527388 1 3
Encounters With Plain Ghosts   ISBN 0 9527388 0 5

Frontispiece   Towards Gaw Hill from Asmall Lane

TALES
FROM THE DARK SIDE

T. M. LALLY

HOMESTEAD

BOOKS

ORMSKIRK LANCASHIRE

Homestead Books,
32 Heathey Lane, Shirdley Hill,
Ormskirk, Lancashire, L39 8SH

British Library Cataloguing in Publication Data:
A CIP record of this book will be available from the British Library.

ISBN   0 9527388 2 1

Cover Design/Composite Illustrations/Situation Plans & 'Plain Ghost Trail' Sources Map: by the author.

Printed and bound in Great Britain by
Centre Print,
Unit 56, Railway Court,
New Court Way, Ormskirk,
Lancashire, L39 2YT.

CONTENTS

These stories are dedicated to E. M. and all those readers who have found pleasure in reading these ghostly tales.

ILLUSTRATIONS

SITUATION GUIDES

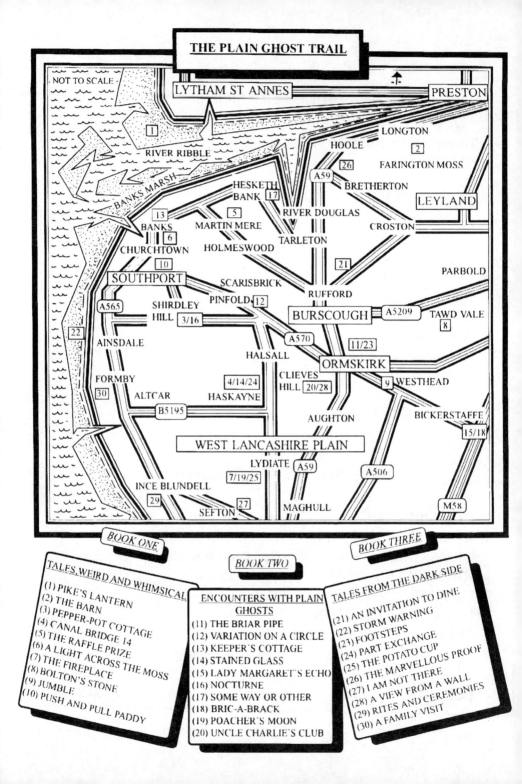

THE PLAIN GHOST TRAIL

NOT TO SCALE

LYTHAM ST ANNES · PRESTON

RIVER RIBBLE · LONGTON · HOOLE · FARINGTON MOSS

BANKS MARSH · HESKETH BANK · BRETHERTON · LEYLAND

BANKS · MARTIN MERE · RIVER DOUGLAS · CROSTON

CHURCHTOWN · HOLMESWOOD · TARLETON

SOUTHPORT · SCARISBRICK · RUFFORD · PARBOLD

SHIRDLEY HILL · PINFOLD · BURSCOUGH · TAWD VALE

AINSDALE · HALSALL · ORMSKIRK

FORMBY · ALTCAR · HASKAYNE · CLIEVES HILL · WESTHEAD

WEST LANCASHIRE PLAIN · AUGHTON · BICKERSTAFFE

LYDIATE

INCE BLUNDELL · SEFTON · MAGHULL

BOOK ONE

TALES, WEIRD AND WHIMSICAL

(1) PIKE'S LANTERN
(2) THE BARN
(3) PEPPER-POT COTTAGE
(4) CANAL BRIDGE 14
(5) THE RAFFLE PRIZE
(6) A LIGHT ACROSS THE MOSS
(7) THE FIREPLACE
(8) BOLTON'S STONE
(9) JUMBLE
(10) PUSH AND PULL PADDY

BOOK TWO

ENCOUNTERS WITH PLAIN GHOSTS

(11) THE BRIAR PIPE
(12) VARIATION ON A CIRCLE
(13) KEEPER'S COTTAGE
(14) STAINED GLASS
(15) LADY MARGARET'S ECHO
(16) NOCTURNE
(17) SOME WAY OR OTHER
(18) BRIC-A-BRACK
(19) POACHER'S MOON
(20) UNCLE CHARLIE'S CLUB

BOOK THREE

TALES FROM THE DARK SIDE

(21) AN INVITATION TO DINE
(22) STORM WARNING
(23) FOOTSTEPS
(24) PART EXCHANGE
(25) THE POTATO CUP
(26) THE MARVELLOUS PROOF
(27) I AM NOT THERE
(28) A VIEW FROM A WALL
(29) RITES AND CEREMONIES
(30) A FAMILY VISIT

AUTHOR'S NOTE

as to the inspirational sources from which the following stories are derived.

Tales from the Dark Side is the third volume in a series of ghost stories set in and around the West Lancashire Plain, and follows the same pattern as the first and second books (*Tales Weird And Whimsical* and *Encounters With Plain Ghosts)* respectively. As with the tales in these previous books the eerie stories in *Tales from the Dark Side* have been inspired by local architectural and geographical features, historical events and folklore.

An invitation to dine is set in Rufford Old Hall, a medieval building built in the 15th century with a Great Hall and richly carved hammer-beam roof, and *Storm Warning* is founded on the events of the tragic lifeboat disaster of 1886, when the barque Mexico, outward bound from Liverpool, was driven ashore off the coast near Southport. *Footsteps* is inspired by the statue of Disraeli, the Earl of Beaconsfield (it was purchased by the Ivy League in 1884 as a memorial to the famous 19th century Prime Minister), recently moved from the busy St. Helen's road junction to its present position in the pedestrian precinct in the centre of Ormskirk. The strange happenings in *Part exchange* take place in Halsall Hall, an ancient building with a peculiar cellar, lately rescued from dereliction and converted into private apartments.

The White House silver collection in the capital of the United States of America and a farm in Lydiate are the setting for *The Potato Cup*, a prize awarded to a lady farmer by the West Derby Hundred Agricultural Society in 1802, and the events in *The truly marvellous proof* take place in Carr House (once the lodgings of a famous 17th century astronomer and lately a Doll's Museum) and Hoole Church. *I am not there* centres around the beautiful church of St. Helen in Sefton, with its fine memorial brasses and wood carvings, while the Devil's Wall (marked on the old Ordnance Survey map) in *A wall with a view* can be found near Gaw Hill and the water reservoir in Aughton. Finally, Ince Blundell Hall (presently a retirement home) with its replica of the Parthenon (originally built to house a collection of Roman antiquities) and unique family chapel, features in the story *Rites and ceremonies*, while the lost village of Argarmeles (long buried beneath the sands near Formby) and the port of Altmouth (washed away in a great storm), with its historical Viking connection, inspired *A family visit.*

When the golden sun gently sinks below the far horizon, and the light gives way to the dark side of night, such haunting elements, that would test even the stoutest heart, emerge from the shadows of the plain to frighten and disturb. A mysterious figure outlined on a lonely hill, a taloned fingerprint on a treasured cut-glass vase, or the relentless step of a late-night visitor crunching up the gravel path, may unnerve the senses and chill the blood — until that long awaited break of day.

Then, as hideous phantoms and insubstantial beings reluctantly depart to that infernal region beyond the unearthly veil, the emerging rays of the dawn-light thankfully return — to banish those menacing shadows to the retreating Dark Side.

But, dear reader, bear this in mind — *your relief may yet be temporary and short lived.*

T. M. Lally.
Shirdley Hill 1997.

12

RUFFORD

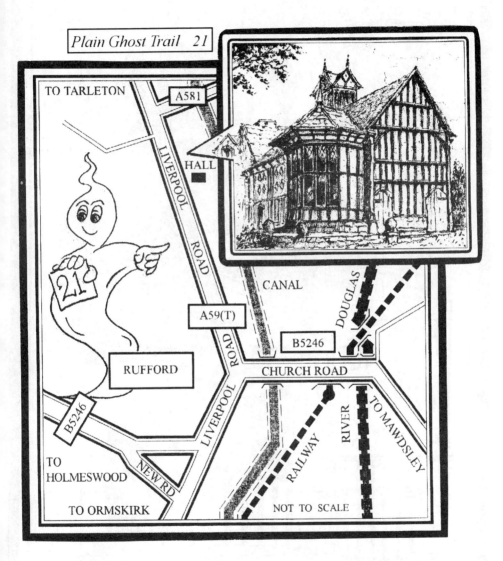

TO TARLETON

A581

LIVERPOOL ROAD

HALL

21

CANAL

DOUGLAS

A59(T)

B5246

RUFFORD

LIVERPOOL ROAD

CHURCH ROAD

B5246

TO HOLMESWOOD

NEW RD

RAILWAY

RIVER

TO MAWDSLEY

TO ORMSKIRK

NOT TO SCALE

[INSET   *The Great Hall, Rufford Old Hall*]

AN INVITATION TO DINE

The two law undergraduates studied the notice on the faculty bulletin board.

"What do you think about the idea, Chris?"

"Yeah, it sounds like a bit of a laugh — trust Spooky Jarvis to come up with something like this."

"Well, I know he can be over the top sometimes, but he does take this sort of thing seriously, so I've been told."

"You mean the "middle of the night bumpers", don't you?" Christopher scoffed. "As far as I'm concerned, Harry, old chap, they're all a bunch of ecto-plasmic weirdos — they'd scare the living daylights out of any misguided ghost who was unfortunate enough to meet them after dark."

"Yes, I know some of them get carried away," Harry countered, "and can be somewhat over-enthusiastic at times, but . . ."

"Over enthusiastic! Is that what you call it?" his companion exploded with laughter. "The Dean didn't think so when he found his cat tied to a broom stick."

"Yes, I heard he threw a fit," Harry replied with a smile, as he recalled the sight of the poor animal dangling from the college roof on a length of rope the previous Hallowe'en, "— but the "bumpers" denied all knowledge of that practical joke. Spooky Jarvis told me it was the college rugger eleven up to their old tricks, as usual."

"Well, may be . . . but the Dean's moggie had a photo of Bettina Smythe-Cooper in a naughty centre fold pose tied around its neck," Chris chuckled, "and she's a prominent member of the "bumpers", as you well know — especially if you saw the photo."

15

"Ah, yes, I heard about that," Harry laughed, dwelling on her shapely figure. "She dumped that prop forward boyfriend of hers immediately afterwards."

At this point it would seem appropriate to expand on the "bumpers" club, prominent or otherwise, of Wentworth Hall, one of the colleges attached to the local university. The "bumpers" consisted of a small group of undergraduates, bound together by a common interest and purpose, that of the world of psychic phenomenon — in other words ghosts. They were preoccupied with anything to do with the supernatural (hence the term "bumps in the night") and Spooky Jarvis was one of the founder members of this peculiar college society. They were the butt of many a joke and prank, especially around Hallowe'en; white sheets, rattling chains and mournful groans featured in the hilarity of the occasion. However, Spooky, despite the slings and knotted sheets he had suffered for his passion, had come up with an idea which had been received with genuine praise. It was an extremely respectable idea, open to all and sundry, and its main purpose was to raise money for the university Rag Week charities. The notice on the bulletin board revealed all.

> *"DARE YOU SPEND A NIGHT IN A HAUNTED HOUSE?"*
> *Can you face ghosts and demons for a worthy cause or charity?*
> *This Rag Week fund raiser (or should I say hair raiser) is planned for the weekend — so why not contact Sydney Jarvis, Wentworth Hall, or any member of the Psychic Society for details of this nocturnal extravaganza and a sponsorship form.*
> *NB. Those of a nervous disposition need not apply.*

Christopher Yealvestan and Harold Bulmer, founders of the university Dangerous Sports and Pastimes Club, certainly did not fall into this latter category: in fact any ghost or demon would be ill advised to cross their paths. There were times when the pair's risky activities placed them in closer contact with the "other side" than was usual in outdoor pursuits: bungee-jumping was their speciality — now that could really be described as "hair-raising".

"Let's find Spooky," said Chris, "and see if he can fix us up with a ghost or two for the weekend."

"Never mind a ghost — I'd rather be fixed up with Bettina Smythe-Cooper instead!" retorted Harry, once again dwelling on her shapely figure.

"Not a good idea, old chap," advised his companion, shaking his head. "Have you seen the size of her latest boyfriend? You could end up haunting the place yourself, if he got his hands on you."

Unfortunately for Christopher Yealvestan someone from the "other side" had a similar idea in mind.

* * *

Sydney Jarvis had spent months organising this supernatural weekend. The Psychic Society had managed to discover a dozen or so houses with ghostly connections in the county (although it had to be said that the "bumpers" had yet to see an actual "real-live" ghost) and the fund raising scheme had been a popular choice with the undergraduates; at this late stage in the proceedings the volunteer list was fully subscribed.

"I think you've left it too late, gentlemen," observed Spooky with a shake of his head. "I've been very surprised by the popularity of the scheme, considering that unfortunate Hallowe'en episode with the Dean's cat and that nude photo of poor Bettina." Christopher and Harry glanced at each other, struggling to control their mirth. "I think all the places have been filled," he continued, thumbing through the sponsor sheets. "Ah . . . You're in luck," he said, uncovering a blank sheet. "There's just one place left — a last minute entry — Ruffwood Old Hall. It only came in yesterday — suggested by a friend of mine. I haven't checked the place out yet."

17

"It doesn't matter, as long as it is haunted," replied Christopher.

"As I said, I'm not sure about the details," Spooky replied. "I haven't come across this property before. It isn't in our society's records, but I gather it's a National Trust property — and Charles Trafford, an old Wentworthian, is in charge of it. That's how we managed to get it on the list." He handed the undergraduates the sponsor sheet: a brief description of the hall and rules for the event were pinned to it.

RUFFWOOD OLD HALL

7 miles N of Ormsley, in the village of Ruffwood on the E side the A59.

Ruffwood Old Hall (replaced by a new Hall on the opposite side of the road in 1798) was built between 1491 and 1523. An east wing, in brick, was added in 1662. One of the finest 16th century buildings in the county, the Tudor hall, timber framed in late medieval style, is remarkable for its beautiful hammer beam roof of five equal bays, and central screen. On either side of this massive screen, richly carved with ornate designs, are the 'speres', solid pillars of oak each hewn from the trunk of a tree. In the West Wing, altered in 1821, there are fine collections of 17th century oak furniture, 16th century arms, armour and tapestries. A Priest's Hole, discovered (along with various religious artefacts) during the alterations, would indicate the presence of a secret chapel in this part of the building, a fitting reminder of that turbulent religious period in the Hall's history. Other rooms on the ground floor are devoted to the Ruffwood Village Museum, an interesting exhibition of country crafts and industries. The Hall, with most of its contents and 14 acres of grounds, was presented to the National Trust in 1936 by the late Lord Haskin.

AN INVITATION TO DINE

SPOOK SPOTTERS' SIT-IN

The following rules must be strictly observed.
[1] Alcohol is prohibited during the sit-in.
[2] Spook Spotters must remain together at all times.
[3] In keeping with the "dare" no electrical or gas light-
ing to be used — candles will be provided by the Society.
[4] Please behave sensibly during your stay and respect
the property and furnishings of the owners.

"Well, it sounds good to me," Christopher replied. "What do you think, Harry?"

"Yes, I'm game," nodded Harry. "The place is bound to be haunted if it's that old."

"I can't help you there," Spooky said with a shrug, "but you're probably right, judging from my experience. No doubt Charles Trafford can provide any ghostly details."

"Well, if he can't deliver a White Lady or Mad Monk," laughed Christopher, "we can always howl round the East Wing with white sheets over our heads instead."

"Hang on a minute, gentlemen!" cried Spooky Jarvis, paling at the thought of the founders of the Dangerous Sports and Pastimes Club sliding down the banisters and swinging from the chandeliers. "You've got to take this seriously, you know. We want to raise money for char-ity — not to bail you out of the local nick."

"Only kidding, Jarvis, old chap," Harry calmed him. "Don't forget Yealvestan's father is a High Court Judge — he'll have us out in no time, won't he Chris?"

"Too true. He plays golf with the Chief Constable and the County Sheriff, you know," Christopher grinned, "— so you see, Spooky, there's nothing to worry about."

"Well — if you say so . . ." Spooky wasn't totally convinced, and handed the sponsor form to Christopher with some reluctance; visions of a wrecked National Trust property flashed through his mind. "I'd

19

take something to occupy your minds, if I were you — it could be a long night."

"I'd like to take Bettina Smythe-Cooper and occupy that Priest's Hole for the night," sniggered Harry, giving Christopher a nudge as they walked away.

Luckily Spooky Jarvis didn't hear this remark: had he done so he would have immediately called the whole thing off. His position in college was, to say the least, somewhat precarious after the episode with the Dean's cat and the broomstick — a stately home sex scandal at this stage of his degree course would be a disaster.

Unfortunately, with hindsight, it was a pity he didn't call it off.

* * *

"You're both Wentworthians, so I've been told," Charles Trafford, the curator, greeted them at the main entrance to Ruffwood Old Hall. "Two more for the Bench, I suppose?"

"Well, you're quite right in my case," replied Christopher. "I'll be joining my father's practice, Yealvestan, Wainright and Partners. I think Harry will want the diplomatic service."

"Yes, I hope so," Harry agreed. "We're in our final year."

"Yealvestans, eh . . ." the curator smiled. "Are you Algernon's Yealvestan's son?"

"Yes. You know him?"

"Oh, yes — we've met on several occasions," Charles Trafford replied. "National Trust affairs, you know — no doubt we'll meet again when you join the firm."

"Probably . . . that's if I'm not collared by a White Lady or Mad Monk tonight," answered Christopher. The curator laughed.

"You needn't worry about a White Lady," he returned. "We don't have one here, more's the pity. However, we can furnish you with a monk — but he's quite sane, so I believe."

"Then you do have a ghost!" Harry exclaimed. "I'm glad to hear it, sane or otherwise."

"Yes, he's our long-standing resident, I'm afraid," responded Charles Trafford with a smile. "A sad apparition, so I've been told — he comes with the Priest's Hole in the West Wing."

'It's a shame Bettina couldn't be here,' thought Harry. 'She'd raise his spirits, for sure.'

"I haven't seen him myself, you understand," the curator continued, "but one or two villagers who worked here in the past when the Hall was occupied have seen a shadowy figure in a grey cowl, the sort of garment worn by monks, in the early hours. He haunts the West Wing and is perfectly harmless."

"What is the ghost of a monk doing in Ruffwood Old Hall?" asked Chris. "Was the place built on the foundations of a monastery?"

"No . . . this is the original building. As far as I'm aware, there are no direct links with the monks of Ruffwood Priory on the other side of the village. I assume it is the ghost of a priest who stayed here during that period of religious persecution in the sixteenth and seventeenth centuries. We do know that a secret chapel was situated in the West Wing. A sealed casket, supposedly containing the relics of some saint or other, was discovered behind the panelling (probably where the altar stood) during alterations in Victorian times. A hidden chamber, or Priest's Hole, in the next room was used to conceal the unauthorized cleric if ever the Hall was raided by the authorities."

"So it's the ghost of some priest who died there?" Harry reflected, "— probably starved to death in his hidy-hole."

"Not at all," replied Charles Trafford. "These priests were hunted down and, when they were caught and arrested, they were sent for trial and usually executed. No doubt you've covered that dark period of our judicial history in your law studies." The law students nodded. "You're more likely to find their ghosts in our county jails," the curator added. "Anyway, first of all let me show you where you'll be spending the night, and then a tour of the Hall before you settle in." The undergraduates followed Charles Trafford through an ante-room into a medieval room.

"This is the Great Hall, once used for banqueting and festive occasions," he declared. "It's one of the finest examples hammer-beam construction in the country, and the wood carving is unique."

The law students gazed round the hall in admiration.

"Is this where we'll be spending the night?" asked Harry, placing his bag on the long dining table. Ornately carved oak chairs, like sentinels on guard duty, lined the table, and their solid upright construction promised a night of extreme discomfort. The curator saw his expression, and swiftly put his mind at rest.

"Yes, it is," he replied. "I'll have a couple of easy chairs sent down — so don't worry — you can lounge the night away in comfort."

Christopher glanced at Harry and heaved a sigh of relief: the thought of sitting bolt upright in one of those chairs for the next twelve hours was worse than bungee-jumping.

"You probably think that the Great Hall looks pleasant and harmless enough in daylight," their host continued solemnly, "— but I can assure you that it is a very ghostly place at night — especially in candlelight. That's why I have chosen it, and I'm sure you'll earn every penny of your sponsorship money by tomorrow morning."

This turned out to be something of an understatement.

* * *

The flickering candle barely illuminated the area around the great arched fireplace. Charles Trafford was right: the Great Hall was indeed a ghostly place, not to mention hostile. As the hours slowly passed by in this silent medieval chamber, powerful influences from the Hall's turbulent past seemed to gather, hovering and prowling in the dark recesses beyond the light; and the students, for all their bravado, could not help feeling twinges of apprehension.

'Forget Bettina Smythe-Cooper and the Priest's Hole,' Harry thought with a shiver. 'I could do with her boyfriend here instead.'

22

Christopher, for his part, relieved the tension with a pack of playing cards and a game of solitaire.

However, as the night wore on and the ghost of the Grey Monk failed to put in an appearance, Harry became restless and bored: he yawned, stretched his arms and rose from his chair.

"Can you remember where the toilets are?" he asked Christopher.

"Just inside the entrance hall, I think," Christopher replied. "Hang on a minute and I'll come with you. The rules are that we stick together."

"Not as far as sharing a gents cubicle, I'm sure!" snorted Harry in mock disgust. "You'll ruin my chances with Bettina, if she finds out." He lit a spare candle, opened the heavy oak door, and disappeared down the passage in a soft glow of candlelight, casting long wavering shadows on the tapestried walls and panelled ceiling. Some moments later Christopher placed the final card in position and completed the game; he picked up his candle and went in search of Harry and the toilet. The rule about artificial light was brilliant idea. The eerie effect of candlelight, combined with the ancient fabric and furnishings, created an intense sensation of unease and apprehension, which would certainly daunt anyone of a timorous or nervous disposition. It began to have an effect on Christopher: he became increasingly anxious and jittery in this ghostly atmosphere. A distant sound, the flush of a modern sanitary unit, reached his ears and quelled his unease, and, shielding the wavering candle with his hand, Christopher hurried forward. Arriving at the entrance hall he saw Harry's candle on the visitor information table: there was no sign of its owner.

"Harry . . .!" he called. "Harry, where are you . . ?"

Harry didn't answer.

"Stop larking about . . ." Christopher pushed the toilet door open. "Come on out of there — you know the rules about messing around."

"Ooooh . . ." The soft moaning sound came, not from the toilet, but from the far end of the entrance hall — from a suit of armour clasping a huge broad sword. "Ooooh . . . Ooooh, Yealvestan . . . Your

23

time has come." Christopher's hair stood on end and he dropped his candle in terror. From behind this suit of armour a grey shape emerged into the candle light. This ghastly apparition shuffled down the hall, moaning and wailing, calling his name.

"I've come for you, Yealvestan . . . I've come for you . . ."

The founder of the Dangerous Sports and Pastimes pulled himself together: he wasn't going to let an old monk get the better of him. He charged forward and grabbed the ghostly figure in an arm lock, wrestling it to the ground. A startled cry rent the air.

"Hey . . .! Ouch . . .!" the figure yelled. "Steady on, you nitwit!" Christopher pulled the grey sheet from the figure to reveal Harry lying on the floor, rubbing his head.

"Calm down, Chris," he cried out. "It's only a joke, old chap."

"Joke . . .!" spluttered Christopher, pale as a ghost, "— only a joke?"

"Yes . . . a joke. I found a dust sheet in the toilet — couldn't resist trying it on," Harry explained. "How was I to know that you'd be taken in by it."

"Thank your lucky stars I didn't grab that broad sword," muttered Christopher angrily, "or you would never have taken your finals."

"Where's your sense of humour?" returned Harry, bursting into laughter: he placed the dust cover over his head and began to shuffle round the entrance hall, moaning and groaning. Christopher had to admit that he did look ridiculous, and started to laugh.

"You know what Spooky Jarvis said about mucking about," he declared, as he relit his candle and went into the toilet. Harry paid no attention to this warning and shuffled off down the passage to the Great Hall, moaning and groaning. Christopher followed some minutes later, but when he reached the Great Hall he found, to his surprise, that it was empty. Rays of silvery moonlight streaming in through the great bay window at the far end of the room bathed the Great Hall in soft eerie light: Harry wasn't there. At that moment, however, he glimpsed a movement through the bay window — it came from the

West Wing. A shadowy figure disappeared momentarily from one window and then reappeared at the next, further along the wing. It had to be Harry, still covered with the dust cover, up to his old tricks, moving slowly from one room to the next.

'He always has to overdo it,' mused Christopher. 'I bet he'll enjoy telling the others about my fright. I'd better sort him out before he goes too far and does something really stupid.' He set off in the direction of the West Wing.

Although Charles Trafford had given a guided tour of the Hall earlier in the day, it now seemed so different in the darkened corridors and narrow passages. More than by luck than design he came upon the entrance to this old part of the Hall: the door stood ajar. Christopher entered the wing and passed through each successive room until he arrived at the bottom of the stairs which led up to the first floor: there was still no sign of his errant companion.

"Harry, you fool!" he shouted. The words echoed eerily through the chambers of the ancient West Wing. "Harry — cut it out!" Christopher climbed the stairs to the first floor, and caught a glimpse of a vague shape bathed in the rays of moonlight streaming in through the mullioned window. It was plain to Christopher that Harry had quenched his candle to create a heightened ghostly atmosphere in the moonlight, and planned to replay his earlier practical joke by hiding in the Priest's Hole — but this time Christopher was prepared for him.

"OK, you gormless Grey Monk," he breathed, blowing his candle out and springing forward "— I'm coming to lock you in. Let's see if you like that!" But the ghostly shape emerged from the panelling and turned — and at this point Christopher executed an emergency stop.

"What the . . ." gasped the shocked undergraduate, his hair standing on end. The figure standing before him definitely wasn't Harry. For a start, he wore a blood-soaked cowl instead of a dust sheet — and the gaping mouth, sightless eye sockets and blood stained face belonged to some one whose last mortal moments had been painful in the extreme. No . . . it definitely wasn't Harry.

"My God — who . . ." cried the petrified student. "Who the hell are you . . .?" The Grey Monk, the blind ghost who, for centuries, had prowled the West Wing of Ruffwood Old Hall, shuffled towards Christopher, guided by the terrified sound of his voice. The arms within the sleeves of the cowl began to rise and the Grey Monk reached out to touch the paralysed student. Christopher was confronted by a further revelation which sent shivers of dismay through his whole being. As well as being sightless, it seemed that the ghost was also 'handless'. . Two bloody jagged stumps protruded from the sleeves and rose to touch his face — *both hands had been chopped off at the wrists.*

The hideous ghost's mouth opened to speak. If that was not enough, Christopher was further stunned by the fact that he was also speechless as well — his tongue had been ripped out. That was final straw. Christopher, aghast at this terrible vision, staggered back in awe and disgust. He hurled the candle at his adversary, and fled from the room. He literally tumbled down the stairs to land at the feet of his erstwhile fellow ghost spotter.

"Blimey . . . What up, Chris?" Harry gulped. He bent down to help Christopher to his feet. "I'm sure I saw a ghost a while back — did you see him as well?" He gazed apprehensibly into the darkness at the top of the stairs.

"Yes . . . I did. For God's sake get me out of here!" the badly shaken undergraduate choked. "It was a terrible sight. The Grey Monk isn't harmless, believe me. Just get me out of here, Harry."

"The Grey Monk, you say . . .?" replied Harry, puzzled and clearly taken aback, but Christopher was on his feet, making for the exit. It had all been too much for the founder of the Dangerous Sports and Pastimes Club. Rag Week and sponsorship money were the last thing on his disturbed mind.

"Well, I don't want to matters worse, old chap," Harry told his friend quietly, after the pair had made their way back through the Great Hall and out into the courtyard, "— but I think Charles Trafford has got it wrong . . ." He hesitated, not wishing to add to his companion's already demoralised state. "From what you tell me, I'm pretty sure this place has more than one ghost."

It would seem that his assertion was well-founded, when he recounted his experience to Christopher on the way back to Wentworth College. Ruffwood Old Hall did have another ghost — if (as it transpired) only on a temporary basis.

* * *

"I'm afraid Charles Trafford will have to rewrite the official Ruffwood Old Hall guide book," Harry began, "and it won't make very pleasant reading, I can assure you."

"It can't be worse than my experience — no way."

"Well, I'll let you be the judge of that," declared Harry soberly, and he went on to recount his own alarming experience.

After his ghostly escapade with the dust sheet in the entrance hall earlier that night, he had left Christopher to return to the Great Hall, still highly amused at the effect of his prank on his friend. He decided to continue his assault on his friend's nervous system (confirming Christopher's appreciation of his nature — "he always has to overdo it") by repeating the haunting process — this time from outdoors. He was sure that the sight of the ghostly monk peering in through the bay window, face pressed flat against the glass panes, would have a similar frightening effect on his already nervous companion. So, when Christopher went into the toilet, Harry nipped smartly out through the front door and round to the Great Hall, where he crept up to the bay window in wait for his friend. To his disappointment, Christopher (or so he thought at the time) was already there, seated at the long oak banqueting table. However, there was something wrong . . . *something was missing.*

Then Harry realised what it was. There was no candle — the figure was sitting at the table, bathed in moonlight . . . *and it wasn't*

Christopher. However, the mysterious figure's attire was very familiar. A long red gown, embroidered cravat and ornate wig pointed to the legal profession, but the black silk cloth draped over the wig confirmed it. It was the figure of a judge — a High Court Judge — and he had recently passed the ultimate sentence ... *death*. That in itself was somewhat alarming — the ghost of a hanging judge seated at the banqueting table of Ruffwood Old Hall, tucking into a splendid meal of Dickensian proportions. This scene was disturbing enough — but it was the objects piled on two huge platters beside this eminent person that shocked and revolted the secret watcher to the core. No doubt, to primitive savages on some South Sea Island, the contents of these platters could be regarded as mouthwatering delicacies — but, to Harry, the sight of a human body, hacked into pieces and placed on two serving dishes, was revolting and nauseating. And what made matters worse — *the judge seem to revel in this situation.*

He munched and drank heartily in the light of the moon, and, all the while, his gleaming cruel eyes darted continually to these gruesome human remains, savouring their bloody and torn condition. At length he rose from the table and crossed the floor, turning to cast a final vengeful look at the 'mortuary' table, before leaving through the door towards the West Wing. The terrible judge appeared some moments later gliding through the ground floor rooms of the wing, and Harry took off back to the front door to warn his friend. He decided that the shocking sight of this gruesome midnight feast on the banqueting table would be really be too much for Christopher's present state of mind. Unfortunately, Christopher had already made his way back to the Great Hall, and had continued on to the West Wing, where Harry had found him lying at the bottom of the stairs.

"The head and body, legs and arms were all there," Harry grimaced, "— but someone had cut off the hands. There was no sign of them on the table."

"I'm glad I didn't see it," replied Christopher with genuine relief, "— and I don't think Charles Trafford would like to know about it either. I don't think that description would go down well in a guide book, do you?"

The vision of dinner with the ghostly High Court Judge filled Harry with revulsion. He couldn't reply.

* * *

"So you didn't make it through the night, gentlemen," Spooky Jarvis scoffed. "Well, that's a shame. Every one else managed to complete the course. Obviously this exercise was too boring for the Dangerous Sports and Pastimes Club."

"If you say so, Jarvis," Christopher shrugged, handing over the void sponsor sheet to the chuckling organiser.

"This is bound to ruin your image, when it gets out," continued Jarvis, savouring the moment. "You know what the collage pranksters are like — and when they find out that you chickened out . . ." He slowly shook his head in mock solemnity, "— and you remember what they did to Bettina Smythe-Cooper and the Dean's cat last year." However, as the pair turned away, there was something about their reserved demeanour and lack of response to his taunting remarks that alerted him — something didn't add up.

"Hang on a minute, chaps . . ." he called. "You don't mean you actually saw a ghost?" The subdued undergraduates made no reply. Jarvis knew he was on to something. "You did, didn't you ? You actually saw a ghost!" His attitude towards the pair instantly changed. "You lucky sods!" he declared. "Trust you two to see one. Our society has always come up with a blank. Damn — I wish I'd been there!"

"Oh no you wouldn't, Jarvis," said Harry. "Believe me — it's not an experience I'd wish on anyone. Take my advice — dump the Psychic Society — take up stamp collecting."

"Ah, come on, chaps — give me a break," Jarvis pleaded. "It's the first chance the society has had to authenticate an up-to-date sighting. It will be totally confidential, I can assure you . . ." Harry looked at

Christopher.

"What do you think?"

"Well, I'm not really sure . . . You know what they're like in Wentworth."

"Listen, boys," Jarvis interrupted. "I can assure you they won't find out about your void sponsor sheet — or your encounter with the supernatural." The students contemplated his suggestion. After all, Jarvis, with his contacts and experience, might be able to come up with some answers to explain the haunting of Ruffwood Old Hall. It was worth the risk

"Well — if you promise not to divulge our experience . . ."

"You have my word!" Jarvis was sworn to secrecy, and the two Spook Spotters related their ghastly experiences of the previous night. As their tale unfolded Spooky Jarvis could hardly contain his emotions. He was positively overcome with joy: at last he had found something he could really get his teeth into. He took copious notes, interspersed with enthusiastic "wows" and "phews", and ended with a solemn promise.

"Gentlemen, rest assured," he concluded, with a gleam in his eye. "I'll get to the bottom of these appearances, even if it means neglecting my revision for the finals."

The High Court Judge and the Grey Monk were in for something of a shake-up. Spooky Jarvis, the dedicated chairman of the Wentworthian Psychic Society, was now on the case — and he meant business.

* * *

"Your not going to believe this, Yealvestan," Jarvis began, "but I think you were the cause of the appearances — a sort of mortal catalyst."

"Me — why me . . .?"

"I'll come to that later," answered Jarvis. "First of all let me tell you about my visit to Ruffwood Old Hall and my conversation with

Charles Trafford. I asked him to show me the Priest's Hole. He told me that this secret compartment behind the panelling was used to hide travelling Jesuit priests, who toured the country to celebrate the Mass in the homes of the catholic faithful. The times of James the First were very turbulent, as you probably know — Puritan unrest and the Pilgrim Fathers — and the Gunpowder Plot which discredited the catholic religion for many years. Later, while checking some old documents in the museum, I came across a reference to a Jesuit priest, who had secretly returned to the county from France in 1626. He was operating in the area around Ruffwood in 1627, and was betrayed, followed and captured by priest hunters and taken to Lancaster Prison."

"So you think the ghost of the Grey Monk could be this priest?" Christopher asked.

"Yes, it looks like it," replied Spooky Jarvis. "By all accounts you were the first to see him at such close quarters — and your description bears out my later research. My next step was the County Archives Office. I searched the trial records for that period — and this is what I uncovered." He opened a folder and handed Christopher a photocopy of a manuscript.

THE LIFE AND TRIAL OF EDWIN GERRARD 1628
Edwin Gerrard was born in 1585, at a time of great religious unrest, and he spent the early part of his life at Brindell, near Prestwood. The Gerrards were fervent Catholics and consequently suffered the penalty for their faith. The house was raided by priest hunters and his parents were arrested and taken to the county jail. Edwin went to Douai College in France and became a Jesuit priest, where he assumed the name Edrich when he was confirmed. He secretly returned to England, where he travelled throughout the county, celebrating the Mass in the homes of the faithful. He was eventually betrayed to the authorities, followed and captured and sent for trial at

31

Lancaster Castle. He refused to recant and was condemned to death, in the words of the judge, to "be hung, drawn and quartered" before the assembled population as a warning to others. A witness account of the execution provides a description of this tragic event.

"The prisoner was bound to a hurdle, his head to the horses tail, and he was dragged through the streets to the gallows. There he was thrown from a ladder, a noose around his neck, and allowed to swing until half dead. He was cut down, disembowelled, and then cut into quarters. His head was placed on a pole amongst the pinnacles of Lancaster Castle and his quarters hung from the battlements at the four corners of the building."

"They certainly "went over the top" with capital punishment in those days," Harry remarked, "— a grand spectacle to entertain the bloodthirsty masses, I suppose."

"Or just another way of keeping the catholic population under control," added Christopher thoughtfully, "and discrediting their faith into the bargain."

"Well, it didn't work in this case," Spooky Jarvis replied. "Unfortunately they chose the wrong man for that purpose — look at this." He handed Christopher another photocopy.

THE MARTYRDOM OF ST. EDRICH

A strange and miraculous occurrence at the execution of the Saint. A witness present at the scene describes "a very brilliant light, extending in a stream from the prison to the gallows like a resplendent glass, falling upon the dying priest, that in the course of my life I have never witnessed the like of it". Edrich Gerrard died a martyr to his faith, and was eventually sanctified.

"It's all very interesting," said Harry, "but it still doesn't prove that this priest is the Grey Monk of Ruffwood Old Hall, does it?"

"Well, that's where you're wrong," Jarvis smirked. "I came across a reference to the martyr and St. Edrich's Church in Ashfield, near here. It seems that one of the gaolers at Lancaster castle at the time of the execution collected relics of Edrich Gerrard, including his hand, which he sent to the Gerrard family."

"His hand . . ." gasped Christopher, startled by this macabre detail. "You mean he had his hands cut off?"

"That's right — the martyr's hand was in the possession of the Gerrard family for centuries and, believe it or not, was supposed to have miraculous qualities. It was said that the hand had the power to cure the afflicted, and it was given to St. Edrich's Church, for, as they say, "public veneration". I gather the mummified hand now rests in a glass case, and is displayed on special occasions."

"But it doesn't explain the ghost which Harry saw in the Great Hall," Christopher continued, "— and what I've got to do with the haunting."

"You will when I tell you the name of the presiding judge at the martyr's trial . . ." Jarvis paused for a moment, savouring the moment. "It was a chance in a million — a stroke of bad luck that you chose Ruffwood Old Hall, of all places," he went on. "The High Court Judge in question was a notorious anti-catholic and an extremely vindictive man, who had himself left the church. His name was Henry Yealvestan — one of the founders of your family law firm, so I believe." Christopher was absolutely nonplussed — the astonished student couldn't utter a word. At this revelation, he just stared, open-mouthed, at Spooky Jarvis.

"Is that right, Chris?" Harry asked him. "Is he one of your lot — Yealvestan, Wainright and Partners.?"

"Yes, he must be . . ." he said dejectedly. "I think the practice was established in the seventeenth century — but I've never heard of a family ghost before."

"Thank God you didn't come across him in the Great Hall, old chap," observed Harry, pursing his lips. "He might have invited you sit down at the banqueting table — and join him for dinner."

"No way," Christopher snorted. "He's definitely one member of the family to be avoided."

"Talking of food," interrupted Jarvis, "— I'm afraid your ancestor's eating habits left a lot to be desired. It's recorded that after the execution, when the body of Edrich Gerrard had been disembowelled and quartered, the Judge had the pieces brought to his table with the venison. He tucked into a hearty dinner, surrounded by the earthly remains of the Jesuit priest."

"Except for his hands," added Harry, recalling the gruesome scene with a shudder. "But I still can't see the connection with Ruffwood Old Hall. You say Chris was a catalyst — that his presence evoked the apparitions — but why in that medieval hall? There's no record of a family ghost, so he says."

"That I can't explain," answered Spooky Jarvis thoughtfully. "I can't fathom the cause or find any reason for the visitations. Charles Trafford accepts that the Grey Monk periodically haunts the West Wing of the Hall, but I'll lay a bet the Haskins built the East Wing because of that supernatural influence — perhaps even moving across the road to a new Hall to escape of the hauntings. However, as far as he knew, there are no recorded sightings of the ghostly Judge. All I can say is that, if your description of that night is accurate, you can think yourself extremely lucky, Yealvestan, that those spectres are confined to Ruffwood Old Hall." Christopher agreed wholeheartedly with this reassuring observation.

"However . . ." Jarvis concluded glumly, "I still envy you both — I'd have given anything to have seen the Grey Monk and the High Court Judge — unsavoury table manners and all."

* * *

Christopher Yealvestan received two letters by the morning post. The first confirmed his examination result — he had passed his finals with honours, and was now set to enter the family practice. The other letter was from Harry, and it contained the usual sentiments and congratulations on his degree. It also contained a newspaper cutting.

CHARITIES BENEFIT FROM STUDENT RAG WEEK
Thanks to the valiant efforts of students from the University, several charities received generous cheques from the organisers of the annual Rag Week events. This year there were some novel fund-raising ideas, and one in particular, aptly named "Spook Spotting", has uncovered something of a mystery. A sealed casket, a religious relic from the museum of Ruffwood Old Hall, has been kindly loaned by Charles Trafford, the curator of this National Trust property near Ormsley, to the university for purposes of research. X-rays of this antique seventeenth century object have revealed a surprising puzzle. It is found to contain the bones of a human hand. Sydney Jarvis, of Wentworth College (and organiser of the popular "Spook Spotting" event in question) thinks that it is the other hand of a Jesuit priest who was executed in 1628 at Lancaster Castle. It seems that this relic was acquired by the staunchly catholic Haskin family shortly after his execution, and the ghost of this unfortunate soul is supposed to haunt the West Wing of the Hall.

There was no mention in the article of Henry Yealvestan, the ghostly High Court Judge.

The following evening the staff of Yealvestan, Wainright and Partners gathered to celebrate the entry of the latest member to the practice. The splendid function suite had been booked and the dining arrangements for the banquet completed. Charles Yealvestan entered the dining room alone, as was the custom with new members of the firm, so that he might greet the assembly from the head of the table as they entered to take their seats. There, he was confronted by a judge, red-robed and be-wigged, surrounded by the remains of a recently executed unfortunate. The hands were missing. The oldest member of this highly respected and long standing legal practice greeted the youngest and latest employee.

"Ah . . . come in, my boy," growled Henry Yealvestan, cruel eyes gleaming in the candlelight, knife and fork poised. "Do come and join me . . ."

There was no reply from the youthful guest of honour — he lay senseless upon the richly carpeted floor.

AINSDALE-BIRKDALE

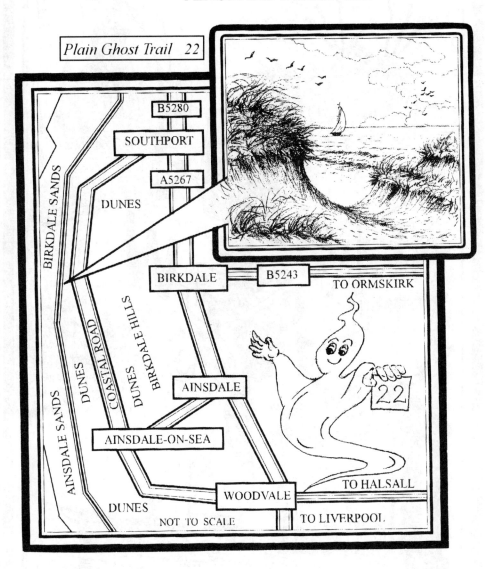

Plain Ghost Trail 22

B5280

SOUTHPORT

A5267

DUNES

BIRKDALE SANDS

BIRKDALE

B5243

TO ORMSKIRK

DUNES

COASTAL ROAD

DUNES

BIRKDALE HILLS

AINSDALE

DUNES

AINSDALE SANDS

AINSDALE-ON-SEA

22

WOODVALE

TO HALSALL

DUNES

NOT TO SCALE

TO LIVERPOOL

[INSET   *The Coastal Dunes*]

STORM WARNING

The vast expanse of sand, wrinkled and salt tipped by the never ending action of tide and wind, stretched away into the distance. Some way off to the south a line of grass-capped sand dunes, interspaced with winding paths and deep gullies, marked the landward side of this sandy terrain. This natural fortification, constructed by the elements and forever shifting and changing, faced a grey sullen line on the horizon to the north, its adversary for centuries — the sea. The sullen mass of grey water advanced daily over this flat expanse to challenge these sandy ramparts for the right of way to the low lying fertile plain beyond, but this malleable barrier stood firm against the onslaught of sea water and wind: between the two a "no man's land" of fine sand ranged for miles in each direction.

The passing seasons exerted their influence on this secluded shore, for during those times when shallow tidal waters swept across its surface it became the domain of fisherman, shrimp and sea bird, while in those brief summer months, when days lengthed and temperatures rose, it resounded to the sound of holiday makers at play. However, in the early morning or late evening, whatever season of the year, it was usually deserted and this was the time of day when Mary Gregson took her customary and solitary exercise — in this case "running". Over the years she had jogged from one end of this shore to the other, clocking up a substantial mileage and wearing out several pairs of trainers in the process.

Whilst out on a run one particular morning in early September, with a light sea mist rolling over the beach and visibility down to a hundred yards or so, she realised that she was not alone. A high pitched sound, muffled by the banks of mist, floated through the air ahead of her, and she halted. The sound abruptly ceased. She jogged on until she made out the shape of someone in the distance — and the figure seemed to be digging in the sand. She drew closer and the figure straightened up: it was a man in long anorak and wellington boots. He held a spade in one hand and a sand-encrusted object in the other: a sack and metal detector lay on the ground beside a deep hole.

"Mornin'," he said. "You're up nice and early."

"Yes, I find it's the best time of day for this sort of exercise," Mary replied, glancing at the metal detector. "Have you had any luck?"

"Not really — just a few coins, tin cans and this piece of scrap metal."

"It looks an interesting shape."

"Well it might be interesting to you," he snorted disdainfully, "but its not worth anything to me — just a bit of old junk."

"Do you mind if I have it," Mary asked. "I think I could find a use for it — it's the sort of shape I've been looking for."

"Be my guest," the man sniffed, handing the piece of metal to her. "It'll save me the job of carrying it back to the litter bin."

The metal sheet, cleaned and polished, turned out to be copper. The shape was cut into the silhouette of a sailing ship and Mary had a replacement for the broken weather-vane on her summerhouse roof.

* * *

The summerhouse in question lay at the bottom of Mary's garden. One generally associates this type of construction with large windows, wooden walls and felt roof, but in this case the summerhouse was a very substantial building of brick and slate — and very old. It belonged to a property which stood on land behind the coastal sand dunes, and was originally the site of an old fishing community. The present seaside town had its beginnings in this area, first settled in the early nineteenth century, but most of the fishermen's cottages had long since disappeared to make way for suburban housing development in the latter part of that century.

"Sea View" had been in Gregson family since those earlier times and Mary's family had inherited the house shortly after her twenty fifth birthday (some three years previously) from a maiden great aunt. Mary's branch of the Gregson family had moved to the south of England in the early thirties and set up business in Maidstone, where she was born. So giving up the family business and moving back to the north of England for the sake of an old house was out of the question. However, when Mary was offered an unforeseen and lucrative promotion in her firm's branch in the very town where the property was situated, she could hardly believe her luck: the problem was solved and she moved into the furnished house within the month.

Mary was single; she found "Sea View" too large for her needs and the furnishings too antiquated for her taste. She had not long settled into this time-warped residence before she began to detect a strange influence around the place. There was a pervading sense of sadness in the rooms which she put down to the previous occupant, her great aunt. Although a noted beauty and much sought after in her day, her aunt never married, and by all accounts became eccentric and somewhat reclusive in her later years. This vague impression of melancholia was sometimes difficult to overcome, but Mary enjoyed life and spent more time out of the house than in. However, "Sea View" did have its advantages: it was convenient for her work and situated in a desirable neighbourhood. It was also convenient for her hobby, long distance running (the London Marathon was high on her agenda).

A rusty wrought iron gate, set into the hedge at the bottom of the garden, opened onto a narrow path used by fishermen in bygone days. This ancient sandy track wound its way through the dunes to the shore. The gate (which Mary deduced from the sound it made) was as old as the summerhouse itself: hinges rasped and grated loudly, and the gate would clang and jangle every time she used it to get to the shore to begin her training schedule. However, she came to the sensible conclusion that because she lived alone it did act, in terms of security, as a valuable form of warning device, should any undesirable approach the house from the vicinity of the shore. The discordant sound became a familiar feature in the immediate neighbourhood, on a par with the whistling milkman and the raucous sea-gull.

This creaking iron gate had a metal companion to keep it company in the rear garden in the form of a weathercock on the roof of the summerhouse. The origin of this quaint meteorological device, with its compass points set on a beautifully scrolled base, was unknown. It had come into the hands of one of the Gregsons when the house was first built and had ended up on the roof of the gazebo (as the family described the summerhouse to visiting guests). However, the years had taken their toll, and the weathercock's spinning days were numbered: it was now very much the worse for wear, having corroded to the point of collapse. Mary's bedroom window looked out onto the rear garden and dunes beyond, and it was all too evident to her untutored eye that the weathercock, hanging at such an awkward angle, was not only a source of visible irritation but a distinct weather hazard as well: one good blow and it would come tumbling down through the roof.

The discovery of the copper sheet, buried for years beneath the sandy shore, came just at the right time, and some weeks later the new weather-vane, in the shape of an old fashioned square-rigged sailing vessel (she had seen a similar design in Folkstone as a child), was hoisted up onto the scrolled compass point base. It looked very smart indeed, and Mary, as she drew the curtains of her bedroom window, daily contemplated the object of her "inspiration" with a certain degree of pleasure. Then, one evening some months later, something happened which disturbed her greatly, and caused a reassessment of "that degree of pleasure".

* * *

The sudden discordant sound of the rusty garden sentinel announced the arrival of an evening visitor as Mary was changing in preparation for her evening run. She went over to the window and looked into the garden: to her surprise she saw that it was empty — there was no one there. She opened the window and contemplated the tranquil scene with a puzzled expression. She had definitely heard the gate open and close. Then something caught her attention.

The evening was dead calm, with no hint of a breeze — so why was the weather-vane slowly circulating? It began to gather speed, spinning round and round until it was almost a blur, and Mary could only stare in wonder at this curious spectacle. Then it suddenly stopped, the prow of the sailing ship pointing midway between the compass points — the bearing was definitely north west. It somehow reminded Mary of the antics of a "pointer", the sportsman's favourite gun dog, casting around until it found the scent of the game bird and then halting to "point" the way. She went down to check the summerhouse and weather-vane, before setting off on her run. The door to the summerhouse was slightly ajar, which caused a moment's apprehension. It was always firmly closed. She cautiously opened the door and peered inside. Except for jumble and assorted garden implements she was relieved to discover that the summerhouse was empty. It was a bit of a mystery, all the same. She checked her stop watch and set off down the sandy path on the first leg of her evening run.

It was a perfect evening for it, and she covered more ground than she had planned: it was time to turn back. Then, as the sun sank beneath a fiery horizon, a stiff breeze sprang up from the north west. The placid surface of the sea became unsettled and increasingly rough, and as she progressed homeward the strong breeze gradually strengthened in severity, whipping up clouds of sand and unleashing sheets of stinging spray from the thundering breakers crashing on the sandy shore. Visibility declined sharply, with huge globules of salt foam rolling across her path, but she battled on against the furious elements, fighting her way through what had now become a howling gale. A loud explosion resounded through the descending gloom, stopping her in her tracks.

'What in heaven's name is that!' she inwardly cried, covering her ears.

And then she saw the light, high in the sky, floating down towards her. It was bright red, and it left a trail of white smoke in it's wake as it fell. She immediately realized what this glowing ball of fire was — a distress flare. In the distance she momentarily caught sight of masts and torn canvas tossing in the grasp of the terrible storm — a vessel in distress. She just stood there, rooted to the spot, absolutely dumbfounded by it all: the flare fell from the sky, twisting and turning in the grip of the howling wind, to crash spluttering into the tumultuous sea.

She set off at a sharp pace, desperate to get home, and within moments found herself in a race, not with elements, but with a stronger force — a supernatural force. Some inner sense, probably acquired from the competition of the race track, urged her to look back over her shoulder, and what she saw drove her forward in absolute panic. Out of the swirling foam and spray she glimpsed a team of horses, lathered with sweat and exhaling clouds of condensed breath, galloping at full speed — rapidly bearing down on her. Even in her terror she was amazed to see that they hauling a large boat on a wheeled contraption, driven on by men in oilskins and sou'westers perched on this carriage. The apparition was no less than a lifeboat from another era. Long distance jogging turned into a hundred metre dash as she sought to outrun this spectre from the past, and she mustered her reserves of strength, put her head down and sprinted away in an effort to win this ghostly race. Her months of training paid off, for, as the storm abated and the wind began to drop, the scudding clouds cleared to leave a starlit sky above. She had outrun the *"unbelievable"*.

The sea breeze faded away and, as a full moon rose over the tops of the dunes to light the deserted beach, she collapsed onto the soft sand in a state of utter exhaustion. The sodden, salt-caked runner eventually recovered to find herself opposite the entrance to the old fisherman's path. She slowly clambered to her feet and dragged herself wearily home. As she drew near she saw the top of the weathervane, illuminated in the light of the moon, above the dunes. The prow of the sailing ship now pointed due south — towards the house.

* * *

The after effects of the ghostly experience put Mary off her stride; jogging on the shore was temporarily suspended. She decided to take a few days off work to recover, and her apprehensive mental state, combined with the extremely inclement weather (it seemed to have set in the very next day), all helped to keep her indoors for the time being: wind howled round the chimneys and rain squalls lashed the windows to reinforce her confinement.

The weather-vane, in the meantime, had resumed its normal activity, and her gaze was constantly drawn to the antics of the copper sailing ship on top of the summerhouse, as it veered this way and that every time the blustery wind changed direction. The days slowly passed by and she became increasingly fidgety and bored: she needed something to do. Looking down on the water logged garden from her bedroom window she recalled the imagined intruder and the open door of the summerhouse. She also remembered the jumbled state of the interior, which was just how her great aunt had left it.

'It must be full of all sorts of junk,' she decided. 'I'll clear the place out — get it ready for the Spring.' And with new this found enthusiasm and energy she immediately set about the task, attacking the accumulation of years of hoarding with gusto.

However, she was soon to discover that it wasn't all junk — quite the opposite, in fact. True, there were stacks of cardboard boxes filled with old magazines and newspapers, and sacks of musty clothing and assorted shoes piled high, which, at first sight, did give an overall impression of leftovers from many a jumble sale: but, as the sorting progressed, she began to uncover items which could be classed as genuine antiques from the Victorian and Edwardian periods.

Porcelain and paintings, hidden beneath dusty mildewed sheets, emerged after years of hibernation into a different age, and one rather large gilt-framed canvas caught her eye. However, it was impossible, in its present state, to make out the subject matter, and she placed it to one side. A large marine telescope, sextant and sea charts from another age, along with other nautical paraphernalia in brass and bronze came to light. A dilapidated life buoy, battered and chipped, with black painted letters ELIZ and ORT the sole surviving remnants from the original name, lay on top of an object which looked like a casement clock until the dirt had been removed from its glass face. To Mary's delight it turned out to be barometer.

'I wonder why my Aunt didn't have it in the house,' she mused. 'It'll go nicely in the hall — and warn me to avoid any storms and freak weather changes in the future.'

As the work progressed, and the room began to take shape, Mary began to realise that the building was not just a common or garden summerhouse, but something far more substantial. She took stock of the sturdy construction, examining the changes in the brickwork and thickness of the rafters, and eventually came to the conclusion that it had been converted into a summerhouse from part of an earlier dwelling which had probably stood on the same spot. She returned to the house with barometer — and made a significant discovery which caused something of a relapse. When the barometer was cleaned and polished she found two inscriptions on the casing. The first one disclosed the name and maker of the instrument.

ANEROID BAROMETER
THOMAS HOLT, LONDON

The second inscription disclosed the name of its original owner.

AWARDED TO COXSWAIN ROBt GREGSON

STORM WARNING

FROM THOSE SAVED FROM THE MIGHTY SEA
IN GRATITUDE — ORIENT SHIPPING COMPANY 1885

The barometer was placed in the hall and Mary's eye followed the line of the weather settings, *Stormy - Rain - Change - Fair - Very Dry* which ranged around the ornate dial — then up to the most significant feature of all (and the cause of the relapse). The beautifully carved and painted model of a lifeboat, mounted on a carriage and pulled by a team of horses, lay on top of this polished Victorian award.

She had seen the ghostly equivalent of this beautiful reproduction charging down on her one dark and stormy night the previous week — — on the shore beyond the dunes.

* * *

The Victorian barometer, in pride of place in the hall, plainly did not function properly. The delicate indicator remained fixed on *Change*, no matter the state of the weather outside. Wind, rain, or sun had no effect on this antique instrument, designed for sophisticated weather forecasts, and (in Mary's opinion) provided the reason for its relegation to the dusty confines of the summerhouse: it was broken and her Aunt obviously thought it was neither use nor ornament. When Mary called in at the jeweller's shop for an estimate for repairs to the family heirloom the salesman took her through to the clock repairer in the workshop: he came to the same conclusion.

"Unlike the mercury barometer," the repairer explained, "your type of instrument, the aneroid barometer, doesn't contain any liquid."

"Oh, really . . . So how does it work?"

"I presume from its age, that your barometer has a circular box with all the air taken out. Atmospheric pressure causes the box to move in and out."

"I see," Mary said with a puzzled expression. "But how does that make the pointer go round the dial?"

"With a complicated system of levers," he replied. "Your barometer probably has a leak in the system, or the levers have jammed. Leave it with me and I'll have a look at it for you."

Mary took his advice and a week later she returned to the shop to collect the antique. She was in for a surprise.

"It defeats me," the clock repairer conceded. "I'm afraid I couldn't find anything wrong with it — it works perfectly."

"Works perfectly . . .?"

"Yes. In fact it is even more accurate than the mercury model, which surprises me even more," he observed. "I'd normally expect a substantial discrepancy in the readings, considering its age and design — but its even more accurate than the latest models." He shook his head in disbelief, as he handed her the barometer.

"I must say it's an extremely fine instrument," he continued, "— a rare and valuable antique. From what you've told me about its origins I just can't understand why anyone would dump it in a shed." When Mary asked for the bill he shook his head.

"There's no charge, my dear," he replied. "It was a pleasure to work on it. By the way, if you ever want to sell it . . ?" Mary smiled and shook her head.

"It has been in the family for years," she said. "I couldn't part with it, whatever the price."

Once again the antique barometer held pride of place in the hall — — and once again, much to Mary's annoyance, it didn't work. For some reason (Mary placed it in several rooms and out in the garden to test it) the pointer remained fixed on *Change* — and the frustrated woman began to have second thoughts about selling it.

Unbeknown to her the valuable antique heirloom would, in the coming days, have "second thoughts" about providing a positive weather forecast.

* * *

The weather improved considerably and Mary decided it was time to resume her early morning training, reserving the evening sessions for the week ends. The next few days passed uneventfully and memories of the ghostly chase began to fade — that is until one fateful Sunday some weeks later.

On that bright afternoon in late November Mary unlocked the gate (it had been padlocked since that eventful night) and set off down the fisherman's path to the shore. The weather was crisp and dry and ideal for jogging, and she had covered a fair amount of distance down the coast when, in a moment of carelessness, she fell, badly twisting her ankle in the process: she turned back and began the painful return, reduced to a slow limp. At this very moment, some miles away in the dark hallway of "Sea View", the valuable aneroid barometer had "second thoughts". It suddenly flickered into life — and the pointer began to move fitfully across the face of the silver dial. It dropped to *Fair*, returned and paused briefly on *Rain* — and came to rest on *Stormy*. In the meantime, the weather-vane in the garden began its mad motion in the calm air, whirling round and round until it too came to a sudden halt — with the prow of the copper sailing ship facing north west.

It grew dark and the weather began to close in. Soon the first breath of chilled air from the north west arrived to lightly caress Mary's cheeks and stir the dune grass — but it didn't last long. From breath to breeze, from wind to gale, the severity of the storm grew, and the fierce gusts knocked her to the ground: the bitterly cold rain lashed down on her numbed body, soaking her to the skin. Gasping for breath she sought refuge from these powerful elements in that natural barrier, the sand dunes. And it was from this place, safe from the crashing waves on the beach below, that she saw, as she shivered and huddled in the lee of a dune, a ghostly scene unfold.

The storm grew in intensity, and the raging sea pounded the shore, hurling sheets of spray and showers of foam high into the air. And into this fearsome turmoil galloped a team of horses hauling a lifeboat on a carriage. Mary watched the spectacle that followed with a mixture of astonishment and awe, rubbing her salt caked eyes in disbelief. In the phosphorescent light cast by the pounding waves the horse drawn carriage was reversed into the thundering breakers and the lifeboat launched into the boiling sea. The crew, in cork life jackets and soaking oil skins that gleamed in this lurid glow, fought to keep the boat on course towards a vessel driven hard aground by the north westerly some quarter of a mile off shore. They had to struggle against the powerful headwind, the boat lifting high and crashing low, to make ground, but the heroic crew persevered and the lifeboat reached the lee of the sailing vessel. The fore mast had long since vanished and tattered strips of canvas, cut to shreds, waved and weaved from the remaining two masts and broken spars. To her horror, Mary glimpsed the unfortunate figures of the vessel's crew clinging desperately to the masts and rigging, as heavy seas pounded the ship mercilessly and huge torrents of water constantly broke over her sides covering the deck in a mass of churning water.

Then she saw a monstrous wave begin to rise, as if from the bowels of this raging mass. It grew and grew, rising high above its enraged companions, and she could only watch helplessly as this huge green wall, foam tipped and jagged, began to curve over the lifeboat like a giant hand. It seemed to pause, as if eyeing its prey, and then with a thunderous roar it crashed down, capsizing the lifeboat — swallowing it and its brave crew in an instant, dragging them beneath the enraged sea. This ghastly development was so dreadful that Mary covered her eyes in shock and dismay.

"My God," the shivering spectator whispered, "— the poor crew." Perhaps some of them had survived. "They were wearing life jackets, after all — and they'll need help."

She staggered to her feet and prepared to descend to the shore below. But her startled eyes met an empty beach, decreasing wind and retreating sea. She stood on top of the dunes surveying a scene of gradual calm and tranquillity.

Some miles from this peaceful scene the weather-vane in the gar-

50

den of "Sea View" veered to the south and rested, pointing towards the house — and inside, in the dark hallway, the polished aneroid barometer of Coxswain Gregson registered *Change*.

* * *

Mary decided to clean the oil painting herself. The heavy gilt frame had long succumbed to the ravages of damp and worm, and its ornately scrolled beading had either disappeared or was flaking and crumbling away: it fell apart in her hands. The painting, in its present state, was a masterpiece of mess and muck. Its surface was encrusted with a mixture of grime and mildew, and the cracked glaze beneath this covering of filth had darkened to the point where the artist's subject was now practically indistinguishable to the human eye.

She had remembered, when she first uncovered the painting in the summerhouse, that there was something about the vague shape of the subject matter which intrigued her: it evoked a compelling fascination which had motivated her to retrieve it from the summerhouse and clean it. And within the hour, after careful dabbing with cotton wool and artist's cleaning fluid, the painting began to reveal the nature of its strange hold over Mary's imagination. A familiar object gradually began to take shape, an object which she immediately recognised from her recent experiences — part of a bulky cork life preserver.

The rest of the painting was gradually exposed to reveal the portrait of a bearded man in sou'wester, oilskins and life jacket. This heroic figure held a life buoy over his left shoulder, with the name "ELIZA FARNWORTH" painted in black letters around its circumference: a stormy sea, ship in distress and the launching of a lifeboat completed the background to this impressive oil painting. Mary gazed at the portrait of Robert Gregson, late coxswain of the "Eliza Farnworth". As to his identity there was no doubt. He held in his right hand an aneroid barometer — the one currently in pride of place in the hall of "Sea View".

* * *

It was nearing midnight by the time Mary arrived home from the staff Christmas party. She stepped from her car — and heard the distant sound. A discordant grating rang through the frosty December night: someone had just come through the gate from the dunes, of that she was certain. She looked into the garden, and in the light of a full moon she saw the spinning weather-vane come to a sudden halt — to point north west. The gate to the fisherman's path stood wide open — and so too was the door of the summerhouse. Mary went back to the car, picked up a wheel brace and torch from the boot of the car and, mindful of her previous experience some weeks ago, approached the summerhouse with extreme caution. She reached the open door: a faint, scraping noise came from within.

"Who's there?"

A sharp gasp of breath rasped through the still air.

"Come out .. ! I know you're in there."

There was no reply. The minutes passed by and Mary, by this time growing impatient, plucked up courage and stepped forward.

"Who are you," she called out once more, trying to control the fear in her voice. "— what do you want?"

She shone her torch through the entrance, and, as the beam of light slowly circled the room, she was relieved to see no sign of an intruder. Then another sharp intake of breath pierced the silence and the trembling beam of the torch swung in the direction of this hair raising sound — searching. It soon found the source. Mary uttered a gasp of dismay, stunned by the vision which rose from the floor into the beam of light to confront her. There, in the interior of this Victorian conversion, she came face to face with a spectre from the same age, the coxswain in the portrait, Robert Gregson. Unlike the heroic subject in the oil painting, this figure was indeed a sorry sight to behold. With oilskins in tatters and life-jacket ripped asunder, bedraggled and dripping with sea water, the formidable coxswain stood before her, swaying backwards and forwards — reaching out to her. Pale lips moved beneath a sodden white beard, and eyes, wide and

52

despairing, stared straight ahead, gleaming in the torchlight.

"All gone . . . all perished . . ."

The hollow voice, hoarse and in great pain, whispered these words, the echo lingering in the confined space. Their eyes met for a second, and the bareheaded apparition, arms outstretched and fingers torn and bloody, lurched forward.

"Help us . . . for God's sake help us . . ."

Mary fell back through the door, tumbling onto the frosty ground outside. She scrambled to her feet, swinging wildly in the air with clenched fists, ready to fight off the crazed intruder.

"Too late . . . all gone . . . all perished . . ."

These mournful words reached her ears again, before gently fading into the freezing night air: Mary stood there, more frightened than hurt, shivering in the pale moonlight. She found the garden empty, the gate closed and firmly padlocked — and the weather-vane facing the house.

* * *

"It was one of the worst disasters in the history of the lifeboat service," Mary's father told her when she arrived in Maidstone for Christmas. "The crews of two lifeboats were lost, you know." His daughter nodded sadly — after all, she had witnessed the disaster, albeit a century later.

"There's an account of it in book somewhere up here," he continued, reaching up to the top shelf of the book case. He ran his finger along the line of titles and pulled out a slim volume, "Sandgrounders of Yesteryear". He opened it and thumbed through the pages.

"Ah, yes . . . Here it is." Mary's father handed her the book.

THE LIFEBOAT DISASTER OF 1886

In the Municipal Cemetery a stone memorial, erected by

public subscription, stands to the memory of the men who lost their lives in the worst disaster since the founding of the Lifeboat Service. The inscription on the southern face of the tomb gives the account of this tragic event.

In grateful memory of Coxswain Robert Gregson and fourteen of the heroic crew of the town's lifeboat, the 'Eliza Farnworth', who together with the crew of the Ansdall-on-Sea lifeboat, perished in a gallant effort to rescue the crew of the German barque 'Mexico', wrecked off this coast on the night of the 9th December, 1886. While erecting here, and at Ansdall-on-Sea, memorials to the courageous bravery of those who perished in this terrible disaster, their fellow countrymen adequately provided for the support of their widows and orphans.

'Greater love hath no man than this,
That man lay down his life for his friends.

The subsequent inquiry into the disaster, although allotting no blame at the time, concluded that the lifeboat failed to right itself after capsizing beneath a gigantic wave. The crew, who were tied to their stations, were unable to escape, except for the coxswain. He miraculously survived the sinking and was washed ashore, where he made his way home, a broken man. He died some hours later. In contrast to this terrible loss of life all the crew of the 'Mexico' were saved and the barque re-floated. The disaster gained widespread publicity at the time and a public appeal to the nation raised a large amount of money for the bereaved families.

"At least some people benefited from it all," Mary's father reflected. "Many of the small cottages of the drowned crew were demolished and replaced with better housing for their families."

54

"Was "Sea View" one of them?"

"Yes. It replaced the Gregson family's cottage," he nodded, "— but they kept part of it — made it into a gazebo in the garden."

"So the summerhouse was the coxswain's home?"

"That's right," her father replied.

'That might explain my Aunt's reason for keeping all that Victorian memorabilia there,' Mary thought to herself. 'Perhaps she herself had seen *him* in the house — and had removed anything associated with the coxswain from "Sea View" and stored it in the summerhouse.'

"I seem to remember that it had a very fine weathercock on its roof," her father continued, "— and I did hear, as a child, that it came from the old lifeboat house on the promenade."

* * *

The distant figure in the early morning mist seemed to be digging in the sand: when Mary approached he stopped and looked up.

"Mornin' young lady," the man in anorak and wellingtons greeted her with a wave of his hand. "— out early as usual, I see."

"Yes, it's the best time of day for training," Mary smiled.

"Ah, yes — I saw your picture in the local paper," the man replied. "You did well to come in the first ten — especially in a big race like the London Marathon."

"Well, I have to say that I was running for a good cause, you know." On that special day, shoulder to shoulder with the cream of the athletic world, she had run the race of her life, aided (so she felt at the time, when she was on the verge of collapse) by some unseen hand.

"That's right," he nodded. "I heard you raised a fair bit of cash for the town inshore lifeboat — and done us all proud, into the bargain."

"We Gregsons have got to do our bit, you know," Mary laughed. "It runs in the family, if you forgive the pun." The man scratched his chin.

"Talking of bits, young lady," he began. "Do you remember that bit of old metal I gave you last Autumn — dug it up somewhere around here?"

"Yes," Mary answered in a quiet voice. "It was made of copper."

"Aye, that's right — copper. My mate told me it was probably off the keel of a lifeboat that was wrecked around here in Victorian times."

Mary shuddered, and drew a sharp breath. If the man's friend was right, it would seem that, thanks to her, part of Robert Gregson's "pride and joy" had followed the coxswain home a hundred years later — a storm warning.

The man rubbed his chin again. "I don't suppose you'd let me have it back, miss?"

Mary looked away and gazed, deep in thought, at the gentle surf running over the fine sand. From that moment when she handed the considerable cheque to the representative of the Royal National Lifeboat Institution the atmosphere in "Sea View" began to change. An abiding sense of peace and happiness seemed to flow through the once melancholy house like an incoming tide. The barometer in the hall began to work perfectly, unlike the weather-vane on the roof of the Gregson gazebo. From that day on (so Mary asserted) it never again pointed to the north west — the coxswain was at rest.

She turned and slowly shook her head.

"No. I'm afraid that is definitely out of the question," she solemnly answered, a warm glow filling her heart. "It has now become a family heirloom — a treasured family heirloom."

ORMSKIRK

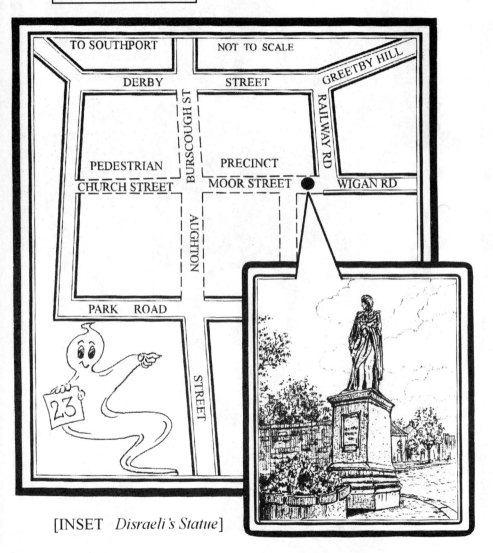

[INSET   *Disraeli's Statue*]

57

FOOTSTEPS

"This is interesting — do you know what it is?"

"No, I'm sorry, Props — I've no idea."

"No idea at all?"

"Absolutely. I can honestly say I've haven't got a clue — it beats me what it's for."

Andrew Fletcher studied the strange object, turning it over in his hands.

"It might come in handy," he said thoughtfully. "What do you think?"

The stall owner shrugged his shoulders. He was well acquainted with Andrew and his purchasing habits, and not a week passed by without a visit from "Props", the pillar of the Ormsley Players. Andrew, the chairman of this local amateur dramatic society, was constantly on the lookout for properties (those bits and pieces so necessary for stage production and essential for the professional touch); hence the stall holder's nickname for him — "Props".

"I really couldn't say," the stall owner answered, shaking his head. Business was slack and takings down, so he was somewhat reluctant to lose a sale. "I suppose it would depend on your next production – – whether you'll need something like this."

"Well, if only I knew what the blessed thing is . . ."

The object of all this speculation was, to say the least, peculiar. Approximately three feet in length, and stoutly constructed in black ebony, it was, to all intents and purposes, a set of narrow wooden spars bound together with strong metal bands. At one end a hinged brass bar, with spiked nodules set along its surface, swung out to

FOOTSTEPS

form a 'T'; and at the opposite end a brass 'U' shaped arm folded out
into a locked position. The small cruciform design was engraved in
the ebony surface, just below the brass 'U'.

However, its main fascination was to be found in the novel construction of the device. It could be extended to varying lengths by
slackening a set of brass wing nuts (rather like the leg of a camera
tripod) and sliding the inner piece (to which the 'U' shape was fixed)
outwards to the appropriate position, according to the desired length.
At the same time another hinged inner spar dropped down, and unfolded into a right angle, connecting the top of the device with its
base, the final assembly resembling a right angled triangle. However, the beauty of this robust device was its compact design and
light weight: Andrew was extremely fascinated by it.

"We haven't decided on the next production yet," Andrew continued. "It's coming up to our centenary and the committee want to
put on something really special — something in keeping with the
occasion."

"Blimey! I didn't think you lot had been going that long," the stall
owner retorted. "Mind you, Props, I've seen one or two of your plays
— and some of the cast did look a bit ancient."

"You've got a d—— cheek!" the chairman of the Ormsley Players
retaliated with feigned indignation. "If the truth be known, mate, you
probably went to school with some of them." His antagonist held his
hands up in mock astonishment.

"Hey . . . hey, calm down, Props — keep your wig on," he laughed.
"Tell you what — make me an offer."

"A couple of quid, then," Andrew replied, slightly mollified by
the suggestion.

"OK — but only if I get a complimentary ticket for the next play."

"Done!" Andrew picked up his mystery "bargain", highly satisfied with the outcome. "By the way, where did you get it from?"

"A house in Scarth Hill Road, next to the park," the stall owner
replied. "The lady is going to have her loft converted — had a bit of

60

a clear-out."

"Is her name Price?"

"That's right — Mrs. Price."

"Well, would you believe it — she's one of our Society's patrons," Andrew sniffed. "If I'd have known that she was chucking stuff out I could have got a few props and this bloomin' thing for nowt!"

However, all was not lost. Andrew bumped into Mrs. Price by the clock tower, and she saw him carrying his recent purchase.

"Ah, I see you've got hold of that weird thing," she said, nodding at the object under his arm.

"That's right," answered Andrew. "It can go in the props cupboard — might even be able to use it in our next production."

"Oh — what's that going to be?"

"We've not decided yet," he replied. "Something special for the centenary. One of Irving's plays, perhaps — or possibly something else from that period."

"Well, now — I might have just the very thing to suit your centenary production," Mrs. Price answered. "Come round later this afternoon. You can decide if it's suitable for the Players."

Before Andrew could reply Mrs. Price, with a "Can't stop — must dash", hurried off towards the railway station, and he was left wondering what the society's patron had in mind.

He was in for a surprise.

* * *

The cover of the manuscript was faded and dog-eared: a frayed blue ribbon, threaded through jagged holes in its spine, just about held the well-thumbed pages together. The title and substance of the work, *"THE WILTON STUDY - A PLAY IN THREE ACTS"*, was scrawled in soft pencil across this yellowed cover. An ill-defined signature below the title disclosed the name of the author — *Ben Margeson*. He had penned a brief inscription which hinted at the inspiration behind the play.

'I sincerely hope, dear friend, that this insignificant and amateur attempt (which, I hastily venture to add, can never reflect the superiority of your genius) pleases you.'

The whole of the manuscript was handwritten.

"I think this might be suitable for your centenary production," Mrs. Price suggested, handing Andrew the tattered manuscript.

"The "Wilton Study" — never heard of it," he replied, thumbing through the sheaves of paper, "— and that goes for the author, Ben Margeson, as well."

"Oh yes, you're perfectly right, Mr. Fletcher," answered Mrs. Price with the hint of a chuckle in her voice when she observed his mystified expression. "You see — no one ever has . . ."

"A completely unknown play — I don't think the committee will accept that, Mrs. Price," snorted Andrew, shaking his head. "You know what they're like. They won't take on anything risky — especially if it has never been performed on stage."

"Did I say it had never been performed?" she said. Andrew nodded.

"Well that's not quite correct," she continued. "It was nearly performed once."

"You mean actually performed on stage?"

"Yes — in Ormsley, as a matter of fact — by my late uncle, Hugh Sherridan-Price." Andrew recognised the name.

"I've heard of him. He was a well known figure in local dramatics in the twenties, wasn't he?"

"Yes, that's right," Mrs. Price said in a more serious tone of voice. "He was so good that many thought he would turn professional and go to London. Unfortunately his acting career was cut short — some form of nervous breakdown, I think."

"So Ormsley lost a budding Olivier?"

"Well, I wouldn't go that far," she returned. "Anyway, Sherridan-Price put this play on at the Working Men's Institute in nineteen twenty five."

"Ah, I remember the old Institute. The Players used it for their performances at that time. Didn't it stand opposite Disraeli's statue?"

"The statue — yes. The place was demolished to make way for the bus station and car park . . ." She paused. "And the play went the same way — demolished in Act Three."

"You mean it only got to the third act?"

"That's right," Mrs. Price replied. "I was told as a little girl that Uncle Hugh collapsed at the end of the act, and the play folded after just one performance."

"So why do you think the "Wilton Study" would be suitable for the Players?"

"Its pedigree, of course."

"Pedigree . . . ?" the puzzled chairman said with a laugh. "It doesn't have one — it's unknown."

"My Uncle thought otherwise," she responded. "He discovered that this manuscript was given to Henry Felton, the celebrated Victorian playwright, by one his inner circle of friends. It's an adaptation of Felton's only novel, "The Study of William Wilton", as a three act play."

"Whew . . ." Andrew whistled. "An original manuscript, an unknown play, and a definite link with Henry Felton — that could be a production and a half. I'll show it to the committee — see what they think." Mrs. Price replaced the manuscript in a dusty leather-bound folder and gave it to the impressed chairman.

"There's one thing that puzzles me," he said, as he left the house. "Why hasn't it come to light before now?"

"Ah, that's where my Uncle comes into it." Mrs. Price lowered her voice. "After his breakdown he never went on stage again. He locked the play away, and refused to let anyone see the it again. When he passed away last year, I got it with some of his papers — and that funny object you bought on the market stall this afternoon."

"Something must have upset him, I suppose?"

"I don't think "upset" is the right word," replied Mrs. Price, slowly shaking her head. "After that one and only performance he would never sleep in an unlocked bedroom again."

* * *

"The Wilton Study" turned out to be something of a disappointment at the play reading: the language was flowery and affected, in keeping with the aspirations of the Aesthetic Movement of the nineteenth century. The melodramatic plot, involving an oil painting which gradually alters to mirror the dissolution of the main character (hence the title "study"), was judged by the play reading group to be rather "over the top" for modern audiences. It was, as one member put it, a "mediocre study in pencil". Nevertheless, the selection committee passed the motion unanimously, subject to some changes in the flowery nature of the script: "The General's Dilemma" and "The Margrove Inheritance" had been selected for the short list, but were shelved in the light of this new and exciting discovery. The centenary performance of "The Wilton Study" was planned for the following December, and the casting committee chose Andrew Fletcher to play the leading role in this premier amateur production.

It was soon after the start of rehearsals that Andrew became aware of the footsteps. The first occasion, he recalled, was late one October night, when he sat in the lounge going over his script in preparation for the next rehearsal. The distinctive sound of footsteps crunching up the shale drive gradually grew louder as the night visitor neared the house and stopped at the front door: Andrew waited for the door bell to ring — but all was silent.

'Whoever could it be at this time of night?' he wondered, putting the script down. After a moment he got up, switched the porch light on, and opened the front door. The light bathed the drive in a yellow glow, casting its rays in a semicircular swathe: but the drive was empty. There was no one there — or so he thought at the time. He was about to close the door when he noticed something which startled him considerably. He saw, in the beams cast by the soft light, a line of faint indentations in the shale surface — a line of footprints stretching from the drive gate to the front door. He wasn't mistaken after all — *someone had just arrived at the door.* But surely the visitor ought to be standing there, because no departing footprints, returning to the drive gate, were visible. It was a mystery which Andrew Fetcher was unable to explain, especially when the same thing occurred some weeks later.

The rehearsals were going well, with an enthusiastic cast settling into their respective characterisations. The main "prop" (or I should say props), and the basis on which the whole plot hinged, was a set of three oil studies of the main character, which meant that the Players' scene painter had to paint a likeness of Andrew on the canvas: the sittings were arranged to fit in with the rehearsals times so that Andrew spent periods on and off the podium during the evening. It soon became apparent that the scene painter was experiencing grave problems with this crucial part of the production; and he rapidly began to lose confidence in his artistic ability.

"Whatever I do I just can't seem to get it right," he complained bitterly to the producer. "When I finish a sitting with Andrew I know I manage to capture a real likeness of him — but the next time I see the portrait it has changed — looks nothing like him — a totally different person." The producer tried to console the distracted painter.

"I wouldn't worry too much about it," he advised. "What with the lighting and Andrew's make up I doubt if the audience will notice."

"It's too much like the actual plot, if you ask me," the artist replied. "There's something about this play — something I can't really explain. The whole thing is beginning to get on my nerves." The producer put it all down to artistic temperament, and diplomatically set his mind at rest.

"It will be alright on the night, mark my words," he reassured the dejected man. "I'm sure you won't let us down."

That evening Andrew experienced a shock to his nervous system, and like the scene painter, he couldn't explain it either. He awoke some time after midnight to the sound of footsteps. This time, however, it was not a crunching sound on loose shale, but the sharp "tap tap" on a lino floor covering: the footsteps were measured and unhurried. Someone was pacing up and down . . . up and down . . . in his kitchen downstairs.

He got up to investigate, cautiously descending the stairs to the kitchen door. Tap tap . . . tap tap . . . the sound grew louder as the feet approached — to stop at the other side of the kitchen door. Andrew could see a vague shape through the frosted glass — the eerie outline of a face pressed hard against the glass. An ugly, hideous face, full of menace and desire, slobbered in the most revolting fashion up and down the pane. Andrew shuddered momentarily at this gruesome sight, and drew back in alarm. He recovered his nerve and prepared to confront this unwelcome visitor. He waited for a moment — then threw the door wide open.

"What's your game! What are you up to, you . . . you . . . ?"

The kitchen was empty, the intruder had vanished, and Andrew, it would appear, was having a conversation with himself: once again his imagination was playing tricks on him. However, the evidence on the lino floor covering demonstrated otherwise. Lines of red marks crisscrossed the floor, the footprints caused by someone who had just come into the kitchen from the wet shale drive outside — and neglected to wipe his feet on the door mat.

* * *

Mrs. Price handed Andrew Fletcher a leather-bound folder: except for the brass fastener, it was exactly the same design as the manuscript folder.

"I forgot to give you this the other day," she said apologetically. "I'm becoming forgetful in my old age, I'm afraid."

"I wouldn't put it down to old age, Mrs. Price," Andrew laughed. "It happens to us all at some time or another — especially on stage."

"Well, I'm sorry it slipped my mind, Mr. Fletcher. I would have brought the folder over sooner, but what with the builders and the conversion . . ."

"I understand perfectly, Mrs. Price," he smiled. "What's in the folder?"

"Some of my late Uncle's papers," She answered. "I thought you might find them of interest, especially with the opening night next week. I think they are mostly old theatre programmes and review cuttings — that sort of thing."

Mrs. Price's comment *"You might find them interesting"* was an understatement, to say the least, as the chairman of the forthcoming production of the Ormsley Players was soon to discover.

The folder contained a host of theatre programmes and papers, review cuttings and letters: it would take, Andrew roughly estimated, a considerable amount of time to wade through them all. However, for the moment he concentrated on the theatre programmes — and came up with the original programme for "The Wilton Study". Inside, tucked into the rear, he found a neatly handwritten memorandum, written by Sherridan-Price (presumably for the programme printer's benefit), on the author of the play.

Please include this extract in the programme - on the third page, below the synopsis.
About the author, Ben Margeson.
The author was the nephew of Charles Margeson, one of London's foremost sculptors of the late Victorian period. He trained in his uncle's studio in Chelsea, and aspired to the stage, socialising with the most celebrated actors and playwrights of the day. He fell under the influence of the celebrated playwright and author, Henry Felton, the president of the Aesthetic Society, and 'The Wilton Study'

was adapted from Felton's one and only novel, 'The Study of William Wilton'. However, the play was never performed and its whereabouts remained unknown until, by sheer coincidence, it came into the hands of Mr. Sherridan-Price, who conceived the idea of performing this obscure play in Ormsley.

A review from the Arts page of the Ormsley Advertiser, dated the 25th of October, 1925, accompanied this printer's reference.

The production of an obscure play by an unknown author presented in the Working Man's Institute created a flurry of excitement in the town last week. However, the excitement was due, not, as one would imagine, to the merit or performance of the work, but to other circumstances. The invited audience, even before entering the theatre, was dismayed to see the desecration of one of our treasured monuments. I allude, of course, to the imposing statue of the Earl of Beaconsfield, and the line of foot prints, painted upon the ground, leading from the statue into the Institute. Obviously some unknown wag, thinking perhaps that the play would merit the company of so distinguished and important a guest, resorted to this novel form of invitation. The invited assembly was not amused.

As to the play itself, I can only say that it was mediocre in the extreme, and fell short (except in one respect) on every aspect of theatrical performance. The one redeeming feature was the portrait of the main character (congratulations to the artist) which was so convincing and lifelike, that several of the ladies in the audience had to be escorted from the Institute. The play came to an abrupt halt, thank heavens, in Act Three, when the stage acter, Mr. Sherridan-Price, for some reason, refused to go on with the performance. The audience was immediately reimbursed, the remaining performances cancelled, and the police are now looking for the 'footprint' culprit.

This highly critical article depressed Andrew, inducing a sense of disenchantment. The words *"mediocre"* and *"fell short of every aspect of theatrical performance"* rose from the print like an accusing finger.

'Had the Players made a error of judgement?' he pondered glumly. 'I hope we haven't chosen the wrong play.'

However, the evening rehearsal helped to restore his faith in the theatrical prospects of "The Wilton Study", and helped to moderate the effects of the adverse criticism of the Advertiser critic: costumes, scenery and props were on display, and the portrait studies, when they were unveiled by the scene painter, were greeted with a burst of applause. The portrait for the third act caused a gasp of astonishment.

"He hasn't managed to capture your likeness," the producer commented, "but I must say the painting looks absolutely magnificent from the back of the hall."

Andrew was in complete agreement. The oil study, to put it bluntly, was absolutely revolting, in stark contrast to the other portraits. The handsome countenance of the character in the portrait in Act One gave way to a face of sheer ugliness in the Act Two study. However, the portrayal of the calamitous deterioration of the character in Act Three had a tremendous impact on the cast. This tremendous study of corruption and mouldering decay, vividly illustrating the complete and utter change from Man to Monster, was executed in thick layers of paint: lurid reds, stark purples, and putrefying yellows created a sense of festering decay and deadly malevolence. The leering, deranged eyes, the rotting teeth and disintegrating flesh, were so realistic, that Andrew could not help wondering what the effect of this monstrous study of human depravity, when viewed in a darkened theatre and in the glow of filtered stage lighting, would have on the audience: *"Several of the ladies had to be escorted from the theatre"* flashed through his mind, and he shuddered at the thought of a possible stampede in Act Three.

Later that night it would seem that there was a stampede in progress outside his bedroom door.

* * *

The footsteps roused him from his slumbers. The vision of that revolting third study had prevented any chance of dropping off to sleep and he had taken a sleeping tablet: it worked — until two in the morning. The noise outside his bedroom door grew in intensity, rising and falling as the footsteps passed the door. Every so often they would stop — and whoever was on the other side of the door would grasp the handle — testing! Then the footsteps would start again . . . up and down . . . up and down — the tap-tap tapping gradually increasing to a crescendo — a virtual stampede. Then, after what seemed like hours to Andrew, the footsteps would suddenly stop — silence.

'First the drive . . . then the kitchen,' he groaned, '— and now this.' He could bear it no longer. He crept to the door, determined to find out who this intruder was — and gently began to ease it open. The sound of the footsteps immediately ceased — the landing was empty — and there was no sign of the intruder. However, the evidence of this nocturnal disturbance lay before his eyes. He saw, bathed in the light streaming from his bedroom, the jumble of shale footprints on the landing carpet, and the line of red marks on the stairs : they were *one way only* — to his bedroom door. He searched downstairs and found no one.

Unable and, to some extent, unwilling to face the prospect of sleep, he sat in the lounge with a glass of whiskey in one hand and the bottle in the other. The contents of the leather-bound folder lay in an untidy heap on the table and he absently began to tidy them, sifting through the papers and programmes, and placing them in separate piles: in the process two letters came to his attention. One had been opened and the other was still sealed.

Dear Hugh,

What a turn-up. I have a part in 'Lord Cecil's Return' — the butler, no less. The play has all the prospects of a long run, so good bye to bread and dripping (not your favourite if I remember correctly). I'll keep my ear to the ground for anything new which would suit you. By the way, I met Gerald the other evening (he thought my performance was outstanding — he was joking as usual) and he asked about the Wilton Study, and whether I planned to do anything with it (don't worry, Hugh old chap — I managed to put off any payment for the moment). Anyway, he told me something quite interesting about Ben Margeson. The fellow was desperate to 'tread the boards' and, in order to impress the 'theatricals', gave an impromptu performance of the Study to some of the members of the Aesthetic Society (he had even managed to get hold of some authentic ceremonial robes for the part).

Unfortunately he only got as far as the first act. By that time the audience was roaring with laughter, and 'Love and Beauty' Felton, their president (it seems the lad was hopelessly infatuated with him — I don't think I need spell it out, do I) gave such a vicious 'crit' of the play, ridiculing it and the pathetic attempts of its author etc. that Margeson, utterly devastated, fled the room in tears. The poor chap hanged himself that very night — dressed in his ceremonial robes, would you believe.

Well, I must away and powder up. The performance

is upon us.

Try to come down to see the play, or at least keep in touch,

Reggie.

PS. I had a rather unpleasant experience the other evening. I'm sure I was followed from the theatre to my digs. There have been one or two street robberies in the neighbourhood recently. I heard the blighter's footsteps but couldn't see him in the fog. Luckily I've still got my service pistol.

The sealed letter was addressed to Reginald Thornton Esq., C/O The Shaftesbury Theatre, London. Sherridan-Price's address was on the back of the envelope and the postmark was dated the 10th November, 1925. The words *"Present whereabouts unknown — Return to Sender"* told its own story. Reggie had never received it, and it had remained unopened for more than fifty years. Andrew could not contain his curiosity — he had to open it. He soon wished he hadn't.

Dear Reggie,

What a disaster! The whole thing has gone badly — a total flop — and my reputation is in tatters. No final curtain, no bows and, to top it all, I am being sued for desecrating a public monument. Some fool (and I have my suspicions who the culprit is) painted a white line of footprints from the statue of Disraeli into the Institute toilet (the ladies convenience, I may add) and yours truly is getting the blame for it (they say it was my idea for a publicity stunt). But that is not all!

It happened in Act Three, Reggie, and it's something which will haunt me from now on. I refer to the part of the play where the audience is confronted with the portrait in its final stage of change. I managed to get a local artist to paint it and his effort was barely adequate (you could say laughable) — or so I thought during the rehearsals. But I tell you, Reggie (and after serving on the Western Front for three years you know that I'm in no way susceptible to fanciful imaginings), that, when the covering was pulled from the portrait, I saw the most ghoulish creature imaginable. The audience gasped (and some screamed) and I absolutely dried up and froze. And then the blackout occurred, plunging everything into complete darkness — but in that brief instant before the lights went out I saw (I swear to you that it is true, my friend) the 'nightmare' stir in the painting and begin to climb out from the canvas!

The light went out and I was embraced by a horrid glutinous mass of stinking flesh — and a slobbering face was pressed against mine — kissing me! The stench made me choke and gasp for breath — and then the foul being whispered in my ear such words that I, even now, cringe from committing them to paper. "Soon, dear one . . . be patient . . . I come soon" — and at that point I collapsed onto the stage.

No one believed me, of course. The portrait was perfectly normal when I forced myself to view it the next day and the cast think I've had delayed shell shock from my trench days. But I tell you, Reggie . . . I would rather face a whole regiment of Huns before I'd sit alone with that accursed painting again.

After this experience I've decided that my acting days are over. I am firmly resolved never to set foot in a theatre again. Speaking of feet, I have to tell you that I am constantly plagued with the sound of footsteps, especially at night — and I have an uneasy suspicion who my visitor might be.

*Thanks for the invitation, but it's out of the question,
I'm afraid,*
   Good luck with your career,
   Best wishes,
   Hugh.
*PS.   I wish I had kept my service pistol, after all. I sense
the footsteps closing in — and I think I might need some-
thing like it soon.*

Unfortunately Andrew did not own a service pistol, or any other weapon, for that matter. Nor had he experienced the rigours and dangers of trench warfare to toughen his nervous system. The opening night was looming, and the full dress rehearsal was planned for the Saturday night. Unfortunately, the feelings Andrew was now experiencing could, in no way, be classed as those of that well-known theatrical affliction, "butterflies in the stomach".

It had to be full blown "stage fright"!

* * *

The cast was assembled on stage, fully powdered and costumed, and the producer rose from the front row of the auditorium to give his customary pep talk.

"You have all done well so far, and the play is looking good," he began. "So let's see if we can't have a complete run-through without any hitches." But, even as he spoke, the sound of footsteps clattering around backstage reached his ears.

"Quiet!" he roared. "Quiet back there!" The footsteps faded away, and the stage manager went behind the backcloth to check.

"No one here . . . Whoever it was has scarpered," he called back.

"Well make sure the exit doors are firmly closed," the producer ordered. "We don't want any more idiots running all over the place."

Unfortunately this happened again during the rehearsal, much to

FOOTSTEPS

the annoyance of cast and stage crew alike. It all had a familiar ring to it and Andrew wasn't feeling at all well, forgetting his lines on several occasions. In the tea break he heard the producer whisper to the prompt.

"I wish we had thought of having an understudy."

"I'm beginning to think you're right," the prompt replied. "I've never seen Andrew like this before. He's usually so competent and reliable."

"Yes, he's always word perfect," the producer agreed. "Something must be upsetting him?"

That *something* struck in the third act. The lights suddenly went out — an ear-splitting scream pierced the air, resounding through the darkened auditorium — and the flurried tap-tap tapping of footsteps echoed from the direction of the stage. They faded away as the emergency lighting came on to reveal the shape of Andrew Fletcher, Chairman and pillar of the Ormsley Players, the leading man in "The Wilton Study" — crumpled up centre stage.

* * *

Two items appeared in the Advertiser the following week. The first was a short paragraph concerning "The Wilton Study".

The centenary production of the Ormsley Players has been temporarily postponed, due to staging problems. Patrons who have already purchased tickets will receive a full refund at the box office.

On the opposite page the second item concerned the town's traffic problems.

"DIZZIE" STEPS DOWN
In keeping with Ormsley's traffic and environmental

schemes the District Council have decided to move the statue of the celebrated Victorian Prime Minister, Lord Beaconsfield, from its present position opposite the bus station into the town's pedestrian precinct. The 20ft monument of Disraeli was purchased by subscription, the bulk of the money donated by the rank and file of the conservative Primrose League (the primrose was Disraeli's favourite flower) and erected in the town in 1884, facing the Ormsley Institute. The imposing statue is the work of the noted London sculptor, Mr. A. Margeson, and is 9ft in height and, with the pedestal, is executed in Portland stone.

Benjamin Margeson, the nephew of the sculptor, was the studio model for the work and wore Disraeli's personal ceremonial robes of office for the sittings (it was the practice to use models or mock-ups when the subject was not available or had died). It was rumoured that the nephew committed suicide shortly afterwards, while dressed in those same robes of office.

The ex-chairman of the Ormsley Players (Andrew had resigned that same night) contemplated the revelation in the latter part of this article with astonishment. He now realised that the problem with "The Wilton Study" was not with its outdated style — but with its location.

'How was Sherridan-Price to know that the author of the play had been the model for Disraeli's statue,' he pondered. '— and then some joker goes and paints a set of footprints from the statue right into the Institute theatre. So the spirit of Margeson takes up the invitation and walks across to watch the first public performance of his play — and makes his very first acting appearance on stage — in Act Three.'

Although Andrew had resigned from the Players, and turned his back on the Thespian scene, he was still plagued by footsteps and whispers in the night.

"Soon, dear one . . . be patient . . . I come soon"

It was plain to see that he was now the object of these ghastly sentiments of affection, and had hardly slept a wink for weeks: he dreaded going to bed at night, and recalled the words of Mrs. Price *"After that one and only performance he would never sleep in an unlocked bedroom again"*. He now understood the reason why. He also discovered the exact purpose of the strange object which had belonged to the late Hugh Sherridan-Price.

When Andrew bundled up the actor's papers and programmes to return them with the manuscript to Mrs. Price, he found a trades-man's bill stuffed down a side pocket of the leather-bound folder: the bill was for ten shillings and sixpence, and attached to it was a pen-cilled diagram and some instructions.

> *(A)   I have left you some excellent hard wood from the pulpit of the old Mission Chapel - please use this wood in the construction of the device.*
>
> *(B)   Make sure the cross engraved in the wood faces the 'U' piece at the top.*
>
> *(C)   The device must be capable of extending to wedge under any height of door handle or latch, and when placed in position should be capable of resisting the strongest force possible and prevent entry into any room.*
>
> *(D)   The fittings should be constructed of the highest quality brass, and the device must be stout enough to with-stand the strongest attack, and yet still be light enough to carry in a suitcase.*

Andrew examined the diagram with growing admiration.

'So he had this contraption specially made up to wedge his bed-room door shut,' he thought. 'I must say it's very original — I think I'll try it out.'

The peculiar device, constructed in wood from the pulpit of a consecrated building, worked perfectly. With the 'U' shape securely lodged under the door handle and the 'T' bracket embedded into the carpet, Andrew sat on his bed contemplating "The Sherridan-Price Patent for the Prevention of Ghoulish and Gruesome Intruders". His spirits rose, and he began to feel like his old self once more.

'Well, it worked for him,' he yawned, '— and he lived for eighty odd years.' Andrew lay back on the pillow, eyelids drooping. Below his bedroom window the distant sound of approaching footsteps, crunching softly on the shale drive, reached his ears: he responded with a gentle snore.

Andrew Fletcher slept peacefully for the first time in ages.

HALSALL

Plain Ghost Trail   24

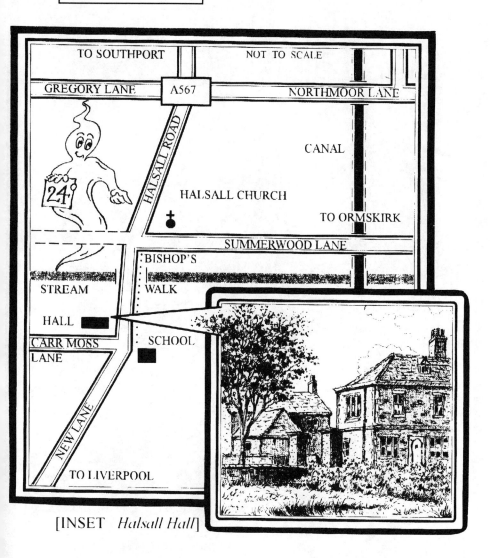

TO SOUTHPORT

NOT TO SCALE

GREGORY LANE

A567

NORTHMOOR LANE

CANAL

HALSALL ROAD

HALSALL CHURCH

TO ORMSKIRK

SUMMERWOOD LANE

BISHOP'S

STREAM

WALK

HALL

CARR MOSS
LANE

SCHOOL

NEW LANE

TO LIVERPOOL

[INSET   *Halsall Hall*]

79

PRESTIGE HOMES
PART EXCHANGE
SCHEME

PART EXCHANGE

The advertisement in the brochure was perfectly clear.

PRESTIGE HOMES PART EXCHANGE SCHEME
*We aim to take the worry of selling your present home off
your mind so that you can move into our select development at Summerwood Court without any fuss or delay. If
you decide to purchase one of our homes using our part
exchange scheme then please let us know as soon as possible so that we can arrange an immediate valuation and
survey report at no cost to yourselves.*

"There — what did I tell you!" cried Joan excitedly. "We can part
exchange our house and move into one of their homes."

"Don't get too excited, dear," her husband replied with a certain
degree of scepticism. "We'll pop up to Summerwood at the weekend
and check the place out, if you like." Robert Mordant couldn't help
feeling, after so many disappointments, that this latest development
would probably turn out to be a complete waste of time like all the
rest.

The Mordaunt's house had been up for sale for over two years,
but a nationwide slump in property values, and the chain reaction
this caused within the system, had ensured that their house would
probably remain unsold for the foreseeable future — that is, until
Joan Mordaunt's telephone call.

"I've just heard they're going to do the old Hall up, Joan," Gaynor
called to tell her the news. "It hasn't been lived in for years, and they

81

were going to pull it down, but some property speculator stepped in and bought the place at the last minute. Got it for a song, so I've been told. Anyway, they're going to convert it into homes, and they say you can part exchange your own house. I'll send you a brochure about it all."

It was the news that Joan had been longing to hear. She grew up in Summerwood, and Gaynor's family lived next door. The girls spent their childhood together, attending the same schools and sharing the same interests: they even worked together in the local agricultural seed company. It could be said that they were constant companions, that is until Joan's marriage and a new life in the south of England severed the relationship. Unfortunately life in the south didn't suit her and she began to miss her old home in Summerwood. Holiday visits to her family and friends only served to heighten this yearning to return to the place so dear to her heart, and when Graham, her son, was born this yearning increased. And then she received the call from her best friend a week after Graham's fifth birthday.

The brochure arrived a couple of days later, and it would seem that, thanks to last minute property speculation and the principle of part exchange, her wish might, at last, come true. And so it did when, later that year, the Mordaunt family moved back to Summerwood, into a *'perfect town house, with four bedrooms, a private parking space, garage, an easily maintained front landscaped garden and rear courtyard. This house has every modern convenience and is built to the highest specification, whilst retaining much of the historical character of a grade two listed building.'*

However, as the Mordaunt family was to discover, there was one aspect of its historical character which definitely was not listed — and, if the truth be known, defied description.

* * *

The substantial red brick building of Summerwood Hall (renamed

Summerwood Court by the development company) stands on an outcrop of sandstone at the edge of a large area of flat agricultural land reclaimed from three ancient lakes. About a quarter of a mile to the south west stands its equally substantial and long time companion, the church of Saint Cuthbert, which dates back to Norman times. The Hall was rebuilt around 1750 (in keeping with the spirit of the times) on the foundations of the ancient manor house of the de Lacy family, whose impressive coat of arms can be seen carved above the arched gateway of the original stable yard, and the new building replaced its outdated predecessor.

These rustic landmarks are separated by a fault in this outcrop of rock and, between the two, a shallow stream meanders its way through a small valley to the flat mossland beyond. In medieval times a water mill stood on this very spot, but it has long since gone and now a solid causeway and bridge carry the road across the site where this mill once stood.

From the lounge of number one, Summerwood Court, (with *"its designer stone fire place and living gas fire"*) Joan could now sit and contemplate this scene of childhood memory with pleasure and satisfaction. Robert, her husband, contemplated a different scene with an equal degree of pleasure and satisfaction. From the cellar of number one, Summerwood Court, he could sit and gaze upon his abiding passion (and one of the reasons which influenced his decision to take up the part exchange scheme) — wines. Robert Mordant was a wine buff, and this underground architectural "leftover" in the foundations of the original manor house fulfilled the exact requirements needed for a wine cellar.

However, this ancient cellar had another qualification besides a constant temperature and lightless atmosphere: it was terraced. A series of steps had been hewn out of the sandstone outcrop along the length of the cellar walls, and a mosaic of pebbles had been set into the floor. The terraced sandstone was ideal for holding the wine racks, and Robert wasted no time in converting this underground room into a "cave" ("That's what the French call wine cellars" he would explain to guests). When the project was completed some weeks later he had the distinct impression that these terraces had originally been designed for that very purpose.

"I don't think cave is the right word for it," Gaynor whispered to her friend when she peered along the dimly lit racks, labelled and filled with wine bottles, and gazed down at the mosaic floor. "It looks more like a shrine to me."

"Shrine . . . Yes, that describes it perfectly," laughed Joan, with a hint of sarcasm in her voice, "— a shrine to his wine tasting buds." (It has to be said at this point that Joan did not share Robert's enthusiasm for the wine connoisseur's bouquet and palette). She didn't care for the taste of most of the wines, much to the annoyance of her husband, and preferred mineral water instead.

"Well, you have to admit that he has made a good job of it all," Gaynor replied.

"I suppose your right," Joan sniffed, indicating the rows of bottles, "— and it has solved the problem of storing all this lot."

Unfortunately, there was a problem which Robert had not foreseen, and which the developers had neglected (or possibly had been unaware of) to mention. It was an age old problem, dreaded by architects and builders alike — water seepage.

It was unusual for a building, standing high above the surrounding land on an outcrop of rock, to have this problem. The water supply for the original manor house came from three wells in the old stable yard. They were sunk into the sandstone and explained the reason why Baron Walter de Lacy had chosen this spot for his family seat in 1305. It seems that, because of a geological peculiarity in the strata, an underground spring lay beneath the Hall, raising the water table above that of the surrounding land; and in times of prolonged heavy rainfall the level of this water table rose.

It so happened that the month of November was extremely wet, well above the national average, and consequently this fluid table rose sharply, allowing water to permeate through the rock — and Robert stepped right into it.

"Joan!" the astounded man yelled, totally unprepared for this sudden complication. "Joan! . . . Come down here — quick." His wife came clattering part way down the stone steps, her son Graham hard on her heels, and peered under the brick arch into the dimly lit cellar.

"What's the matter?"

"Just look at this floor!"

"I can't see anything wrong with it."

"The water, woman," declared the exasperated man, "— just look at this water."

"I can't see any water, dear," replied his startled wife.

"Neither can I, mummy," her son agreed.

"Can't see any water! You must be blind." However, there was nothing wrong with Joan's eyesight. By some peculiar trick of the light falling onto the pebble mosaic floor it was impossible to see the surface of the water from that angle, and only when she came down the remaining steps to the level of the cellar floor did she see the watery covering.

"My God, you're right!" she exclaimed. "Has a water pipe burst?"

"No, it hasn't," her irate husband snapped. "I'm pretty sure that it's water seepage with all this rain we've been having." He surveyed the cellar with a despondent air. "Well, if it gets any higher, and ruins my wine, Prestige Homes can start thinking about another part exchange." Graham took a different view: he immediately jumped into the water and began to paddle up and down the cellar.

"Look, mummy!" he cried excitedly, "— my own paddling pool."

The sight of their five year old son splashing about in the water relieved the tension, and the parents burst into fits of uncontrollable laughter.

"Oh, Graham," spluttered his mother, "— come out of that water at once. You'll ruin your shoes." Graham took no notice and continued to paddle up and down; and then suddenly he stopped.

"Oooh, look, daddy!" he cried, bending down and staring into the water, "— bubbles."

"Bubbles?" his father answered. He lifted his son out of the water. "What do you mean — bubbles?"

"Down there, daddy," pointed the sharp-eyed five year old, "— bubbles in the pebbles." He was right. His father saw a small stream of bubbles rising from the pebble floor.

"Is the floor punctured like my bicycle tyre, daddy?" the child asked.

"I don't know about a puncture," Robert answered, "— but I think your mother might be right about a pipe, after all."

"I told you it was probably a burst pipe, dear," Joan nodded. "Let's get rid of the water before we do anything else." They all set about the task with mops, buckets and cloths, and an hour or so later the pebble floor was cleared and the paddling pool reverted back to a wine cellar, much to Graham's disappointment.

"I don't think there's a pipe under here, Joan," her husband observed ruefully.

"There must be," she replied. "What makes you think it isn't burst pipe?"

"Because there isn't any sign of more water coming up through the pebbles, is there?" Joan had to admit he was right.

"There must be a bubble factory underneath, daddy," a wide-eyed Graham innocently suggested, "— full of goblins making bubbles for your bottles of wine."

"No, I don't think so, darling," his mother smiled, and suppressed a chuckle. Somehow, the thought of little underworld creatures injecting Robert's vintage wine with masses of bubbles was hilarious. She picked Graham up, and carried him from the cellar. "We must leave daddy to find out what it really is, while I change your wet shoes and socks." Robert was left to ponder the situation.

"Goblins making bubbles for my wine, indeed," he muttered to himself. "I wish it was as simple as that."

Unfortunately, Robert's wish was not to be granted — it was not to be as simple as that.

* * *

He looked down, wide eyed, at the hole in the floor.

'What can it mean?' he thought, scrutinising the rough cut slab. Earlier, during the preliminary inspection of the floor he had observed a simple crucifix design incorporated into the swirling mosaic pattern of the pebbles: the bubbles had appeared at this point, at the intersection of lines of this cross. Robert had carefully prised away the pebbles in this specific area and had uncovered a stone slab set into the rock foundation of the cellar. It had the de Lacy crest and several words incised on its rough surface.

Robert wiped the slab with a cloth, but the letters were ill defined and he had great difficulty in reading the words. He resorted to a piece of paper and a soft pencil, and proceeded to make a rubbing of the stone surface. Within minutes he had completed the task: the words appeared to be in French.

ÉCOUTE BIEN - DÉPLACE PAS
FAUT REPOUSSER Â JAMAIS LES ODIEUX
H de L

"I've haven't the faintest idea what it means," Robert observed, when he showed the rubbing to his wife. "Have you . . . ?"

"No, I haven't, I'm afraid," Joan answered. "It's obviously something very old belonging to the original manor house, and if someone has gone to all that trouble of putting it there — then there must be some reason for it. I'd leave it where it is if I were you."

"Well, I can't see any harm in lifting it up," her husband countered. "That's where the bubbles were coming from."

"Well, don't say I didn't warn you," Joan replied, as Robert went down to continue his excavation. He returned minutes later, clutching an object wrapped in the cloth.

"Just as I thought," he said with a smirk. "There's nothing sinister about that slab. It's covering an old culvert, that's all."

"A culvert under the house?"

"Yes . . . It was probably a drain for the old manor house — designed to carry away any excess water from the cellar. I'll put a grid there instead."

"What's that you've found?" Joan asked her husband, pointing to the cloth.

"Oh, this was underneath the stone slab." He unfolded the cloth and placed a wreath-shaped piece of metal on the table.

"It looks like holly set around a cross," Joan observed, "— metal holly."

"Holly is right," Robert agreed, "and if you pass me the metal polish I think you'll find that it is silver." And so it was. The pair gazed at the silver wreath of holly set in a crucifix in rapturous astonishment.

"It must be worth a bob or two," Robert said in undisguised admiration. "It's a beautiful piece of workmanship."

"It is, dear," his wife breathed. "It will look lovely as a Christmas decoration, don't you think?"

"That's a good idea, Joan," he replied. In the meantime, Graham had examined the silver ornament.

"Why did the goblins leave it there, daddy?" he asked, "— and how do they make bubbles with it?" Robert laughed, and picked up his son.

"Don't be silly, old chap," he chuckled. "There aren't any goblins or bubbles down there."

"Mind you, he has a point, dear," Joan declared. "I wonder why anyone would put a beautiful piece of silver in an old culvert. It does make you think, doesn't it?"

"Some superstitious nonsense, I don't doubt," he replied. "You know what they were like in those days."

Joan wasn't convinced.

* * *

"Look, daddy . . . The goblins have put some bubbles in your wine bottles." The child stood at the end of the cellar, pointing up to the wine racks.

"Don't tell your mother that, old chap," his father snorted, "or she'll give up her mineral water and drink my wine cellar dry. Anyway, the bubble goblins have gone now. Daddy has fixed the floor."

"But they still come back to put the bubbles in the wine, daddy," insisted Graham, continuing to stare up at the bottles. His father was about to ignore his son's childish observations, when he saw what was causing his son's fanciful remarks.

'Was it a trick of the light — or the way the bottles were racked?' Robert blinked in disbelief — but his son was right in one respect. Someone had been tampering with his precious wine bottles. The fingerprints around the neck of the bottle were unmistakable in the light covering of dust. He carefully withdrew the bottle from the rack and carried it upstairs, preceded by the clamour of "Mummy, mummy — daddy's bottle has been bubbled by the wine goblins!"

"Have they, my darling?" his mother laughed, giving the excited child a hug. "Aren't they naughty — fancy putting bubbles in your daddy's dry old wine." Then she saw the serious expression on her husband's face. "I was only joking, darling. Your wine isn't all that bad."

"I wouldn't be too sure," Robert answered sharply. "What do you make of this?" He placed the bottle on the table and pointed to the fingerprints around the its neck. Joan bent down and examined the marks. She turned to her son.

"Have you been playing with your daddy's wine bottles, Graham?" she asked the wide eyed child. Graham slowly shook his head. "You know you must not go down into the cellar, don't you?" Graham slowly nodded. "And you know that you must always tell mummy the truth, don't you?" Graham nodded again. Joan looked at her husband.

"Little "busy fingers" has probably been at work," she concluded. "We'll have to put a lock on the cellar door, dear." Robert was not convinced by her theory.

"I don't think the lad is to blame, Joan," he replied, turning to his son. "Give me your hand, old chap." Robert took his son's hand and placed the tiny fingers over the marks around the neck of the wine bottle. "See what I mean, Joan — these prints were made by a hand much larger than Graham's, and fingers are longer — look at the shape of the tips . . ." Joan scrutinised the marks, and pursed her lips.

"Mmmm . . . They are very odd, now you mention it," she said, trying to visualise the hand which had made them. "They look like talons or claws rather than fingers — whoever made these certainly wasn't our Graham."

"I think your right on that score," her husband replied. "And your right about the lock on the cellar door as well — and it's not just for Graham's benefit either."

Unfortunately, as Joan was to learn a week later, the lock proved useless. Graham's teacher spoke to her about the forthcoming Christmas party.

"There's a fancy dress competition, Mrs. Mordaunt," the teacher informed her at the school gate. "Your Graham tells me that he wants to come to the party as a bubble goblin — he's really thrilled about it."

"Oh dear, I know," Joan replied. "He's got a vivid imagination, you know."

"I do indeed," she said, "— and it shows in his paintings. They are so imaginative for a child of his age, and I have to admit that I have never seen paintings like his before. He says they are the bubble goblin who comes up from the cellar to visit him." Joan was completely taken aback by this revelation.

"The bubble goblin comes up from the cellar — and visits him?"

"Yes. He's always talking about it — and I must say that some of the other children are quite frightened by his paintings as well."

On the way home Joan questioned her son about his imaginary visitor: Graham's factual description of the bubble goblin was disturbing, to say the least.

"He doesn't wear any clothes, mummy," the child giggled, "— and he has horns and pointed ears — and a long tail and funny feet."

"Are you sure you aren't making him up, darling?" Joan asked him with a degree of panic in her voice. "You must have seen a picture of a goblin at school."

"Oh, no, mummy, I'm not making him up," declared the excited child. "I'm going to play with him at his house soon." His alarmed mother turned pale and didn't answer. 'It has to be his vivid imagination,' she thought. 'He has to be making it up.'

The finger prints in the house told a different story. Her husband was the first to discover them.

"Over here, Joan!" he cried, "— on the coffee table." The faint imprint of a long taloned finger on the glass surface was just visible with aid of a torch. Others soon came to light — in the kitchen, on the stairs, and, to their horror, in Graham's bedroom. The pair just stared at each other, speechless.

"The bubble goblin is coming to play with me tonight, daddy," Graham told his startled parents, "and I'm going to help him put the bubbles in your wine." He smiled and picked up his glass of milk, adding "Would you like to come too?"

Mr. and Mrs. Mordaunt refused their son's kind invitation, and went off in search of something stronger than milk.

* * *

The baby alarm was tried and tested, and helped to allay the rising apprehension of Graham's parents. They sat in the darkness, fully dressed, listening to the soft breathing of their son in the nursery. The hours went by and, except for the occasional noise of passing traffic on the main road, all was silent. Just after two in the morning this silence extended to the baby alarm. The breathing had stopped.

"My God, I can't hear him!" cried Joan, and dashed to the nursery, her husband close behind. The bedclothes lay on the floor and the bed was empty. Graham had gone.

"The cellar!" yelled Robert, and they raced out of the room and ran down the staircase. Ahead of them their son skipped down the cellar steps, hand in hand, with something out of a horror comic. The creature had horns and pointed ears, perfectly matching their son's description, and the bottom half of its body resembled that of a goat, with long tail and cloven hooves. The creature's leathery skin glistened in the torch light and long taloned hands pulled the boy along. However, the face of this devilish creature, held in the beam of the torch light, was so venomous and cruel, its luminous red eyes so vindictive and mad, that its intentions were not that of child's play. The cellar door was open and they arrived in time to see their son's body disappearing down the drainage hole in the pebble floor — down into the culvert below the house. In a nick of time Robert grabbed his son's feet and tried to haul him back.

"Hang on, old chap!" his father cried in a panic. "We'll soon have you out." But Graham refused to budge.

"That creature is holding on to him!" Robert shouted in despair. "For God's sake, Joan, give me a hand before I lose him." They both strained and pulled, gasping for breath — and, slowly but surely, the body of the senseless child emerged from this gruesome cavity. One last supreme effort and he was free, and he popped out like a cork from one of his father's wine bottles. A foul smelling stench rose from the dark culvert, and the sound of scampering feet, echoing round and round in the culvert, slowly faded away into the distance.

Graham's sinister companion had decided to call it a night — and

Mr. and Mrs. Mordant had decided to call a doctor. There would be no more bubbles for the time being.

* * *

Most of the guests had arrived and the party was in full swing by the time the Mordaunts knocked on the door of number five, Summerwood Court. Their hosts, the Baxters, had just moved into number five, the last unit to be completed in the development, and they had invited the residents in the other units to a house warming party.

"Sorry we're late," Joan apologised to Mrs. Baxter. "The baby sitter was delayed."

"No problem . . . Joan, isn't it?" Mrs. Baxter declared. "Come in. You already know the rest of the Court, don't you." Joan and Robert nodded, and mingled with the gathering. The evening passed by pleasantly enough, and, in the course of conversation, Robert's next door neighbour brought up the subject of his wine cellar.

"Have you finished it yet,?" he asked.

"Yes, it's all fitted out," Robert replied.

"Well you certainly worked hard at it — all hours of the day and night. We can always tell when your down there. We often hear your little boy scampering up and down."

"It almost sounds as if he is running about under the house, you know," the man's wife added, "— but you do keep him up late, don't you? Sometimes we hear him playing well after midnight." Joan paled at this remark: the vision of her son's recent experience could hardly be described as "play". She quickly changed the subject, and Robert beat a swift retreat to the kitchen. There he heard Mr. Baxter talking about the de Lacy family and the history of the old manor house. He seemed remarkably well informed, and Robert decided, when the opportunity arose, to ask him about the stone slab from the floor of the cellar. Some minutes later he took Mr. Baxter to one side and told him about the problem of the waterlogged cellar and the culvert.

"I made a tracing of the words," he said to his host. "Perhaps you can explain what they mean. I'll just nip home and get it." On his return he handed the tracing to Mr. Baxter.

ÉCOUTE BIEN - DÉPLACE PAS
FAUT REPOUSSER Â JAMAIS LES ODIEUX
H de L

"What do you make of it?"

"This is interesting," he began. "It's in French, of course, and H de L is probably Hugh de Lacy. "*Écoute bien, déplace pas*" — I'd translate that as "Take heed - do not remove". The next bit "*Faut repousser â jamais les odieux*" means something like "In order to keep the Damned out for all time.""

"What do you think it means?"

"It's perfectly clear to me," Mr. Baxter answered solemnly. "The de Lacys of Summerwood Manor were the direct descendants of the Norman barons who came over with William the Conqueror — that's why this warning is in French."

"A warning?"

"Oh yes, it's a warning all right," declared Mr. Baxter. "One of them, Hugh de Lacy, left a warning in your cellar. In my opinion you shouldn't disturb anything until you find out more about it — and even then I'd be very wary of tampering with something which has been there for centuries."

"You think so?"

"I do," he replied. "My advice is to put that stone back where you found it, and put up with occasional damp cellar."

Robert took his advice and the next day the grid was removed and the stone slab and pebbles replaced in their original positions. Unfortunately it turned out to be a case of "barring the stable door after the horse had bolted" when Joan met her neighbour some days later.

"Is you husband still working on his wine cellar?" she asked Joan, "— only we heard him working late last night." Joan was at a loss for words. Her son's comments added to her growing anxiety.

"Mummy, I don't want to play with the bubble goblin any more," he declared.

"Don't be silly, Graham," she said firmly. "There isn't a bubble goblin."

"But he came to play with me last night," Graham insisted. "Will you ask daddy to make him go away?" His perturbed mother tried to put his mind at rest.

"Of course I will, darling," she consoled him, "— just as soon as Daddy comes home from work." She broke the news to Robert as soon as he arrived home: he went straight to the cellar. Loose pebbles littered the floor, and the stone slab lay beside the dark hole. Gazing down into the black culvert below, he realised that banning his son's playmate from the house would be easier said than done.

* * *

"Mummy . . . Mummy, I've seen the bubble goblin today!"

Graham ran up to his mother at the school gate, bursting with excitement.

"Calm down, Graham," Joan scolded the agitated child, "and stop being silly."

"But I did, Mummy . . . I did!" Graham's teacher came to the gate.

"Oh, he's been so unsettled this afternoon, Mrs. Mordaunt," she explained. "We went across to the church to practise for the carol service and when he saw one of the gargoyles on the church roof he became so excited that he wouldn't go into the church. He has driven us mad with his bubble goblin ever since. He just can't stop talking about it."

Joan apologised for her son's behaviour and ushered him away. Graham was so agitated that she decided to stop by the church.

"Now, darling," She asked her son, "— can you show me where

you saw your bubble goblin?" she asked her son. The boy, without any hesitation, set off through the grave yard to the north side of the building. Graham halted by the chancel and pointed up to the parapet.

"There, Mummy . . . up there!"

Joan looked up at the weathered stone carving, jutting out, immobile and lifeless, from the wall above, and drew a sharp breath of astonishment. She had recently seen that same gargoyle in her husband's wine cellar — and it had been far from lifeless. She gazed up at the stone carving, remembering the horns, pointed ears and cloven hooves. In this instance, however, the stone gargoyle was embracing a hooded figure (obviously a monk) with an expression of fiendish pleasure: long taloned fingers grasped its companion in a deadly everlasting grip.

"Why is he holding that man?" her son asked. "Is the bubble goblin playing with him now?"

"I don't know, darling," his mother replied, shuddering at the memory of that night when her own son was held in such a vice-like grip. "Perhaps daddy will be able to tell you."

In the event, the answer to the child's question didn't come from his father, but from the latest occupant of Summerwood court, Mr. Baxter.

* * *

"It is probably true to say that these old church carvings (and the same thing applies to some stained glass windows) are often based on the superstitious notions of the craftsmen of the time," Mr. Baxter explained. "They let their imagination run riot and carved figures with feathered bodies, birds' claws and fiends' heads in stone outside (and wood inside) the church. Some parts of the inspiration for these carvings are pagan in origin, and predate Christianity."

"So the carving of the gargoyle on the church roof is just a figment of some medieval stone mason's imagination?" asked Robert.

"Not necessarily," Mr. Baxter replied. "It is possible that the carving you refer to has some basis in truth — the monk (or Christianity) in a struggle with a demon (or Paganism). Before taking up the Prestige Homes' part exchange offer I did some research on the place, rather than leaving it to the solicitor. By chance I came across an old text in the archives office concerning the de Lacys and this church. Sir Raymond de Lacy returned from the crusades with some strange (some say pagan) ideas about cultivation and, in particular, wine. He planted a vineyard and was so successful that the monks at Myerscough Priory (their wine harvest failed regularly) became jealous. They were a powerful order and resorted to devious means, casting doubt on Sir Raymond's farming ability and planting suspicions of sorcery in the minds of the local hierarchy and the nobility at court. Anyway, the outcome was cut and dried. Sir Raymond was removed to France, and the estate went his younger brother, Sir Hugh de Lacy."

"I understand the monk in the stone carving," Joan remarked, "but what has the gargoyle got to do with the business?"

"Good question," Mr. Baxter replied. "The monks were right about one thing — and that was Sir Raymond's method of cultivation. While in the Middle East fighting the Turk he learned of the ancient Greeks and their Gods. Dionysus was their god of wine, and Greek farmers held various rites and rituals in his honour. It seems Sir Raymond brought some of these ideas home with him and put them into practice in Summerwood."

"So that horrible creature originally came from Greece and had something to do with Sir Raymond's wine cultivation?"

"Not just from Greece, Mrs. Mordaunt," laughed Mr. Baxter. "Our own pre-Christian legends have a similar basis. In the summer the woodland king, or "Green Man", and his followers (like the gargoyles on the church roof) ruled the season of plenty, but, as winter approached and the seasons waned, his adversary the holly king gained the upper hand." At the mention of the word "holly" Joan looked at

97

her husband in astonishment.

"Holly!" they uttered in unison.

"That's right — holly. Holly, mistletoe and the oak tree feature in the old Celtic pagan beliefs and superstition, and it seems that the early Christians used holly wreaths to ward off those mischievous woodland spirits. You must understand that, in an age of superstition and envy, it's no wonder Raymond de Lacy's successful vineyards attracted attention — especially if the monks had discovered some visible link with paganism."

The Mordaunts understood that *visible link* only too well — there were fingerprints on Robert's wine bottles to prove it.

"So you see — your mysterious stone slab, in what was the original wine cellar of the de Lacy manor house, has all the trappings of those old superstitious beliefs," Mr. Baxter observed. "It would be interesting to find out why the de Lacys put that culvert under your cellar in the first place — and where it ends."

* * *

They gathered round the hole in the floor, each holding a bucket filled to the top with water: the water contained a red dye, which, in the dimly lit cellar, had the appearance of blood.

"This should do the trick," said Mr. Baxter, as he slowly poured the red liquid into the cavity. "I'm sure that we'll find the outlet down by the stream near the causeway. Your turn now, Mrs. Mordaunt." Joan emptied her bucket, followed by her husband: the blood red water splashed and gurgled as it flowed away into the darkness. They dropped their buckets and dashed off on their quest. The spectacle of three adults puffing and panting across the causeway, scrambling and sliding down the grassy bank to the bed of the sleepy stream caused some astonishment and hilarity amongst the passengers in the local bus as it passed by. Like excited children in search of buried treasure, they splashed up and down the stream, scanning the bank in front of the Hall for any tell tale signs. Minutes passed by and still there was no sign of the red dye.

"I don't think it is going to work," Robert sniffed in disappointment. "I can't see any sign of it." They stood for while contemplating the bushes and tall grass covering the steep bank. It would seem that the gamble was a failure — until Joan glanced down at her feet. There, on the gently flowing surface of the water, was a narrow line of red dye stretching away to a clump of reeds in the distance.

"It's here!" she cried. "Look — it's coming from the reeds over there."

They splashed across to the spot, and sure enough a trickle of blood-like fluid emerged from the bank, just above the water line.

"This is definitely where the outlet is," Mr. Baxter proclaimed with obvious satisfaction, "but it has been covered up for some reason."

"Maybe the bank collapsed," suggested Robert, bending down to examine the undergrowth. "It looks as if it is seeping out from the rock."

"Well, there is only one way to find out," Joan announced. "We'll have to do a spot of digging."

"Good idea, Mrs. Mordaunt," Mr. Baxter agreed. "We'll come back after lunch and poke about a bit — see if we can find anything of interest under there."

They certainly did. It didn't take long for them to discover, when they began to excavate the bank later that afternoon, that they had found something very peculiar hidden there. All manner of sea shells and assorted pebbles came to light, and, as they dug further into the bank, they began to uncover pieces of coloured mosaic. They rested for a while and Mr. Baxter eyed the recess, deep in thought.

"I think we've stumbled across a man-made cave," he began. "You can see the chisel marks where the rock face has been cut away."

"You're right," Robert replied." "The same type of chisel marks are on the rock terraces in the wine cellar." Joan scrutinised the gaping hole in the bank, and pondered over a piece of coloured mosaic.

"Well, do you want to know what I think it was?" she asked. Her companions nodded. "Well . . . I think it was a grotto. There used to be a grotto here — and for some reason it has been sealed up."

"A grotto . . .? That's it!" Mr. Baxter declared. "I've heard of "well dressing", and I suppose that grottoes and shrines were popular in those times as well. Now why was this grotto covered up?"

They found the reason some half an hour (and vigorous elbow work) later, when the perspiring trio found the outlet of the culvert in the rock face. Something was jammed inside it, firmly blocking the entrance. At first they thought it was a circular metal plug, for it was almost a perfect fit. However, after part of the culvert had been chipped away, Robert was able to grip the edge of this metal plug and slowly pull it from its resting place. Out into the light of day, after centuries sealed in the culvert, emerged a statue. It was covered in a coating of mildew and fungus, and was accompanied by a nauseating stench, so familiar to the Mordaunts. There, in front of amazed hunters, lay the figure which had been forcibly abducted, centuries earlier, from its home in the Mediterranean by Sir Raymond de Lacy, to cooler alien climes, to stand in the grotto of Summerwood Manor. That debauched companion of Dionysus, the Greek God of Wine and Revelry, the satyr of ancient mythology and the *visible link* with Sir Raymond de Lacy, stared up at them with unblinking malevolent eyes. Its stone counterpart was currently on view on the parapet of the village church. The horns, pointed ears, tail and cloven hooves belonged to the night visitor in the cellar of number one, and in its taloned fingers it grasped a bunch of grapes and a wine cup: it was clear that the fingerprints on the wine bottles came from these same taloned fingers — from the secret playmate of their son, Graham — the bubble goblin.

* * *

The latest acquisition of the museum was on public display inside a glass case in the main foyer. An explanatory leaflet was available from the information desk.

THE SUMMERWOOD SATYR

The Summerwood Satyr is a genuine antique bronze sculpture, originating from Ancient Greece, probably in the area around Athens. Sir Raymond de Lacy brought the statue back from the crusades, and evidence has recently been uncovered to suggest that he built a grotto in the grounds of Summerwood Manor especially for the satyr. A culvert linked the grotto with the wine cellar of the manor, and was used for drainage in periods of prolonged rainfall. However, there is also evidence to suggest Sir Raymond performed some obscure ritual, in keeping with the Antique cult of resurrection and rebirth. Wine was poured down the culvert which then flowed from the grotto into the cup which can be seen in the hands of the satyr. This practice ceased when his younger brother Hugh de Lacy succeeded to the estate.

The Satyrs of Greek and Roman mythology were deities of woods and mountains, and dwelt in grottoes, groves, fountains and streams. They were the drinking companions of Bacchus (sometimes identified with Dionysus) the God of Wine, and spent their time pursuing nymphs, drinking wine, playing the flute or bagpipes, and generally indulging in mischief and orgies of one sort or another. However, anyone who spurned their master, or the rituals of his cult, were tormented to madness and destruction, and early Christian travellers went in fear of the woodland satyr. These creatures had a powerful influence on the superstitious medieval mind and figured prominently in the imaginary of the craftsmen of that age.

Number one, Summerwood Court (thanks to the Prestige Homes part exchange scheme) also had a new acquisition — in the form of new occupants. The original owners, the Mordaunts, worried by the sinister influence of the de Lacy inheritance on the mind of their son, Graham (not to mention his fixation about bubbles), had decided to part exchange their home and move elsewhere. What with the memories of the sitting tenant and the constant reminder perched up on the church roof, somehow the village of Summerwood had lost its appeal for Joan. As an added precaution they took the silver holly wreath with them — just in case of any *hidden extras* in the part exchange scheme. The new occupants in turn had made some changes to the house. The wine cellar was scrapped in favour of an adult play room, and a model railway (the abiding passion of the new owner) installed there instead. The lady of the house also installed one of her passions (collecting 'objet d'art') in the hallway. The shining marble figure of a wood nymph now graced the entrance lobby. A plaque on the polished wooden base described it.

ECHO THE WOOD NYMPH
an Oread deprived of speech by the Goddess Hera. Echo could only repeat the last words that were said to her.

"Oh darling!" the lady of the house called from the entrance lobby. "Oh darling . . . oh darling . . . oh darling . . ." The sound rose from the depths of the cellar, and echoed through the rooms above.

An irate master of the house stamped up the cellar stairs, muttering something to the effect that "those blasted echoes are driving me mad", and confronted his wife.

"Someone has been messing about with my trains — they're covered in sticky fingerprints!"

"Oh dear, I was just about to tell you the same thing, darling," she declared in alarm. "Someone has been fondling my lovely nymph — just look at those nasty black fingerprints on her breast!"

LYDIATE

Plain Ghost Trail   25

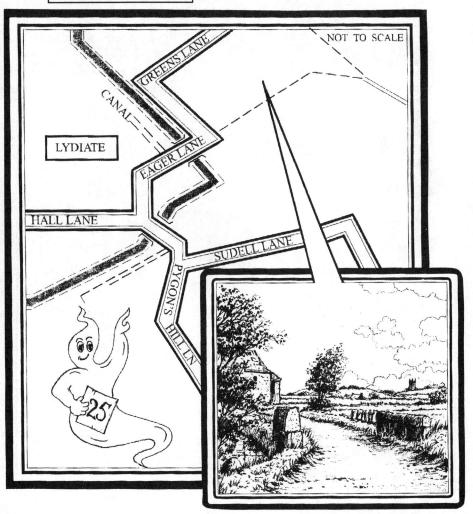

NOT TO SCALE

GREENS LANE

CANAL

LYDIATE

EAGER LANE

HALL LANE

SUDELL LANE

PYGON'S HILL LN

[INSET   *Farmland, Lydiate*]

THE POTATO CUP

"Have you heard the news about Peter Watkinson?"

"No . . ."

"He was rushed into hospital yesterday."

"Good Lord! I was only talking to him last week."

"Yes — I must say it gave me a bit of surprise when I heard about it."

"What's the matter with him?"

"Something of a mystery, so I've been told. He was found at the edge of Dark Wood early in the morning — out of his mind, so they say."

"That doesn't sound like Peter — he's a pretty level-headed sort of chap."

"That's what I thought at the time — until I heard about the blood."

"The blood . . .?"

"That's right. He kept babbling on about not having any."

This strange and chilling detail added a macabre dimension to the unfortunate mental breakdown of my old friend, Peter Watkinson, and I recalled the last time I saw him. Now, with hindsight, I realise that his premonition of some dreadful and imminent catastrophe was all too real.

"I can't shake off the feeling," he confided in a low voice, "that someone or something is following me."

The haunted expression in his eyes, coupled with the nervous tension in his bearing only served to highlight his unfortunate mental condition.

This explanation for his unsettled state of mind was, at the time, somewhat unbelievable — but after this latest news . . .

* * *

Dark Wood lies at the end of a narrow, badly rutted farm track, bordered by rampant weeds, brambles and overgrown hedges: it is hardly ever used. This wood is all that remains of a very old plantation, its origins dating back to the eighteenth century, and its tangled mass of branches and dense undergrowth present a foreboding and unsettling prospect to any traveller who happens to stumble across it: the locals avoid it, believing it to haunted — hence its title, Dark Wood.

This solitary thicket stood on land belonging to Pygon Farm, an equally ancient building, ringed by tall poplars and thorn bushes. The farm consisted of a house, barn and assorted outbuildings, and its origins could be traced back to the Middle Ages, when it held a prominent position in the manorial setup of this period.

However, since that time the house itself had seen many alterations and changes, the last being around the turn of the nineteenth century, in sharp contrast to its rustic companions. The ancient barn, in particular, had remained undisturbed since those early times, save for the addition of some storage bays to house the farm machinery. Unfortunately, its sorry appearance emphasised its extreme age: the roof sagged under the weight of heavy stone slabs, and the weathered brick walls and sandstone quoins were in dire need of repair. The owner of Pygon farm, faced with the cost of expensive restoration, had reluctantly decided to put the old barn on the market. The description in the estate agent's window described it as *"a delightful barn with character and potential for conversion into a desirable private dwelling, suitable for the discerning buyer who yearns for the peace and quiet of the traditional English countryside"*. Peter Watkinson, engaged to a distant cousin of mine and soon to be married, was that *discerning peace-lover*.

And so this tranquil spot, isolated from the hustle and bustle of modern life, became the rustic setting for a sequence of events which ended in the madness of my close friend. I have managed to piece together these various events from his notes and letters, and later from his own lips, when he had partially recovered from his ordeal. It seems that this sequence began part way through the conversion, or to be more exact, with the mysterious discovery in the rafters of the barn.

> *'Work on the main structure progressing slowly — weather and late delivery of building materials partly to blame — Bill (the joiner) found something under the roof, between the stone slabs and supporting timbers.'*

This entry in Peter's progress report for the month of April was the first indication of something out of the ordinary, and, in my opinion, the start of the sorry business. It seems that the joiner, during the process of replacing rotten timbers in the corner of the barn roof, came across an unusual object carefully hidden between the wooden beam and the stone roofing slab.

> *'Climbed up to the eaves and saw what Bill had found — looked like a pewter cup, possibly a chalice — rather battered and dinted, and wrapped in a bit of old cloth — may be a piece of a woman's shawl — not worth much.'*

This unusual find caused a flurry of heated debate as to ownership and speculation as to the reason for its secret concealment, but the excitement soon faded under the pressure of work deadlines and deteriorating weather conditions: the chalice was thrown unceremoniously into a cardboard box. Two days later, while checking the opposite corner of the barn roof, the joiner found another object carefully hidden beneath the stone slabs.

> *'Bill is getting a bit worried — he has found something*

else — looks like a knife — has a bone handle and curved blade — it was wrapped in a similar piece of shawl — he thinks that it smacks of witchcraft — I must say my curiosity has been aroused.'

This growing curiosity led to further debate and speculation. A chalice and knife found in two corners of the barn: perhaps the other corners of the barn would reveal more hidden objects.

'Decided to check the other corners — hunch proved correct — two more objects found — I think Bill could be right, after all.'

The entry went on to describe the items, and I, for my part, had to agree with the joiner's original conclusion: it did smack of witchcraft.

'After carefully lifting the slab we found some sort of medallion — had a weird design engraved on it — and in the final corner we found a small wooden box — it contained a button, bits of hair and a ring.'

The joiner had definite opinions about the next stage of proceedings.

'Bill says I ought to get rid of the stuff — burn the lot — says he wouldn't have it in the house if I gave it to him — told him it was superstitious nonsense, but still curious about the stuff — will sort it out after the barn is finished.'

It was clear from this entry that Peter had decided to ignore the joiner's sensible advice. Thereafter, the entries dealt with mundane details concerning the general progress of building work; that is, except for an entry underlined in red ink.

> *Found a rusty hook in the central joist in the main struc-*
> *ture underneath the roof— bits of mouldering rope hang-*
> *ing from it — possibly for hoisting heavy sacks or weights*
> *— floor beneath badly stained.'*

Two letters were fastened to this page with a paper clip. They were both addressed to Peter and came from the Regional Archive Department and his solicitor respectively. They made interesting reading, and prompted much speculation on Peter's motive for his original inquiries. The first letter was dated the 24th of April.

> *'Dear Mr. Watkinson,*
> *Thank you for your letter of the 20th of April, concerning*
> *the history of Pygon Farm. As far as I can ascertain from*
> *available records the farm belonged to the estates of the*
> *De Lyle family and subsequently passed to the Helsell*
> *family through marriage during the Reformation Period.*
> *This family was staunchly catholic and the estates were*
> *sequestered at the end of the Civil War. However, Pygon*
> *Farm remained in the hands of Maria Helsell, but her*
> *tenancy was short-lived. The property then passed to the*
> *Cruckshead family and remained in their hands until the*
> *line died out in the nineteen twenties. I shall be in contact*
> *with you if any further information comes to light.*
> *Yours sincerely,*
> *J. Butterworth*
> *(Assistant Archivist-Regional Service)'*

'Why did Peter want to know about the origins of Pygon farm?' I wondered. 'Normally his solicitor would check through the deeds of the property for any discrepancies or problems.' The second letter, from his solicitor, confirmed my train of thought. It was short and to the point.

> *'Dear Mr. Watkinson,*
> *With regard to your recent enquiry I am unable to find*
> *any details of occupancy for the years 1780 to 1815. For*
> *some reason the relevant papers are missing, but I can*
> *assure you that this does not, in any way, affect the legal-*
> *ity of the purchase of Pygon barn.*
> *Best wishes,*
> *David Tait.'*

My friend Peter Watkinson, secure within the psychiatric wing of the local hospital, held the key to the mystery, but his present mental condition ensured that it would remain locked inside his mind for the foreseeable future.

In the meantime, it would seem that the converted barn at Pygon Farm was unoccupied. I recalled Peter's words — *'something or some-one is following me'*. Perhaps the barn had a new tenant after all . . .?

* * *

'What a turn-up!'

I gazed in absolute amazement at the fine silverware arrayed on the shelves behind a polished glass door. The brass plaque on the base of the door described it as

THE VERMEIL COLLECTION
(donated by Mrs. Amy Groves, Long Island. 19...)

The rosewood display case stood in the Diplomatic Reception Room in the White House, home to the President of the United States of America. This part of the Presidential Executive Mansion, refurnished in the classic style of the late 18th and early 19th centuries, housed the silver collection, and was one of several rooms containing paintings, sculpture and furniture spanning the period of early settlement of the Colonies up to the present day. The various historical collections, gathered together by the Fine Arts Committee, were open to the public on certain days of the week, and, by sheer chance, the visit of "Heritage Trail Holidays - U.S.A." to Washington, D.C. on this particular day (I had planned this trip to America the previous year) included a tour of the White House as part of the travel itinerary: this was to be the final excursion of the holiday before returning to England.

The object of my undivided attention lay on the middle shelf, in the centre of a set of silver cups, but, in fact it was the label which had initially caused my astonishment.

THE POTATO CUP
Pygon Farm, Liddiate, Lancashire.

I thumbed swiftly through the exhibition catalogue for the relevant descriptive page and found the annotation.

'The Vermeil Collection, chiefly English and French covering a wide span from Renaissance to the present, was donated to the White House by Mrs. Amy Groves, of Long Island, New York. The influential Groves family line stretches back to Independence times, and this donation of these items of silverware illustrates the Georgian style so popular in that era. The silver cup (center shelf, left, footed cup, marked by Robert and Samuel Hennell) known as the Potato Cup, originated in England and was presented to Mary Cruckshead, of Pygon Farm, Liddiate, Lancashire, by the Agricultural Society of the Hundred of West Derby in 1812. It is made of silver, classified as

vermeil by the nature of its colour and workmanship.
'Vermeil' is a French term for silver gilt (i.e. silver with
an applied surface varnish of gold to give a reddish lus-
tre to the gilding). No record exists of how this unusual
cup came to America, but it has been in the Groves fam-
ily since the mid-nineteenth century.'

It seemed incredible that a direct link with Pygon Farm stood before me in the White House, of all places, thousands of miles from its
original home: and equally more incredible was the date, 1812. I recalled the lost records mentioned in the solicitor's letter to Peter —
'for the years 1780 to 1815'.

'It would seem that Mary Cruckshead was the tenant of Pygon
Farm in 1812, which certainly falls between those dates,' I calculated.
'Could this award by the Agricultural Society of the Hundred of West
Derby have anything to do with Peter's inquiry?'

The closing bell sounded, echoing through the rooms, and our
group concluded its tour of the White House: unfortunately the guide
was unable to help with further details about the Vermeil Collection.

"Gee, I'm sure sorry, sir," she apologised. "I don't have a clue
about the cup's background, but you gotta admit it's a great colour —
that darned cup gets a deeper red every year."

Some months later I found out why.

* * *

On my return to England I decided to follow up the "Agricultural
Society of the Hundred of West Derby" connection, and so I got in
touch with the local history society: The secretary was very helpful
and through her efforts I obtained details of the Agricultural Society's
Annual Meetings which covered presentations and awards going back
to the beginning of the nineteenth century. There I found the Society's
awards for 1812, and in amongst the notifications and rewards I found

the name Mary Cruckshead. The award stated.

'No: 4 The reward of a silver cup - value 5 guineas -
for the raising of the greatest quantity of potatoes, of
the best quality, from the same land, in the same year,
not less than two acres.

I was immediately struck by two facts: she was the only woman prize winner on the list, and she owned the farm, which was rather unusual in those days. She undoubtedly had a gardener's touch to produce such a yield of potatoes, when one considers the primitive machinery, lack of modern fertilizers and pest control methods of those times. *So what was her secret?* Perhaps the assistant archivist, in the meantime, had uncovered more information about the farm. I decided to phone Mr. Butterworth.

"Hello. I'm calling on behalf of Peter Watkinson," I began, recounting the circumstances of my friend's illness. "I wonder if you have uncovered any further information on past tenants of Pygon Farm?"

"Yes, as a matter of fact I was going to get in touch with Mr. Watkinson about a previous owner at the time of the Civil War," he replied. "Her name was Maria Helsell, and she was a spinster who inherited Pygon Farm from her uncle. Unfortunately, because of her single status she didn't have a protector, and so was vulnerable to many social pressures. During her tenancy the land which she had inherited became very fertile, which considerably increased its value. Many cast envious eyes on the farm, but she refused to sell and held out against all those landowners who wanted to get their hands on that valuable land. Unfortunately she was denounced for practices involving sorcery, and was tried and executed by burning at the stake. Her farm and adjoining acreage became the property of the Cruckshead family, her chief denouncers and staunch supporters of Cromwell and the Commonwealth."

"So you think the farm was obtained in a rather unsavoury way?"

"Yes, I would think so," he answered, "— and the local people had the same idea as well. I gather that they avoided Dark Wood whenever possible. It was said that the kindling for Maria Helsell's burning came from trees in that wood; so over the years, what with strange sounds and sightings, it acquired a sinister reputation."

"Wasn't there another single woman, and called Mary Cruckshead," I asked, "who owned the farm at the beginning of the nineteenth century?"

"Now, you do surprise me," the archivist replied. "Where did you come by that information?" I proceeded to recount the details of my holiday and the discovery of the Potato Cup.

"Well, that is absolutely remarkable," he enthused. "The whereabouts of that cup has remained a mystery since the early nineteenth century."

"Well, I can tell you where it is now," I laughed. "It's in a polished glass case in the White House. But what happened to Mary Cruckshead?"

"I'm afraid there are no farm records for the period prior to 1815," replied Mr. Butterworth. "However, your information about the Potato Cup would indicate that, for some reason, this tenant left England and settled in America."

"And I suppose that's when the Groves family acquired the cup."

"That's possible," he replied. "Now that I have this latest information I'll check out our contacts in the United States. I'm sure that they'll come up with something on the Groves family."

'And possibly the reason why Amy Groves donated the cup to the White House,' I thought to myself. In the meantime, a note arrived from the hospital: it was from Peter's doctor. It seemed Peter's health had improved and he wanted to see me — urgently.

* * *

"Thank god you've come," the patient whispered from his bed. "I'm afraid I did something very stupid — and I don't know what to do about it." Although well on the road to recovery Peter was a changed man: his recent traumatic experience had definitely left its mark. His eyes still had that haunted expression, but his gaunt features and constant nervous twitching were recent additions. He had developed an unfortunate habit of searching the faces of all who passed the room, so that he was always in a constant state of alertness — *as if watching and waiting for something or someone.*

"We found some bits and pieces in the roof of the barn," he continued in a low voice.

"Yes, I know — I read about it in your journal."

"One of the pieces was a medallion and . . ." Peter shuddered and halted, reliving the experience. "I took a fancy to the damned thing, even after Bill's warning about sorcery — wore it on several occasions."

"That was a daft thing to do," I snorted. "You shouldn't have meddled in that sort of thing — you never know what could happen."

"Nothing did," he replied, "— at first, that is." The next part of his story was somewhat garbled, mainly because of the Dark Wood episode, so I'll try to relate the events in the correct order.

It seems that one evening, a few days after the weird discoveries, he placed the medallion around his neck, and, glancing across the farmyard, saw a woman standing by the window in one of the upstairs rooms of the farm. He was immediately captivated by her handsome features and long tresses of dark hair beauty which fell over her shoulders. And what's more, she was staring intently at the barn. Peter was bewildered. The owners of the farm were away at the time, and the house was supposedly empty, so who could she be — and what was she doing there? He decided to investigate. The sun was setting over Dark Wood as he crossed the farmyard and unlocked the front door: the house was silent. In the failing light he called out — and a voice, sensuous and inviting, fulfilling his earlier vision, floated down from above.

"Enter . . . come . . . come to me. . . ." The whispered words faded
away into the dark recesses of the house. He searched the building,
cautiously entering each room, hoping to meet the sensuous creature
— but, to his disappointment, all was silent, all was empty. He had a
restless night, disturbed by dreams of Dark Wood.

Some nights later, as he drove up the misty lane to the farm, he
saw the mysterious creature again, flitting across the farmyard, caught
in the glare of the car headlights. To his astonishment, considering the
cold weather, he saw she was naked, except for a shawl (in retrospect
the same as the cloth wrappings in the roof) which partly covered her
shapely figure: she momentarily paused and beckoned seductively to
him — then swept away through the swirling mist and entered the
barn. He jumped out of the car to follow her and dashed through the
door, vainly searching for the lovely creature. The barn was silent and
empty. And then he recounted the final episode.

The very next evening (Midsummer's Eve) he was working late in
the attic and heard a voice, soft and light, below. He thought at first
that it was singing some obscure melody, but, on paying more attention, realised that it was actually chanting — a weird sound, rising and
falling like the wild wind, with the words all jumbled up. He crept
down stairs, just in time to see the same naked, shawl-draped vision
pass through the door into the farm yard, and some spell-like impulse
drew him on, urging him to follow her.

The pale rays of a full moon bathed the land in a soft glow, high-
lighting the white skin of the naked intruder, and the moving figure
turned down the lane towards Dark Wood, gliding swiftly over the
rutted uneven track. Anyway, he was close on her heels when she
entered the trees, seemingly unhindered by the tangle of branches and
dense bushes. Not to be outdone, and driven on by a primitive desire
for this lovely creature, he struggled through this mass of tangled vegetation and eventually reached the centre of the ancient wood. There,
within a small clearing, stood the skeleton of an old oak tree. There

was no sign of his quarry. The woman had vanished — but only for a moment.

"And then I saw her," Peter declared with a shudder, "rising out of the ground mist from the base of the tree — absolutely starkers."

"I bet you thought it was your lucky night," I gasped.

"You've said it," he agreed. "I told you she was good looking — and she was — all over! I just stood there, rooted to the spot, held in a trance, grasping the medallion around my neck. And then she stirred and began to move towards me, smiling and chanting softly 'Come, come to me . . . come to me'. I knew what she wanted from the way that she beckoned to me with her long fingers, and I was ready to reciprocate in every way. I was totally under her spell — until she brought her other hand from behind her back, and I saw what she was holding."

"What?"

"A knife — the carved dagger we found in the roof. And then the mist cleared and I saw a stained leather bucket and length of rope lying in the roots of the old tree. I had seen those sort of stains before — and at that moment I knew what she really wanted, and what that rusty hook in the barn roof was for." He paused, trembling at the memory of this appalling confrontation. "She came closer, overpowering my senses, but somehow, call it a supreme effort of will, I somehow managed to break away from her sensual power: I turned and bolted, my assailant close on my heels. The wood was filled with a wild primitive sound, of screeches and cries rising and falling, and I could feel her cold breath on the back of my neck as I reached the edge of the trees — but I got no further."

He placed his face in his hands and composed himself for the next gruesome detail. "They rose out of the mist," he whispered, "their pale arms reaching out, their bony fingers grasping and clawing at my legs. They were creatures with lifeless eyes and open mouths filled with squirming maggots — and they were trying to pull me to the ground. She was behind me and they were in front — there was no escape.

The terrible sound rose to a crescendo, making my senses reel, and I began to sway unsteadily under this onslaught of ghastly sight and horrifying sound. The medallion hung like a heavy burden around my neck, its weight pulling me down to the damp earth. I tore it from my neck and flung it at those hideous beings, before collapsing to the ground as the first rays of daylight broke the night sky. And that's were I was found — at the edge of Dark Wood."

He looked up at me, waiting for a derisory comment, expecting an exclamation of disbelief, but, although it all sounded so incredible, I refrained from any disparaging reply.

"That's not an experience I'd like to go through," I replied, "or wish on anyone else." He sensed that I believed him, and breathed a sigh of relief.

"And now I don't know what to do about it all," he continued.

"But you got away in the end."

"For the moment — but I'm sure *she* won't give me up. I'm sure I've seen her in here, in the ward, at night, and heard her chanting — calling my name and waiting for me to join her."

"It's your imagination," I reassured him.

"I don't think so. The only way I can think of stopping her," replied Peter, shaking his head, "is to get rid of those things from the barn. I should have taken Bill's advice in the first place. So now I'm asking for your help."

"What had you in mind?"

"I know it's asking a lot — but will you go back and bury that awful stuff under the old tree in that infernal wood. I'm sure that awful place holds the key to this nightmare, and this way I hope she'll be confined to that dismal spot for ever."

I didn't like the idea, but, for the sake of my friend's sanity, I promised to do as he asked. When I agreed to his proposal I could see the relief and gratitude in his face, and he became more relaxed in his bearing and manner, as if a weight had been lifted from his shoulders:

I left him in a happier frame of mind.

My mind on the other hand was greatly perturbed at the thought of the coming challenge.

* * *

The distant hills lay in a blue heat haze, basking in the warm rays of the midday sun, crowning a perfect country setting. But even at this time of day, at the height of a glorious English summer, with the sound of insect and bird mingling with the gentle rustle of golden corn in a light breeze, Dark Wood stood sullen and foreboding: no wonder the locals avoided it. I drew near, and with some reluctance, and, I have to admit, growing apprehension, entered this silent place, seemingly devoid of natural life. After what seemed an interminable length of time, twisting, turning and fighting my way through the dense foliage, I reached the centre of the wood — and the old tree. It was exactly as Peter had described it. In the daylight it looked equally as menacing, and I too sensed the presence of something unnatural and hostile; Dark Wood's reputation was fully justified. I recalled Peter's haunting words — "*someone or something watching me*".

I began to dig down, my spade striking the tangled roots, and, after some feverish moments of energetic spade work, to my horror I uncovered something which caused me to leap back in shock. Bones, burnt and blackened, remnants of tattered shawl-like cloth, mixed with dry earth and bits of what looked like a leather bucket, saw the light of day for the first time in centuries: I stood looking down at a human skull, the earthly remains of some long forgotten enchantress (or should it be guardian) of Dark Wood.

'Did I hear the whispered words *"come to me . . . come to me"* and a cold breath of air on the back of my neck?' It took all my will power to stay put, but I steadied my nerves, placing Peter's "findings", wrapped in the shawl remnants, into the deep cavity with the other incumbent: within minutes I had buried the lot. However, as I flattened the loose earth with the spade, stamping it down with my boots, a piercing shriek rent the air. I can only describe it as the painful scream of someone deprived of power and influence, or of a spell being countered or broken (although now I think it was my imagination) and I had no desire to wait for a second vengeful cry. I turned swiftly and fled from that evil place in absolute panic. Only when I at last reached my car, and had partially recovered from the experience, did a thought, disconcerting and frightening, surface in my mind.

The medallion still lay somewhere in Dark Wood, unfound and unburied — a continuing threat.

* * *

Some months later I received two letters: one was from Mr. Butterworth, and the other from Mrs. Groves. The first letter revealed a strange coincidence.

> *'Thanks to your information regarding Mary Cruckshead my American contacts have been in touch. They inform me that she probably arrived in America in 1815, and some time later met and married an American widower, Charles Groves, moving to his farm in New Hampshire. However, for some reason known only to herself, she took all her personal records with her, which explains their absence here. Another piece of information might interest you. In my research into the farm I uncovered a rather unusual coincidence. Believe it or not, in tracing the family line on the female side I found that Mary Cruckshead was a direct descendant of Maria Helsell, who was burned for sorcery in the 17th century. So you can see the irony of the situation — Pygon Farm came back to that family in a round about way.'*

The second letter revealed a further and more disturbing coincidence. It was from Mrs. Groves, and began with the usual sentiments. It then went on to explain the reason for her generous donation to the White House collection.

'The silver (I don't think it's vermeil at all) cup came into my late husband's possession on the death of his uncle in New Hampshire. It originally came to the Groves family by way of an English woman, Mary Cruckshead (she married a Groves at the beginning of the last century). The cup was found in an old trunk, along with various papers and accounts from a farm in England, and, for some reason, had never been displayed with the rest of the family silverware. I now think I know the reason why. From the very first I didn't like the feel of it (how can I put it — something of a slippery slimy feel that made my flesh creep). And its blood red colour put me off as well, but my husband, George, thought I was over-sensitive. Anyway, at his suggestion, I placed it with the other silver (the family had collected some fine pieces over the years) — and guess what happened? Over the next few months the silver pieces next to the cup began to turn red! Once again George said I was imagining it, but I wasn't to be put off. I took a closer look at those old papers in the trunk, and reading between the lines it was obvious from the farm records that the place was getting Mary Cruckshead down (there's a note about itinerant labourers going missing — and she keeps referring to a place called Dark Wood). Then, stuffed right down in a side pocket of one of the account books I found an old scrap of parchment (check out the enclosed photocopy). After reading it I came to the conclusion that the Potato Cup had nothing to do with potatoes — but something a deal

*more sinister. I heard about the First Lady's silver collec-
tion, and when George died I offered it to the White House
(I'm not a Democrat and don't care much for that bunch
up there — so I hope that darned cup upsets them). I was
glad to get it off my hands and out of the house.'*

I examined the enclosed photocopy and came to the same conclusion as Mrs. Groves. The faded scrawl was in verse, and although it
was unsigned the date and initials would suggest that it was composed by Maria Helsell. It had remained hidden somewhere in Pygon
Farm for centuries, along with the other sinister (or should I say sac-
rificial) items, until they fell into the hands of Mary Cruckshead, her
descendant. And then *she* went on to win the Potato Cup.

*Oh Wanderer, behold ~
A sterile earth so forlorn, so bare,
This barren soil no crop woulds't yield
'til upon t'great oak in yon wood there
Such spells to pagan Pan were seal'd*

*Oh Wanderer, lo ~
A sacrifice at length cometh forth
At midnight on Midsommer's Eve.
So dust to dust and blood to earth,
Ah, thereafter such fruits. Pray do not grieve,*

*Oh Wanderer, nay ~
For those from earthly coils releas'd
Beneath this bounteous harvest land.
Their vengeful souls cry out for peace
In Dark Wood. Go! Lest thee too be damn'd
M H 1653*

* * *

When Peter was fit and well enough to travel he immediately broke off his engagement to my distant cousin (his recent and ghastly encounter with an enchanting member of the fair sex put paid to all thoughts of marriage) much to the chagrin of both sets of parents and friends. He sold up and moved abroad.

"I'm looking for some place without trees and old stone buildings," he confided in me at the time. However, for his peace of mind I neglected to tell him about the present whereabouts of the medallion. He has remained a confirmed bachelor ever since, and has assured me on several occasions that he will never, under any circumstances whatsoever, visit the capital of the United States of America.

With this emphatic declaration I find myself in complete agreement, and, for my part, I have given up eating potatoes.

HOOLE-BRETHERTON

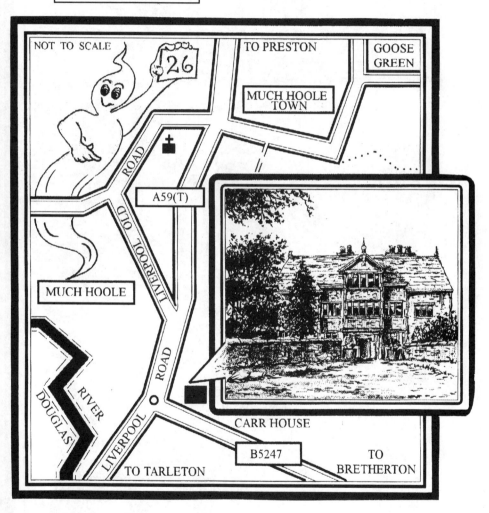

Plain Ghost Trail   26

NOT TO SCALE

26

TO PRESTON

GOOSE GREEN

MUCH HOOLE TOWN

A59(T)

LIVERPOOL OLD ROAD

MUCH HOOLE

LIVERPOOL ROAD

RIVER DOUGLAS

CARR HOUSE

B5247

TO TARLETON

TO BRETHERTON

[INSET   *Carr House, Bretherton*]

THE TRULY MARVELLOUS PROOF

An ear-splitting scream pierced the night and reverberated through the peaceful house, waking Mrs. Rowland from her slumbers with a terrific jolt. Startled and alarmed by this horrifying shriek the dismayed woman sat bolt upright in the darkness, gathering her senses. A faint sound, a muffled sobbing, eddied through the still night air, filling her with dread: she knew that sound well. Leaping from her bed she rushed out of the room onto the landing, straight to the door of her daughter's bedroom. Mrs. Rowland flung the door open, fumbling, in her panic, with the light switch — and stood aghast at the appalling scene which confronted her eyes. Mary, her seven year old daughter, crouched in the far corner of the room, her hands clasped tightly over her eyes, sobbing and shaking uncontrollably in her thin floral nightdress. The floor of the bedroom was strewn with a jumble of Christmas decorations, 'stocking fillers' and presents, intermixed with pieces of clothing, which Mrs. Rowland immediately recognised by their shape and size. They were the torn remnants of her daughter's favourite doll. However, the most chilling aspect of this frightening scene lay scattered around the trembling child.

The doll's arms and legs had been ripped from its torso, and the head had been pulled and twisted from the body, attached only by a slim thread. It stared up, wide eyed, at Mrs. Rowland.

There was no sign of the malevolent "Father Christmas".

* * *

Some months earlier Mrs. Rowland had received a parcel. The enclosed letter explained its contents.

> *'Dear Alison,*
> *I have just had a clear-out of my father's attic. You prob-*
> *ably know that he's moving into a retirement home — he*
> *can't manage on his own any more. Anyway, I found some-*
> *thing from my childhood up there and thought that Mary*
> *might like it for a Christmas present. It's in a bit of a*
> *state, I'm afraid, but no doubt you can do something with*
> *it, knowing your flair with the sewing machine.*
> *Love to all the family,*
> *Margaret.*
> *PS. You must come down for a visit soon — it's a long*
> *time since we've seen you and Mary.'*

The *something* turned out to be leather-bound box, stained and discoloured, with tarnished brass corner plates, hinges, carrying handle and lock. Its age was further accentuated by what appeared to be a faded design, possibly a crest or coat of arms, on the scored lid. Her daughter Mary eyed this antiquated piece of leather, wood and metal with some reservation.

"I don't think I like it," she observed, holding her nose. "It doesn't smell very nice, does it, mummy?"

"I'm sure it's going to be something you'll like, silly," her mother replied. "Aunty Margaret thinks so, anyway." Mary still wasn't convinced.

"I think it looks like a coffin."

Her daughter had a point. The old box did, in some respects, resemble a miniature coffin; and it did smell very musty into the bargain. Her mother banished the thought and laughed.

"Shall we open it and see what Aunty Margaret has sent you?" she replied. "Now where is the key?" Alison searched in the envelope and the parcel paper, and came up with a blank. It seemed that the key was missing, and the box would remain locked for the time being. Her sharp-eyed daughter resolved the dilemma.

"What's that black stuff," Mary asked her puzzled mother, "— underneath the box?" Alison rubbed it with her thumb.

"It's sticky tape," she cried, "— and here's the key!"

The key turned easily in the lock, and some moments later Alison and her nervous daughter gazed down at the contents of the mysterious container.

"Well, I never . . ." Alison paused in amazement.

"Ooh, look, mummy!" Mary squealed in delight, her initial aversion to the "coffin" evaporating in an instant. "It's a dolly!"

The incumbent was, indeed, a doll, dressed in fashionable clothes of bygone times. And Mary was right about her first observation. The box, like a coffin, was specially formed and lined in velvet, and, as Alison carefully prised the doll from the box, she realised, from the way the doll adhered to the velvet interior, that it had lain there, undisturbed for many years. Its clothing, released at last from the restricting confines of the box, emitted a musty, pungent odour which caused Mary to wrinkle her nose in disgust.

"Phew . . ." she gasped. "It smells nasty, doesn't it, mummy?"

"Yes. That's because the doll is probably very old and has been in the box for a long time," her mother replied. "But not to worry — we'll soon have it smelling nice and clean. You can help me to wash it." Mary, overcoming her repugnance, quickly warmed to the idea.

"Can I hold it, mummy," she begged, " — please let me hold it."

"Well, all right — but be very careful," her mother replied, gently placing the doll in her daughter's outstretched hands. "We don't want to break it, do we?"

Mary shook her head. "And Aunty Margaret would be upset too," she added wisely. The dark, unblinking eyes of the doll, staring up at Mary through wisps of fine hair, seemed to agree with this childish observation. "What shall we call her?"

Alison pondered the question for a moment. Her daughter had

several dolls and soft toys in her bedroom, with a variety of names to suit their special characteristics. Fluffy, Snuzzles and Chumps were perfectly respectable names for modern synthetic toys, but did not seem entirely appropriate for a refined, aristocratic doll from another age.

"We ought to choose a sensible name for her," she mused. "Something with style—something elegant." Mary was of the same opinion, and gazed at the doll, contemplating the upturned face.

"I know, Mummy," she said thoughtfully. "Can I call her Lady Sarah?"

"Now that is a good choice," her mother agreed. "I must say, she does have the look of royalty about her."

Unfortunately, the doll's royal status did not exempt her from the ravages of age and neglect: Lady Sarah was decidedly unwell. Mary was the first to notice it, for, when she began to remove the refined clothes from the doll, she noticed that one of the doll's arms was extremely loose where it joined the body.

"Look, mummy," she cried, "I think her arm is going to fall off." Her mother examined the arm, and came to the same conclusion.

"Oh dear," she said. "I think you're right. We'll have to leave the doll as it is, just in case we damage it any further."

Mary was crestfallen. She had taken a shine to Aunty Margaret's present and this news came as a blow. Her disappointment showed in her dejected expression.

"If Daddy came home," she sniffed, " he would mend it for me."

The mention of "Daddy" was something of a red rag to Mrs. Rowland. The behaviour of an selfish, violent husband, with all the attendant unhappiness and misery which he caused her, had resulted in a breakdown of the marriage. "Irreconcilable differences", to quote the divorce papers, didn't scratch the surface of what she had gone through, and Mary's occasional reference to her "Daddy" only served to revive memories of those unhappy times. He was, however, devoted to his daughter, although, as Alison surmised from the way he often touched and looked at her, possibly for the wrong reasons. He had not agreed with the court's decision to award total custody of the child to the mother, to the extent that Alison felt he was, in his present state of mind, quite capable of resorting to abduction to get his way. Mary could end up living in some far flung continent. So, when it came to her daughter health and happiness, Mrs. Rowland was an extremely protective mother.

"Oh, I don't think he could, Mary," Alison replied, remembering how useless her "Daddy" was around the house.

"Then, why can't we take Lady Sarah to the doctors and have her arm mended?"

"I wish we could," Alison sighed, "but there aren't any doctors for this sort of thing, I'm afraid."

"Couldn't we take her to the hospital instead?"

Alison was about to reject this plea when the word "hospital" jogged her memory. She remembered something she had read in a magazine. It was, she recalled, an article about repairing and renovating dolls and dolls' houses, and the caption *'Bretherton House Doll Museum and Surgery'* briefly flashed through her mind. She picked her daughter up and gave her a hug. "You're quite right, darling," she smiled, " we can take her to hospital after all."

Lady Sarah was about to enter an age of modern medicine. Her treatment, however, was to have grave repercussions for Mrs. Rowland and her daughter.

* * *

Alison found the advertisement in the trade section of the Countryside Journal.

BRETHERTON HOUSE DOLL MUSEUM

This unique museum contains a comprehensive and exclusive collection of dolls and related toys, past and present, including British, American, French, German and

*other carefully selected dolls from around the world. Why
not come along and enter this fascinating and enchanting world of dolls and miniatures. Traditional model
houses, furniture and accessories are also on display. Our
impressive Dolls' Hospital offers a specialised repair and
restoration service and we can advise on all aspects of
the miniature scene.*

Open Monday-Saturday, 10.00-5.00.
Closed all day Wednesday.
Ample free parking.

Lady Sarah made an immediate and profound impression on the museum guide, an elderly lady of ample proportions and homely disposition.

"My word, young lady," she breathed, addressing Mary in a hushed voice, "this is a very unusual doll." She carefully lifted the doll out of the box. "In fact I haven't seen anything quite like it before," she continued. "Has she got a name?"

"Yes — Lady Sarah," Mary replied in a serious voice. "And she is very poorly. I think she has hurt her arm."

"Ah, I see what you mean," the guide nodded, examining the loose arm. "We'll have to ask the Doll Doctor to have a look at her."

"Will he make her better?"

"I'm sure he will," her mother reassured her daughter, and the homely museum guide confirmed her opinion with an encouraging nod.

"He has cured many dolls, so don't you worry your little head about it. If your mummy would like leave your telephone number with me, I'll call you when Lady Sarah is well enough to come home."

Mrs. Rowland took her daughter's hand, and Mary left the museum in a happier frame of mind.

* * *

Alison received the call a fortnight to the day later: It had been a trying time. Her daughter's constant questions about the doll's state of health and homecoming had driven Alison "up the wall". Mary had behaved like a worried parent, dashing to answer the telephone on every occasion. But now Lady Sarah was ready and well enough to come home, and Alison decided to surprise Mary, when she met her out of school, by collecting the doll that very day.

The museum guide seemed genuinely pleased to see her — perhaps too pleased.

"Oh, I'm so glad you could come so quickly, Mrs. Rowland," she exclaimed, leading her to the ground floor Bretherton Room. Antiquated items and domestic implements from the past adorned this exhibition room, and paintings and prints hung from the panelled walls, displaying the history of the house and its previous owners. Alison was puzzled by the guide's tone.

"Is there a problem?"

"No — not at all . . ." The guide hesitated for a moment, somewhat flustered. "Mr. Fell, our curator and restorer, would like to see you for a moment," she quickly continued, but Alison sensed there was definitely something wrong. "If you would like to go up to his work room on the top floor and wait for him, I'll let him know that you've arrived." Alison turned and began to climb the carved wooden staircase.

"Oh, I forgot to mention that Mr. Fell found something in the doll," she continued, reaching under the cash desk. She brought out a white envelope. "He asked me to give it to you, just in case you happened to call to collect the doll on his day off." Alison took the envelope and opened the seal, releasing a pungent odour which she immediately recognised. The musty smell from the interior of the Lady Sarah's box floated through the air, and the guide immediately covered her nose with her handkerchief.

"It smells awful," she spluttered, turning her head away in disgust.

"Did he say what he found in the doll?"

"Well, he did say that it was something very unusual," the guide replied, recovering from the nauseous smell. "Not the sort of thing you would expect to find inside a doll."

Alison held the envelope at arms length, and carefully tipped the contents on to the cash desk. A malodorous piece of parchment, creased and stained, slipped out in a cloud of dust. Alison gingerly picked it up and smoothed the faded paper.

"It's in such a bad state, I can hardly read it," she muttered. "What do you make of it?"

"It looks like a jumble of letters and numbers to me," the bemused lady replied. "Don't you think it looks a bit like algebra?"

Alison examined the faint characters and came to the same conclusion. Both sides of the parchment were covered in mathematical calculations, and she recognised one set of symbols from her school days.

"I'm sure I know this one," she murmured. "$-x^2 + y^2 = a^2$. That's Py-someone's funny theorem, isn't it?"

"Pythagoras . . . ?"

"Yes, that's him," Alison nodded. "Isn't it about the hypotenuse and the squares on a triangle being equal — something like that?"

"Oh, don't ask me," the mystified guide replied. "It's all 'double dutch' to me, I'm afraid. Perhaps Mr. Fell can help you with that."

Alison replaced the parchment in the envelope, and climbed the stairs to a long passage which gave access to the various rooms housing the doll collections. A decorated sign above each door described their particular contents. *'Ancient Dolls'*, *'Ritual and Religious Dolls'* and *'Early European Dolls'* on one side of this passage faced *'19th century Dolls'* and *'Modern Dolls'* on the other, each room containing glass display cases, wall charts an associated memorabilia At the far end she came to a rope barrier with a notice hanging from it.

NO ADMITTANCE - STAFF ONLY

Beyond this barrier a smaller flight of stairs led up to what could be described as the attic section of the old house, now isolated from the public and untouched by the designers and decorators of the museum below. Here she found herself in another age, in a part of the building unchanged by the passing years. The passage was dark and gloomy, and a pervading smell of dank wood and mildewed fabric gave the impression of gradual decay: It was decidedly spooky and Alison could not help but shiver with apprehension. The door at the far end opened slightly, allowing a shaft of light to pierce the gloom of this forbidding part of Bretherton House. She hurried to the door and knocked briefly. For a moment she thought she heard a movement, a soft shuffle, beyond the door — but all was quiet. She pushed it open and entered the room. A soft light filtered through an open window the cold November day was waning.

"Mr. Fell . . . ?"

There was no reply.

Alison gazed around the room, and her eye was drawn to a strange contraption at the far end, facing the window. She walked towards it, her curiosity overcoming her nervousness: the sound of her footsteps on the bare wooden floor boards echoed around her.

'It looks like a primitive telescope,' she thought, contemplating what seemed to be some form of astronomical apparatus. The primitive telescope rested in a rough cradle, mounted at one end of a rough wooden beam, and a large wooden board was fixed to the opposite end. A piece of parchment was pinned to this board, and the whole apparatus was aligned with the horizon. Alison was quick to realise the purpose of this weird design, for, as the setting sun's rays broke through a cloud-filled November sky, they passed through the lens of the telescope and projected an image of the sun onto the parchment at the far end of the wooden beam. 'It must be an old toy brought in for repair,' she concluded.

However, as she turned to leave she also noticed that the room itself was cluttered up with junk. Dusty cardboard boxes and packing cases lay stacked against the walls, and shelves, piled high with assorted items, were fixed precariously to the walls. It would seem that this room was used for storage and stock, rather than repair work. And then a soft noise alerted her senses, and, to her astonishment, she realised she was not alone. She spun round — and saw a mysterious figure bending over the telescope.

"Ah . . . " Alison drew a deep breath. "Mr. Fell . . . ?

The figure straightened up, and turned towards her. It was a young man in his early twenties, dressed in very odd attire, which Alison ascribed to the outlandish garments popular with the modern generation. He was tall and gaunt, with unkempt hair which fell in long strands over his shoulders and face. The deathly pallor of his complexion gleamed beneath these straggled wisps of hair, giving an impression of extreme ill health, and his deep-set eyes fixed her with a steadfast gaze. He had the air of an scholar, accentuated by his flowing academic gown and cravat, which, in no sense of the imagination, could be described as the working attire of a repairer and restorer of broken dolls.

"You . . . you startled me, Mr. Fell," Alison stammered, regaining her composure. "The museum guide mentioned that you wanted to see me."

The sickly young man stared blankly at her. He remained motionless and silent.

"She told me that you had found this in my doll," she continued, under the growing impression, from his blank expression, that he was either stupid or drunk. She took the faded parchment from the envelope and held it out. "I think it's some sort of algebra, and I wondered if you knew what it meant."

The effect of the parchment on the silent figure was astonishing, to say the least. In an instant his whole bearing was transformed. His eyes burned with rage, and a hoarse cry burst from his lips.

"My calculations!"

He glared at the terrified woman.

"Where in heaven's name did thee find them?"

"In my doll — the one with the broken arm."

136

"A doll . . . ! A doll?"

He didn't seem to understand what she meant, or what a doll was; but one thing was plain to see. He wanted his "calculations" back, and he intended to get them. He sprang forward, arms outstretched, intent on a violent solution to resolve the matter, but Alison reacted with speed born of absolute panic and fear. In an instant she leaped back, narrowly avoiding the grasp of his long ink-stained fingers, and spun round. Fleeing from the room, she made her escape down the dark passage and stairs, only to trip over the rope barrier at the bottom. Alison tumbled in a sprawling heap onto the museum floor.

"Are you all right?" A friendly voice brought her to her senses, and strong hands helped her to her feet. "Whatever's the matter?" The voice and hands belonged to a middle aged man, with receding hair and a jovial face. "You look as if you've seen a ghost."

"I don't know anything about ghosts," Alison snorted, "but that Mr. Fell needs locking up. He's just flipped his lid up there!"

"I beg your pardon, madam," the man retorted, somewhat taken aback by this heated remark. "I'm Mr. Fell — and I can assure you that I haven't "flipped my lid", as you put it!"

"But you . . ." Alison paused totally confused. "I mean *him* up in the workroom — I thought he was Mr. Fell."

"Well, as far as I know, there is no one else in the attic section," the man replied confidently, "— that is, unless a member of the public has strayed up there by mistake."

"He didn't look like your normal member of the public to me," Alison asserted with a toss of her head. "In my opinion he's an escaped lunatic hiding up there."

"I'm sure you're mistaken," the real Mr. Fell spoke in a reassuring voice. "Let's go up and find out, shall we?"

Alison reluctantly agreed, and followed him back up the stairs. He opened the first door at the beginning of the passage, and went in.

"There . . ." He turned and beckoned her into the room. "What did I tell you — there's no-one here."

137

"This isn't the room," Alison replied with a snort. "It's the one at the end of the passage — the one with the funny telescope in it." She pointed to the far door, and Mr. Fell demeanour changed.

"Ah, you mean the old storeroom," he replied in a serious tone of voice. "You say a telescope?" He obviously knew something . . .

"Yes, a funny telescope with a board at the end — pointing out of the window," she continued. "And when that lunatic saw the old paper that you found in my doll, he turned really nasty."

"Ah, I see." His expression changed at the mention of the doll and parchment. "So you are Mrs. Rowland. I wanted to have a word with you about your doll. But first, just let me check the storeroom." Alison followed him. To her amazement and relief, when Mr. Fell cautiously opened the door, she found the storeroom empty. There was no sign of either the telescope or the intimidating stranger. "Well . . . you can see for yourself," he continued, "— there's no one here." Alison was perplexed by the whole affair.

"I'm beginning to think you might be right about that ghost, after all," she remarked, completely puzzled by the whole affair. "You probably think I need locking up."

"Nonsense," Mr. Fell replied, observing the baffled expression on Alison's face. "Anyway, you look as if you could do with a strong cup of tea." He took her arm. "Come along, and I'll explain as much as I can."

Moments later Alison sat in the 'doll hospital' workroom, clasping a mug of hot tea, while the curator settled down to tell his tale. He began with an explanation on the origins of Bretherton House, before it became a museum.

"The house was built for James Bretherton, a wealthy landowner, at the beginning of the seventeenth century. He had two sons, John and Charles. John inherited the property, and his brother became a merchant in Holland — Amsterdam, I think. As a matter of fact the bricks for the old village church came from the ballast in his ships, which docked in the River Westland. You can see some of the family portraits in the Bretherton Room on the ground floor."

"Yes, I saw them. They looked a dusty old bunch to me. And the house is much older than I imagined, too," Alison commented. "Have there been many changes?"

"As a matter of fact, there haven't, which is surprising in a house this size," Mr. Fell answered. "Considering the Brethertons have lived here for centuries, you would think some alterations would have occurred. But the place is virtually in its original state, inside and out."

"And the doll museum . . . ?"

"Ah . . . Well, the museum did need some slight alterations—lighting, plumbing, that sort of thing, but the attic section wasn't disturbed."

"Oh, I see . . . But how did it become a museum?"

"One of the Victorian members of the Bretherton family was rather eccentric — collected dolls," he chuckled. "The collection, which came from all over the world, grew over the years, and developed into a small private museum, using a couple of the rooms on the ground floor. Other toys were added, and a dolls' hospital as well, so that the house was eventually taken over by the dolls . . ." He paused for a moment, and then added, "That is — except for one room."

"Let me guess," Alison quietly remarked. "The storeroom . . . ?"

"That's right," Mr. Fell nodded, "and, considering your unfortunate experience this afternoon, it would seem that you met another long-standing resident of Bretherton House. Judging from your description I'd say that you made the acquaintance of Master Jeremy Horrox."

"Has he worked here for long?"

Mr. Fell laughed. "You could say that, I suppose. He been here, on and off, since 1639."

"You mean I . . ." Alison halted, trying to come to terms with the obvious conclusion. She stared at him, open mouthed.

"Saw a ghost . . . ?" Mr. Fell replied. "Yes, that's right. He has only been seen once or twice over the centuries, and there are no portraits or sketches of his appearance, so we don't really know what he looked like."

"So how do you know it was him?"

"The telescope, Mrs. Rowland — the telescope confirms it," he declared. "You see, Master Horrox was an astronomer, the founder of English astronomy in fact. He made an very important discovery concerning Venus and the Sun, amongst other things, and he set up his telescope, which he designed especially for the purpose, in that very room to record it."

"So you think my description of that funny contraption proves it, then?"

"I think it does," Mr. Fell surmised. "But one thing still puzzles me. By all accounts, Horrox was a religious, scholarly man, with a pleasant and kindly disposition — so your description of the angry lunatic in the storeroom certainly does not fit him."

"But he only changed when I showed him what you found in my doll."

"Ah, your doll . . ." Mr. Fell got up and reached up to a shelf. "I almost forgot about your doll. And here is another interesting discovery. Your doll is a very rare example of its type — very rare indeed." He placed the leather-bound box on the work bench: renovation had changed its appearance out of all recognition. "As you can see, I managed to get some colour back into the case, but unfortunately the coat of arms, a French design, I think, was too far gone to repair." He opened the lid, and Alison gasped in delight at the restored Lady Sarah. Mr. Fell had certainly worked wonders with the doll and costume.

"Isn't she lovely," Alison cried, picking up the bright and shining doll. "What a marvellous job you've made of it. Mary will be so thrilled when she sees it —— she won't be able to put it down." Mr. Fell accepted this praise with a slight gesture of his hand.

"I'm sure she will be delighted with the doll, Mrs. Rowland," he agreed, "but I don't think you know what you are holding there." He looked at her gravely. "Do you know how much the doll is worth?"

"Why, no . . . It's just an old childhood toy which belonged to my aunt. It has been in her attic for years."

"Well — I'm talking four figures here," he said, "and possibly more."

"You mean thousands of pounds?"

"I do indeed. In my opinion, this was one of the first dolls to be manufactured in glazed stoneware, with movable glass eyes — and this one has a wig made out of human hair."

"Human hair . . .?" Alison's surprise amused the curator.

"Yes, human hair," he chuckled. "You're probably thinking of those dolls which are used in witchcraft ceremonies and black magic."

"Yes, I was," Alison nodded.

"Well, you're right in that respect," he continued. "Ritual dolls were used in black magic, probably as symbols of living people, in order to gain power over others, either to influence or destroy them. They used hair from victims for this purpose."

"So my doll could be one of those?"

"Don't worry, Mrs. Rowland. I don't think it was," he assured her. "In fact, it really wasn't intended to be a children's toy at all."

"That sounds a bit odd," Alison frowned.

"I suppose it would, especially to a child," Mr. Fell replied. "Let me explain. Your doll is a perfect example of a Lady Doll, which was very fashionable in the seventeenth century, especially with the European aristocracy. These dolls were very popular with rulers and influential people of that time. They were used as gifts, and were very much sought after." It seemed Alison's daughter had chosen the right name for her doll after all.

"So it might have belonged to a King or Queen, and that probably explains the crest on the case?"

"That's right," Mr. Fell nodded. "This doll is in very good condition for its age. In fact I'd lay a bet that it has hardly ever been taken out of its case, and has probably lain in one attic or another for centuries, totally undisturbed. It's a pity you don't know more about its background — it would certainly add to its value."

"I suppose I could get in touch with my Aunt and find out," Alison suggested. "Perhaps she can shed some light on its history."

"Well, don't be surprised if it once belonged to someone like Marie-Antoinette. In the meantime I would take very good care of it, if I were you — keep it safe."

Alison was so excited at the prospect of owning such a valuable antique that she almost forgot about the parchment.

"And the old paper . . . ?"

"Ah, of course — the hidden parchment," Mr. Fell replied. "Now that is a real puzzle. Someone went to great lengths to hide that item in the body of the doll, and it would still be undiscovered today, if the arm had been put back correctly in the first place."

"What do the numbers mean?"

"Some sort of mathematical calculations, I think," he pondered. "I'm afraid you'll have to seek another opinion on that. But remember, with antiques you can never tell — that old parchment might turn out to be even more valuable than the doll."

Alison settled the bill and thanked him.

"Don't mention it," Mr. Fell replied with a smile. "By the way, if you have some time to spare, call in at the village church. You can see the memorial to Master Jeremy Horrox there — that's if your up to seeing him once more today."

"I don't think he'll follow me to church," Alison laughed. She left Mr. Fell at the workroom door, and returned to the ground floor. The guide accompanied her to the museum entrance.

"I don't mind telling you, Mrs. Rowland," she confided, "I'm glad you're collecting the doll. Ever since you brought it in, the atmosphere in the museum has been — how can I put it . . . ?" She searched for the right word. "Unsettled. Yes, that's how I'd describe it — unsettled, especially upstairs in the storeroom . . ." She paused, and nervously glanced up at the storeroom window. "We have a ghost, you know."

"Yes," Alison nodded. "Mr. Fell has told me all about it."

"Well, I never believed all that nonsense," the lady sniffed, "but after these last couple of weeks I'm not so certain, what with all the strange noises and whispers upstairs. Do you know, I'm sure I heard some one shuffling about up in the storeroom the other afternoon and the window was left wide open!"

'I can believe it,' Alison thought to herself. Shivering in the damp November air, she made her way back to her car, and, as she drove past the old building on her way out, she saw the vague image of Mr. Fell waving to her from the storeroom window. However, it was only as she turned onto the highway that she realised something very odd.

Mr. Fell didn't wear a cravat . . .

* * *

St. Michael's was, in every aspect, the epitome of a quaint old English Parish Church. It nestled in a secluded corner of the isolated village, surrounded by a well-kept graveyard and ringed by mature trees, now bare of their summer foliage. Winter was on hand, and the pale, watery sun gave no sustenance to their lifeless, straggling branches. Yet the church retained its warmth and charm. Mellowed brick, stained glass and an ornate gilded sundial helped to create a benevolent ambience. The inscription above this primitive time piece provided a fitting comment on this seasonal rustic picture.

WITHOUT THE SUN I AM SILENT

As Mrs. Rowland entered the nave of this ancient church, the antiquated clock stirred and whirred, and, with a clanking worthy of an old beam engine, struck two, its resonant chimes vibrating through the rafters and empty pews. The fading light which filtered through stained glass tracery windows fell upon a lady arranging flowers beside the chancel arch. Alison hesitated for a moment, not wishing to intrude, and the flower lady looked up and smiled.

"Can I help you?"

"I hope so," Alison replied. "I was told at the Doll Museum that

143

there is a special memorial in the church — to a . . . ."

"To Jeremy Horrox, our famous astronomer," the lady declared. "You mean the Horrox memorial?"

"Yes, that's the one."

"Well, his commemoration window is in the side chapel over there," she said, pointing towards the altar, "and his memorial plaque is on the north wall by the clock tower door. You'll find a leaflet about the church on the stall by the font." The lady turned back to her flower arranging. "I'll have to lock the church in a few minutes," she continued, "— sign of the times."

"Yes, I know," Alison agreed. "I won't be long. I just wanted to see the memorial out of curiosity."

She walked down the aisle to the side chapel, and stood before the stained glass window. She did not recognise the man in the glass design, but the long flowing gown and cravat were familiar. However, the golden image of the sun on a draped cloth, and the various astronomical instruments surrounding the famous astronomer did not, in any way, resemble the objects which she had recently seen in the museum storeroom. The weird telescopic device was plainly absent. She picked up a visitors leaflet on the way back to the memorial plaque by the tower, and flipped through the notes until she came to the section on the famous astronomer.

THE HORROX MEMORIAL CHAPEL

The side chapel and memorial window were added to the church in 1859, thanks to the indefatigable efforts of Richard Brickle, the Rector from 1848 until his death in 1881, and the sundial and clock were erected by the parishioners. The eminent 17th century astronomer Jeremy Horrox lived in this parish from 1639 to 1640. He was probably engaged as a tutor to the children of the Bretherton family, and was a lay reader at the church. It was in this remote Lancashire village that the seed of

British astronomy was planted by this twenty year old youth, already burdened by poverty and dispirited by lack of books and implements. Unknown and obscure, his persistence, courage and great genius overcame these obstacles, and it was on Sunday, 24th of November, 1639, using a primitive telescope (the one in the stained glass window is of a later Victorian design) that he observed the Transit of Venus in Bretherton House. This observation was to have a tremendous impact in astronomical circles. For more information about his life and times see the booklet Graced by God, available from the Rector or Churchwarden, price 1.00p (Tel: 01772 34623).

The date *"24th of November"* made an immediate and profound impression. 'That's today's date,' she thought, speculating on the day's events as she walked back to the north wall memorial. 'Was there a connection between my recent ghostly encounter and this great astronomical discovery — and why single me out? Was it just a coincidence that I came to collect Lady Sarah on this day of all days?' She gazed up at the marble plaque by the clock tower door, trying to decipher the inscription in the semidarkness. What Alison read caused her some disquiet.

MASTER JEREMY HORROX
GRACED BY GOD
born 1618 died 1640
His fertile imagination, his ardent enthusiasm in the pursuit in Mathematics and Astronomy, all seem to foreshadow a career of uncommon brilliancy, which a premature and sudden death on 25th January in his twenty second year sadly brought to a close.

HINC ILLÆ LACHRIMÆ

145

Alison was quick to see the reason for her disquiet.

'He died shortly after his discovery,' she thought, '— and it was very sudden . . .'

At that very moment something alerted her senses: she was not the only visitor in the church. Out of the corner of her eye she noticed that the door to the tower was slightly ajar, and that she was being closely observed. In the deepening shadows she glimpsed a tall figure. Eyes fixed her with a penetrating stare, and a cruel face, swarthy and bearded, exuded animosity and menace. Their eyes met for an instant, and Alison froze, unable to break away from his hypnotic gaze: a feeling of helplessness and vulnerability swept over her. The mysterious watcher receded into the darkness, and the door silently closed. The spell was broken, but this brief experience left Alison with a deep sense of foreboding.

'Where had she seen that face before?'

At that moment the lady flower arranger approached from the chancel. .

"I'll have to close the church now, my dear," she said apologetically, leading Alison to the porch door.

"But what about the man in the tower?"

"Man in the tower . . .?" The lady looked at Alison with a puzzled expression. "I think you must be mistaken. There is no one else here, my dear." And with that she locked the heavy oak door.

* * *

Mary was delighted with the rejuvenated Lady Sarah. However, she wasn't as delighted with her mother's decision to keep the doll in the safe confines of the box.

"But I want to play with her," she wailed. "Why can't she be with all the other toys, mummy?"

"I know, dear," agreed Alison, desperately searching for some excuse to prevent the valuable doll sustaining further "injuries" from

146

Mary's boisterous friends. "We have to be careful she doesn't come to any more harm, darling. In fact, her doctor, Mr. Fell, says that she will need lots of rest."

"But she will be very lonely." Her mother had an idea.

"Why not keep Lady Sarah in your bedroom, safe in your wardrobe," she suggested. "You can talk to her every day — and then she won't be lonely."

Mary, after some deliberation, reluctantly agreed, helped, no doubt, by that season of childish wonder and anticipation, Christmas. She was to take a prominent role in the school Nativity, which also helped to take her mind off the disappointment. Her teacher, Mrs. Jones, was delighted with her acting ability, and Alison, in the course of a conversation with Mrs. Jones, found out that her husband was also a teacher of mathematics. She mentioned the old parchment.

"Do you think your husband could tell me what it is?"

"I don't see why not," Mrs. Jones replied. "He's really keen on anything mathematical — problems and equations — that sort of thing. Send it along with Mary tomorrow."

"I'll do that," Alison declared. "It's just curiosity on my part."

"Well, you know what they say about that?"

"I'm sorry . . . ?" Alison blinked, puzzled by the remark.

"Curiosity killed the cat," the teacher laughed, and Alison recalled her unpleasant encounter at the museum.

"Oh . . . I see what you mean," she returned, but didn't find it so amusing. As she left the classroom with Mary, another well-known saying came to mind. 'I hope *"many a true word spoken in jest"* doesn't apply, as well,' she mused.

But, as events turned out, *"Pandora's box"* would have been a more realistic substitute.

* * *

Mary came out of school clutching a brown envelope.

"Mrs. Jones says it is for you, Mummy," she cried. "Is it a Christmas card?" Other parents, waiting by the gate to greet their children, looked quizzically at Mrs. Rowland.

"No, I don't think so, darling," her mother replied, shaking her head. "I think it's from Mr. Jones." This observation raised one or two eyebrows and some whispers on the problems and pitfalls of divorced women. However, Alison had guessed correctly. The envelope did contain the parchment, together with an accompanying letter.

> *'Dear Mrs. Rowland,*
> *I am returning your strange discovery — my wife told me that you found it in a doll. You were right in assuming that it is a set of calculations, and from what I was able to distinguish from the faded paper I came to the conclusion (with my limited knowledge of this old fashioned style of working out) that it is either a very clever hoax by a maths university graduate (the algebra is too advanced for the general mathematician) or a really exciting discovery which would solve an age-old problem — and make you very rich. I don't suppose that you have heard of Fermat, a famous mathematician. Well, there is a prize of 100,000 marks for anyone who can prove his last theorem, and I think your old parchment might contain the calculations to do it. Many have tried over the centuries, and the proof has eluded them — that's why I think it could be an elaborate hoax.*
> *Regards,*
> *Bill Jones.*
> *PS. Call me on 01772 8302131 if I can be of any further help.'*

The contents of the letter puzzled Alison.

'An elaborate hoax, prize money and a famous mathematician,' she mused. 'It has to be a practical joke.' However, on reflection, Alison recalled the effect it had on the ghostly astronomer of Bretherton House. 'He said the calculations were his — and *he* certainly wasn't joking.' Later that evening she decided to call Mr. Jones.

"Thank you for the letter, Mr. Jones," she began. "I wonder if you could tell me more about that mathematician Fer . . . ?" She had forgotten the name and began to read through the letter again.

"Fermat . . ." Mr. Jones answered. "Pierre de Fermat — a French lawyer who studied ancient Greek mathematicians and the theory of numbers. He became interested in Pythagoras and his theorem — the equation $a^2 + b^2 = c^2$ or the three four five triangle."

"Ah, you mean the one about the sum of the squares on two sides of the triangle," Alison replied. "I did that in geometry at school."

"Equals the sum of the square on the third side. That's right. I'm glad to hear we teachers haven't been wasting our time," he chuckled. "Anyway, Fermat said that numbers to the power of two could add up, but not powers of three, or, as we say, cubes. And this also applies to fourth powers and so on. Just before he died he wrote that he had discovered a truly marvellous proof which demonstrated his own theorem, but did not leave any working calculations to back it up."

"When did he discover this proof?"

"I think it was around sixteen thirty," Mr. Jones replied. Alison grasped the significance of the date. Master Jeremy Horrox was alive at the same time. "So you see mathematicians have been trying to prove Fermat's last theorem for nearly three hundred years. A prize of ten thousand marks was set up by a German University to go to any mathematician who could find the proof of the theorem."

"And you think my parchment was a trick to claim the prize?"

"Probably . . ." Mr. Jones paused. "But they'll have to be quick about it. There's a time limit to claim it. The proof has to be found by the year two thousand and seven — so there isn't much time left."

"And if the parchment is genuine?"

"You would become a rich, not to mention famous, woman. It

would be interesting to find out where your doll originally came from. That might help to solve the mystery. Good luck in your treasure hunt."

The word *rich* was sweet music to a divorced woman living off intermittent maintenance payments and welfare benefits. Alison resolved to hunt the "treasure" as soon as the Christmas and New Year festivities were over. Unfortunately, circumstances beyond her control brought the starting date forward.

On Christmas Eve Alison was awoken by piercing scream, which echoed through the house. She leaped from her bed and dashed to her daughter's bedroom, to be confronted by a dreadful sight. Her daughter, Mary, crouched in the far corner of the room, her hands clasped tightly over her eyes, shaking uncontrollably in her floral nightdress. The floor of the bedroom was strewn with a jumble of decorations, presents and 'stocking fillers' intermixed with articles of clothing, which Mrs. Rowland quickly recognised by their shape and size. They were the torn remnants of Lady Sarah, her daughter's favourite doll. However, the most chilling aspect of this frightening scene lay scattered around the trembling child. *Lady Sarah's arms and legs had been ripped from her torso, and her head had been pulled and twisted from her body, attached only by a slim thread. The doll stared up, wide eyed, at Mrs. Rowland.*

There was no sign of the malevolent "Father Christmas", or more to the point, the "Father of English astronomy".

* * *

Christmas, that season of merriment and goodwill, was, in effect, totally ruined. The scene of wilful vandalism and destruction had turned Alison's dream of fame and fortune into a nightmare of self preservation, and left her daughter, Mary, with a fearful dead of Santa Claus which would remain with her for many years to come. Furthermore, it would seem that, if Mary's recollection of the horrifying confrontation was to be believed, the jovial figure of childhood fantasy and commercial propaganda came *in pairs* .

"But there *were* two of them," Mary sobbed, clinging tightly to her mother, "— and they hurt Snuzzles, Lady Sarah, and all my other toys. I don't like Christmas any more." Her mother eventually managed to calm the stricken child, and gradually a picture of what took place in her bedroom began to take shape.

Mary had difficulty dropping off to sleep, what with the excitement of that special evening and the prospect of meeting the "man himself", and possibly his reindeer, Rudolph. However, the person standing at the end of her bed, when she awoke in the early hours, was not who she expected. Even in the glow of the street light, which filtered through the curtains, she could see that he was much too young to be Santa Claus, and he didn't even carry a sack of toys over his shoulder: the absence of red tunic, black fur-lined boots and a white beard just added to the disappointment. His gown was black and he was very pale, and, although he startled Mary at first, she said she wasn't afraid of him.

He smiled, held out his hand, and asked in a gentle voice if he could see her doll, Lady Sarah. Mary went to the wardrobe and took out the box. She opened it, and at that moment another figure appeared behind the pale man. This sudden appearance so alarmed Mary, that she dropped the box, tipping the doll onto the floor. With an awful moan, the pale man faded away, leaving her at the mercy of this second intruder. He glared at the distraught child with menacing eyes and reached down for the doll. Without uttering a word he tore it apart, flinging arms and legs onto the floor. However, it seemed that he didn't find what he was searching for, and in his rage he set about all the other toys, scattering bits and pieces all over the place. With no avenue of escape Mary sank to the floor, sobbing hysterically. And when he came up empty handed with the toys, he focused his attention on the huddled child. He crept slowly towards her, his wild eyes glistening in the orange glow of the street light. He bent over her, his hands reaching out to grasp her, and she let out an almighty scream of terror. Moments later her mother burst in and switched on the light. The fearsome spectre had vanished.

"I knew *he* wasn't Santa Claus, Mummy," she whispered, "— because he had staring eyes and a nasty black beard."

Alison turned pale at this childish observation. She recalled the face behind the tower door of St. Michael's church.

* * *

Aunty Margaret was thrilled to see Alison and Mary.

"I was so pleased when you said you would come down for a visit," she enthused as she welcomed the weary pair. "I thought you sounded rather tired on the telephone."

"Yes, it has been rather stressful recently," Alison commented. 'That has got to be the understatement of the year,' she thought ironically.

"Well, I'm glad you could make it — it's so nice to see you both for Christmas . . ." Aunty Margaret paused and looked at Mary. "My word, you're very quiet today, young lady," she said, bending down to speak to the child. Mary remained silent, and lowered her eyes. "What did Father Christmas bring you?"

Mary reacted instantly by clinging to her mother and burying her face in her dress. A muffled "I don't like Father Christmas any more" was barely audible.

"Oh dear," Aunty Margaret gulped. "I didn't mean to upset her have I said something wrong?"

"No, not at all . . ." Alison cuddled her daughter. "She's just a little upset at the moment, but it will soon pass, now that she's here."

Later that evening, Alison tucked Mary up in bed with Aunty Margaret's childhood teddy bear for company, and rejoined her aunt downstairs. There she began her treasure hunt, but she needed some clues. She broached the subject of the doll.

"It was very good of you to send the doll to Mary," she said. "She was thrilled with it."

"I'm so glad. It's been lying in the attic for years."

"Where did your father get the doll?"

"He brought it back for me from the war," Aunty Margaret replied. "Though I have to admit that I didn't take to it."

"Why was that?"

"There was something about it that made me uneasy — those unsettling vibrations children sometimes pick up. I'm rather sensitive in that department — a mental metal detector, I suppose. Silly really, but I definitely felt there was something from the doll's past lurking inside, waiting to get out." Alison knew exactly what she meant, and that *something* was now definitely *out*.

"Anyway, we'll go and see my father tomorrow," she continued, "so you can ask him yourself — that's if he can still remember after all these years."

To his daughter's astonishment and Alison's delight the old soldier's memory on the subject of the doll was as sharp as a razor, when they met him the following afternoon. He had great difficulty with the general swirl of everyday modern life, but those traumatic wartime memories, of events and places long past, were as fresh as the day they occurred.

"We were pushing up through France," he declared hoarsely. "Jerry was on the run and we were close behind, but he tried to slow us down with mines and booby traps." Mary stood by the armchair, eyes full of wonder, listening to the old soldier.

"What are boobies, Mummy," she whispered, "— do soldiers eat them?" The old man heard the question and burst into a cackle of laughter.

"*They* eat soldiers, buttercup," he grimaced, "— when they go off!"

He proceeded to explain the principle of booby traps and to recount his wartime experiences. He was a sapper in the Royal Engineers, and his particular job was highly dangerous. His speciality was clearing buildings and defusing booby traps and mines laid by the re-

153

treating German Army: and on this particular day they came across an old French chateau on the outskirts of Paris. It had been damaged by shell fire, and he was sent in to check the rooms, searching in all the cavities and recesses for explosives. Part of the ground floor had been destroyed, revealing a cellar, and when he lowered himself down through the gaping hole he found himself in a sort of crypt. Memorial plaques lined the walls, and he came to the conclusion that it was a burial vault. One of these wall plaques had been partly shattered by the shell's explosion, revealing a cavity, and he decided to check it out.

"I reached in, my fingers working round this hole, feeling for a trip wire." The soldier's voice dropped to whisper, intent on frightening the solemn child. "I felt old bones and pieces of cloth, rotted with age and then what do you think I found?" He peered at Mary. "Well, young lady . . . ?"

The child trembled, and clutched her mother's hand.

"A booby," she whispered back.

Alison and Aunt Margaret burst out laughing. The tension, so carefully built up, was ruined, and the old man snorted in disgust.

"No — not a booby. Damn it — she got me at it now!" He glared at the anxious child, and eventually recovered his composure. "My fingers felt something solid," he continued. "It was a box covered with grime and dirt. I wiped the top and saw a design on it — like the one on the remains of the memorial plaque."

"It was the doll's case," Alison interrupted with excitement.

"It was," he nodded. "I brought it back for Margaret, although I never told her where I had found it. She never seemed to want to play with it, so I put it up in the attic." He looked at Mary and smiled. "But I'm glad you like it. You must promise to look after it." The little girl shook her head.

"Lady Sarah is very poorly, and has to go back to hospital," she declared slowly. The tea bell rang and the old man yawned. It was time to leave.

Mary left the room with Aunty Margaret, and Alison remained with the Margaret's father for a moment. She needed the "x" for her "treasure map".

"Can you tell me," she asked the old soldier, "— where exactly in France was this chateau?"

"I couldn't honestly say," he replied. "After Normandy we were on the move all the time, and the officers had the maps."

"And the name on the plaque . . .?"

"It was badly smashed up," he replied. "Just the word PAS, and a date— sixteen hundred and something, I think."

His final comment was rather unnerving.

"I think I know why Margaret never played with the doll," he surmised. "When I first touched the box I thought something moved inside it. And then I thought it was a baby's coffin. Our Margaret must have felt something was queer about it as well."

Alison shivered. She remembered Mary's first impression of the case, and Mr. Fell's disclosure of the wig made from human hair.

Perhaps the old soldier's first impression was right, after all.

* * *

"Just look at this mess," Aunty Margaret exclaimed. "I didn't expect Mary to be so untidy!" Alison entered the bedroom, closely followed by her daughter.

"She isn't — quite the opposite in fact," she countered. However, the state of the room gave her quite a shock. "I don't know what to say . . ."

Mary's upturned suitcase lay on the bed, and her clothes and the contents of the bedside cabinet were scattered around the room. Alison came to the obvious conclusion. "I think that you've been burgled?" Mary, on the other hand, didn't think so.

"Look, Mummy," she cried in a distressed voice. "*They* have come back again." She pointed to an arm of the teddy bear sticking out from

155

the heap of clothes. Aunty Margaret picked it up.

"How could any one do this to a child's toy," she snorted with disgust, collecting the other pieces of the mutilated teddy bear from the pile. "They must be sick!"

"I'm afraid it isn't burglars, Margaret," Alison answered in a subdued voice, "— it's something far worse." She went on to tell the angry woman about Lady Sarah and the traumatic events of the previous weeks. As the story unfolded her Aunty looked at her in disbelief.

"I can't believe it," she replied, shaking her head. "I played with that doll as a child and I never had any trouble with it. Considering the number of years it has been up in the attic, you'd think something would have happened before now."

"I don't think it's the doll," Alison said thoughtfully. "I'm sure it's that old parchment, hidden inside Lady Sarah for goodness knows how long. Its discovery has triggered off this awful business."

"Then you ought to find out as much as you can about that astronomer, and the place where my father found the doll's box," her Aunty advised. "May be you could find a link with the parchment. I'll try and find out more about that chateau in France, while you check the astronomer." Alison, relieved that her Aunty had believed her story and grateful for her offer of help, agreed to the plan without question.

"I'll get in touch with the Rector of St. Michael's Church right away," she decided. "He has a set of booklets about Jeremy Horrox."

"And I'll chase up father's old cronies at the British Legion," Aunty Margaret replied. "I'm sure some of them are still knocking around." However, there was one aspect of the ominous business which could not be avoided.

"I don't think we have much time left," Alison warned her aunt.

"Why do you say that," her Aunty laughed, "— I don't think ghosts are bothered about time, do you?"

"In this case I'm not so sure. Jeremy Horrox died suddenly on the twenty fifth of January, soon after his famous observation at Bretherton House."

"Well, in my opinion he's not the problem — it's that other fellow you've got to worry about," Aunty Margaret declared. "He seems to be the dangerous one —— probably had something to do with the astronomer's death as well, I shouldn't wonder." A vision of the half-hidden, sinister figure in the doorway of St. Michael's tower flashed through Alison's mind. 'What if the bearded intruder decided to take Mary to pieces in his search for the parchment.' She could not help but tremble at the thought of her daughter's predicament.

"I'm sure I've seen his face somewhere . . ."

* * *

The booklet arrived at the start of the New Year. It was a slim volume of twelve pages, with an illustration of the astronomer's memorial window on the cover. The booklet briefly covered the life and times of Jeremy Horrox, dwelling mainly on his achievements in mathematics and astronomy. Alison scrutinised the pages, marking the relevant passages.

> *Unfortunately there is no record of his personal appearance, but we do know that Jeremy Horrox died on the 25th January 1640. Again, we are unable to give the exact details of his birth other than to presume that it was around 1618. His life spanned the build up of that turbulent time in our history, the Civil War, and although his family were Puritans, he probably was not a supporter of the Parliamentarians. He spent four years at Emmanuel College, Cambridge prior to returning to Bretherton to take up a position of tutor to the Bretherton family, who were wealthy landowners and merchants. His mathematical calculations and astronomical predictions were well in advance of his time and it can be said that he was the forerunner of Newton, Flamstead and Halley.*

In the next passage Alison found the link between the astronomer and France, and uncovered the identity of the sinister bearded man in the church tower.

> *Horrox, in his passion for calculating numbers, studied the Greek mathematicians Pythagoras and Diophantus and their respective theorems and solutions to equations on numbers. The difficulty in studying mathematics and astronomy was exceeding great at that time, for he had no teacher and very few books. His position as tutor placed him in contact with Charles Bretherton, the brother of his employer. He was a prosperous merchant in Holland, and this connection with the continent opened a valuable avenue to the work of other scientists in France and Germany. Through Charles he obtained the Rudolphine Tables of Kepler and the hypotheses of Landsberg.*

The accompanying illustrations of Bretherton House and portraits of the family solved the mystery. At last Alison remembered where she had seen the sinister figure before: it had been on the wall of the Bretherton Room in the museum. The face of Charles Bretherton was imprinted on her mind. The cruel face, penetrating eyes and black beard were unmistakeable. It was the face in the tower, and, judging from her daughter's description, the malevolent "Father Christmas" in Mary's bedroom. 'But was there any connection between him and the death of the famous astronomer?'

> *There is no information about the death of Jeremy Horrox, other than it took place on January 25th 1640, and was sudden and unexpected. A planned visit to a supporter and colleague in Manchester on the 26th came to light in one of his letters, and it was evident that the astronomer had just made an exciting discovery, one "which would*

confound those who deny the will of God as the cause of all things" and that the " harmony of creation is such that small things constitute a faithful type of greater things". In this, his last communication, he left no calculations or clue to the exact nature of this momentous discovery, and his close confident, Charles Bretherton, who was one of the last people to see him alive, could shed no light on these enigmatic statements.

However, Aunty Margaret could.

"I've managed to get something on that old French chateau," she told her niece. "It was originally part of a convent called Port-Royal-des-Champs."

"What sort of convent?" Alison wondered what a convent full of French nuns had to do with a Lancashire astronomer.

"I've no idea, I'm afraid."

"So we're no further on with solving the mystery of Lady Sarah?"

Her Aunty shrugged. "I suppose so — but if that parchment is genuine, then there's still a small fortune to consider."

The *treasure* was the least of Alison's worries. It was the two *pirates*, hot on her trail, who perturbed her.

* * *

"Some one went to great lengths to hide that item in the body of the doll."

Alison recalled the words of the museum curator. She studied the faded parchment, trying to find the connection between the calculations of an obscure astronomer and the last theorem of an influential French mathematician. She asked her Aunt.

"I wonder if Pythagoras has anything to do with it?"

"I'd try the local library, if I were you," Margaret suggested. "They're bound to have something about him in the reference section." Alison took her advice.

The librarian was very helpful.

"If you would like to wait here for a moment," she said, "I'll see what we have on Pythagoras." She returned with a large, leather-bound encyclopedia. "I think you'll find what you're looking for in this volume."

Alison glanced down the index, and the title *'FAMOUS MEN OF MATHEMATICS'* caught her eye. The contents of the chapter solved the puzzle, but added a further macabre dimension to her predicament.

> ## PYTHAGORAS
> The famous Greek philosopher and mathematician was born on the island of Sámos, but left to settle in Crotona, southern Italy where he founded a religious movement, later known as Pythagoreanism. The Pythagoreans believed immortality and the transmigration of souls, claiming to be the reincarnation of people of earlier times, with memories of their previous existences. Their studies of odd and even numbers, and of prime and square numbers, resulted in the scientific foundation of mathematics. The hypotenuse, or Pythagorean, theorem was their great discovery in geometry, and centuries later a French mathematician, Fermat, discovered a proof which confirmed the Pythagorean theorem, that no other numbers of a greater power than two would satisfy the equation.

'If my parchment is genuine,' Alison mused, reaching the bottom of the page, 'they have got the wrong man. No wonder Jeremy Horrox wanted his calculations back.' She turned the page.

> The Pythagoreans also studied the planets. Their astrological investigations marked an important advance in

this sphere, for they were the first to perceive that the planets revolved at intervals round a ball of fire. They equated this to music and called it the harmony of the spheres. Philosophers and scientist in later ages would call it Sacred Geometry, and in certain cases it was used by practitioners of the Black Arts in their quest for power and immortality.

"The Black Arts". These words struck home, and a vision of Charles Bretherton flashed, once again, into her mind. 'He looked like the type of person to be involved in that sort of thing,' she thought. 'But what about Fermat?' She checked in the index, and found his name.

PIERRE DE FERMAT

The renowned French mathematician was born in Beaumont-de-Lomagne in 1601. He was extremely interested in the theory of numbers and their powers and made certain discoveries which placed him in the forefront of this science. His studies anticipated the advances in algebra and analysis, and his interest in Pythagorean numbers led to his last theorem. He claimed to have proved that there was no such power higher than a second power that could extend the hypotenuse theorem of Pythagoras. He wrote in the margin of a book "I have discovered a truly marvellous proof which this margin is too small to hold". A prize of 100,000 marks was established in 1908 to be awarded to anyone who could find this proof. His close friend and confidant, Blaise Pascal, helped to formulate the theory of mathematical probability which was to become so important in today's society.

'Blaise Pascal . . . Could this be the PAS on the shattered memorial plaque — the 'x' on my treasure trail?' Alison, with growing excitement, turned to the index. And there he was, on page seventy.

BLAISE PASCAL
Blaise Pascal was born in Clermont-Ferrand in 1623 and is regarded as one of the great intellectuals of Western history. A philosopher, mathematician and physicist, he was a mathematical prodigy, inventing the first mechanical adding machine when he was 19 years of age. A staunch Roman Catholic, he was drawn to Jansenism, a movement of religious reform, and entered the spiritual centre of this sect, situated in a convent at Port-Royal-des Champs, near Paris. Their religious interpretation, a belief in absolute predestination whereby the faithful will either be saved or damned, but only a selected few will be 'chosen' to receive salvation, brought them in conflict with the state and church of the day. His interest in algebra and geometry brought him in contact with others of influence on the continent, including Fermat, another mathematical genius of his day. Together they gathered and exchanged information from various sources, and formulated many theorems. However, no evidence or calculations can be found to indicate that Pascal assisted in finding the proof for Fermat's Last Theorem.

'Well, that's wrong for a start,' Alison thought. 'The calculations were in a doll — in his tomb. And what if one of their sources of information was Charles Bretherton, and he had given the Lancashire astronomer's calculations to Fermat. May be that was what he meant when he wrote those words on the margin of his book — *I have discovered a truly marvellous proof.*' She recalled another of the museum curator's comments.
"These dolls were often given as presents to influential people."

'Did Fermat need a second opinion, and decide to hide the calculations in the doll and send it to his friend?' Alison speculated, mulling the problem over in her mind. She remembered that Mr. Fell had assured her that the doll had no ritual magic significance. 'On the other hand, there was the human hair — so could there be a more sinister intention behind this secrecy?' Alison returned to the chapter on Pythagoras, and considered the evidence.

'Was there a similarity between Pascal's religious sect, Jansenism, and Pythagorean doctrine,' Alison speculated, 'and, more to the point, had the two mathematicians believed in the Pythagorean version of immortality and the transmigration of souls?'

There was nothing in the chapters to indicate this. Time was running out, and she came to the conclusion that one person held the key to the mystery — Charles Bretherton.

* * *

"Can you tell me anything about Charles Bretherton?"

Standing on the steps of Bretherton Doll Museum, one bitterly cold morning in January, Alison asked Mr. Fell this important question. A wintery blanket of crisp white hoar frost swathed the old house from top to bottom, and the morning sun had yet to break the stranglehold of freezing banks of dense mist. The curator ushered the shivering visitor through the old oak door into the warm entrance hall.

"I was surprised to get your call, Mrs. Rowland, especially in this weather," he said. "From the tone of your voice it seemed very important."

"Yes, it is," she declared.

"And why the interest in Charles Bretherton," he asked, showing her into the room where the Bretherton portraits were on display.

"I think I've seen him."

"Not another ghost!" The curator stepped back in astonishment.

"You've seen him — where?"

Alison told him of her visit to St. Michael's church and her brief encounter with the figure behind the tower door. She pointed up to one of the portraits.

"That's definitely him."

"Are you sure?" The astonished curator stared in some disbelief at the solemn visitor. "Perhaps it was a trick of the light?"

"Could you mistake a face like that?"

"Well . . ." He paused, gazing up at the cruel face of Charles Bretherton. "You might be right in that respect. He was, by all accounts, a very interesting character. I'll put the kettle on and tell you what I know about him, over a cup of tea."

Mr. Fell's account of Charles Bretherton, the bearded figure in the tower, held the missing pieces of the puzzle, and, as far as Alison was concerned, settled the matter of the doll and Jeremy Horrox.

"I think I told you on your last visit that John Bretherton had a brother who was a merchant in Holland."

"Yes, I remember something like that."

"Well, initially it wasn't by choice. The nation was in a bit of a pickle at the time, building up to the Civil War, and he had to get out of the country in a hurry because of a scandal. He set up shop in Amsterdam."

"What was the scandal about?"

"It was rumoured that he practised the ancient art of alchemy."

"Alchemy . . . Isn't that something to do with making gold?"

"Yes," Mr. Fell nodded. "The goal of the alchemist is to turn base metals, such as lead, into gold. It has fascinated scientists for centuries and is considered to be the ultimate in scientific achievement."

Alison still couldn't see any connection between the astronomer's calculations, a Pythagorean theorem and making gold from a lump of lead. 'It just doesn't make sense,' she thought to herself.

"Only, in the case of Charles Bretherton, it wasn't gold that he was interested in," the curator went on. His next comment gave Alison the

164

link she had been searching for. "No, it was the elixir of life — he wanted to reverse the process of ageing."

"Immortality!"

"That's right," he smiled. "He conducted his experiments in this house, in the very room where Jeremy Horrox later made his famous observation. And it is said that the alchemist tried every avenue, turning to the ancient world for inspiration." Alison had her link with Pythagoras.

"How was he found out?"

"Charles was careless with his equipment. A servant found ancient symbols of the alchemist's tree of knowledge, and mathematical calculations, and took them to his elder brother, John, the master of the house. In the prevailing climate of suspicion and religious mania anything smacking of sorcery would be investigated by the authorities and severely dealt with. So you can see that it would be only a matter of time before Charles was denounced and arrested."

"So his brother shipped him off to the continent at the first opportunity," Alison surmised, "and he started a business in Holland?"

"Yes. He eventually returned to Bretherton House as a respectable merchant and benefactor. He provided the bricks for St. Michael's church," Mr. Fell replied. "And that's when he met Jeremy Horrox. When he realised that Horrox was a genius in the field of algebra and geometry he went out of way to ingratiate himself with the young tutor, using his connections with the influential continental guilds to obtain scientific papers and books for the astronomer."

"Perhaps he thought Horrox would help him with his calculations and secret experiments," Alison commented.

"Well, I'm sure he was disappointed if he did," the curator retorted. "Horrox had studied Divinity at Cambridge University, and probably intended to go into the church when he was older. He was a lay preacher at St. Michael's, so I don't think he'd get involved with alchemy and sorcery, do you?"

"I suppose not," Alison agreed, "— not willingly, anyway." She guessed that the "truly marvellous proof" had altered the situation. Charles Bretherton saw the potential of such a powerful mathematical discovery in his quest for immortality — and had to get hold of it by fair means or foul.

"Unfortunately the astronomer suddenly died," Mr. Fell continued. "And I do mean *sudden*. He was fit and well one day, and dead the next."

"That's what I'd call suspicious circumstances."

"Just so," Mr. Fell agreed, "—especially when we find that Charles Bretherton was supposedly the last person to see him alive. After the tragedy Charles returned to Holland, and rarely visited Bretherton House after that."

'But he still hangs about St. Michael's,' Alison thought to herself. In her mind it was obvious that Charles Bretherton had murdered the young astronomer for his "marvellous proof". But he still needed to check the accuracy of the calculations, and that's where his scientific connections came in handy. Secrecy was paramount and what better way to send it than as a gift of a doll, a popular present at that time: no one would suspect this novel method. In order to set his seal of ownership on the doll and parchment he resorted to his knowledge of the Black Arts. He made the wig for the doll out of locks of his own hair. He sent the gift and "proof" to Fermat for verification.

'Realising its importance and suspecting its "owner", Fermat could easily have decided to ask his friend, Pascal, for a second opinion,' she mused. 'Just before he died Fermat passed it to his friend, but, because of those troubled religious times, and the danger of being associated with the Black Arts while a member of a fervent religious sect, Pascal saw the gravity of his situation. Fermat had died, and he sought an equally secret hiding place for the doll — his own prepared memorial for the "chosen" in the convent of Port Royal.' In the meantime, Charles Bretherton waited patiently for the return of the "truly marvellous proof". It never arrived.

And so, if Alison's speculations were correct, the secret within

Lady Sarah lay there, safe and secure, for centuries. The only evidence of the proof was a scribbled note in the margin of a book of a famous French mathematician. A world war, a house-proud daughter and a child's concern changed all that. The secret hiding place of the truly marvellous proof was finally revealed when Lady Sarah went for treatment into Bretherton House Doll Hospital, and, by sheer coincidence, the very place where it had originally been conceived — and now Jeremy Horrox wanted it back.

"Well, that's about it, Mrs. Rowland." Mr. Fell stood up, concluding his story. "I haven't heard of any ghostly visitation in St. Michael's, so I suppose you could put it down to imagination." He walked down with Alison to the entrance hall, and his parting comment explained Charles Bretherton's grim determination to recover the astronomer's marvellous proof.

"On the other hand," the curator smiled, "— talking of immortality. It was said that, when Charles Bretherton returned for his brother's funeral some twenty years later, he hardly looked a day older that when he left all those years before."

* * *

Alison had to make a snap decision.

The 25th of January loomed, with the inevitable and possibly final confrontation with the alchemist and the astronomer of Bretherton House. Whether the parchment was genuine or not, or worth all that money, she felt that, for peace of mind and her daughter's safety, she had to get rid of it. She decided that the best place for it was Bretherton House. She would donate the valuable Lady Doll to the museum.

'The "marvellous proof" will be back were it should be — with Jeremy Horrox,' she decided. 'And if Charles Bretherton wants it, he'll have to sort it out with the astronomer.' She set about reassembling Lady Sarah, inserting the parchment in the body of the doll before refitting the arms, legs and head. The wig was a problem. In order to counteract any potential danger from contact with the alchemist's locks of hair she wore gloves when fitting the wig. The torn clothing was expertly repaired and the completed doll placed in the case. Alison was pleased with the result.

'The doll looks as good as new,' she thought. Lady Sarah stared up at her, and when, in that brief instant before finally closing the lid, Alison thought she saw the doll blink and smile, she knew she had made the right decision.

* * *

The next morning Mary began to sneeze and cough, and a high temperature confirmed the onset of a bad cold.

"You're not well enough to go to school today, darling," Alison consoled her tearful daughter. "You'll have to stay at home, while I run down to the chemist for some cough mixture." Her next door neighbour kindly offered to keep an eye on the sickly child, and Alison departed to collect the medicine. On her return she was eagerly greeted by her daughter.

"Mummy . . . mummy!" cried the excited child. "Guess who came to see me?" Alison had no idea, but the kindly neighbour soon put that right.

"You had a visitor just after you went out, Alison," she declared. "Your "ex" called with a Christmas present for Mary." Alison's heart sank at this news. Visits from Mary's father usually meant trouble, Christmas or not, and he usually didn't bother with presents or cards. He was up to something — but what?

"Yes, he brought a doll's house for me, Mummy," her daughter added, "— and I told him all about Lady Sarah."

"I'm sure he wouldn't be interested, darling," Alison declared in a rather bitter tone.

"Oh, but he was, Mummy," she replied. "He said it wouldn't be long before I could go and stay with him and his new girlfriend."

Alison turned pale, gripped by a wave of panic. She'd had a premonition that something like this would happen one day, and she felt powerless to do anything about it.

"And when I told Daddy how poorly Lady Sarah was," continued the jubilant child, "he said he would take her away and make her better." His ex-wife sat down in a daze, slowly recovering her composure. The "truly marvellous proof" was now in the hands of another, and she had lost a small fortune. However, she had gained something far more valuable — her child.

Time was running out but not for her. Alison gave her daughter a big hug and smiled.

"What a splendid idea!"

* * *

The Evening Gazette lay on the kitchen table. Three items in the newspaper were circled in red.

OBITUARIES
Luke Rowland, suddenly, on the 25th of January.

BRETHERTON HOUSE DOLL MUSEUM
We are pleased to announce the latest addition to our collection. It is a unique "fashion', or 'lady' doll of the 17th century, and has been generously donated by Mrs. L. Rowland. It is one of the few examples of this type to survive, and is a highly sought after doll. The museum also contains a comprehensive and exclusive collection of dolls and related toys, past and present, so why not come along and enter this fascinating and enchanting world of traditional dolls' houses, furniture and accessories. Our impressive Dolls' Hospital offers a specialised repair and restoration service and we can advise on all

169

aspects of the miniature scene.
Open Monday - Saturday, 10.00 - 5.00
Closed all day Wednesday.
Ample free parking.

SITUATIONS VACANT

Owing to the recent illness of the present occupant a va-cancy has arisen for an assistant curator at Bretherton House Doll Museum. The applicant should possess an open mind and be totally at ease working in old premises. Good prospects and remuneration for the right person.
Apply with C.V. to:-
Mr. Fell,
The Curator,
Bretherton House.

The child maintenance payments had ceased, and Alison was in dire financial circumstances. She was in desperate need of suitable employment — but this was one job which she would never dream of taking, no matter how good the prospects and remuneration.

SEFTON

Plain Ghost Trail   27

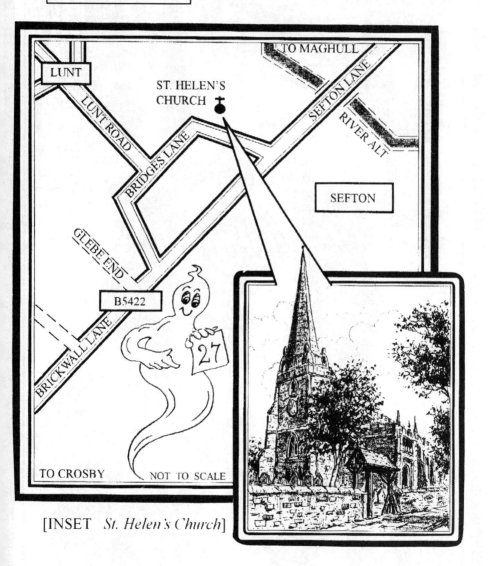

[INSET   *St. Helen's Church*]

I AM NOT THERE

Some months ago I received a rather unusual gift from Alec, my next door neighbour.

"I picked it up at a car boot sale," he informed me, handing me a battered wooden case over the garden fence. "It was dirt cheap and I thought the box would come in handy for the garage — but when I opened it up I thought it would suit your line of work." The line of work in question was Art and Design, and in particular painting in oils, with a leaning towards still life subjects. Alec always kept a look-out for any interesting items which fell within the scope of my hobby, and I had received some interesting bits and pieces over the years. This latest gift, however, was to have a marked effect on "my line of work", which required concentration and attention to detail. A tremendous improvement in draughtsmanship and style of execution were immediately apparent to anyone who saw my work at that time (but more of this later).

The case was of sturdy construction, and probably home-made. It had a hasp lock and hinged lid and was sectioned off to hold tubes of paint, brushes and all the various accessories required for the practice of oil painting. There was one additional item which made it somewhat unique in the concept of an artist's paint box. It had a stand, easel and seat combined within the framework of the case. Its construction was exceedingly clever and well thought out, allowing four adjustable legs to unfold from the base, and an easel to open out from within the lid. It also held a folding canvas stool and, more to the point, the whole construction was extremely light for its size. However, it still had a home-made feel about it, and the overall concept

173

seemed to reflect the artist's own ideas and requirements. My neighbour had indeed picked up a cheap bargain — unfortunately it would cost me much more than a couple of pounds, to say the least.

* * *

The case really suited me. This surprised me, considering my first negative impression of its battered condition. But the more I looked at it, testing the easel, folding down the legs and stocking up the tubes of oil colours, the more I became fascinated by it, and I couldn't wait to try it out. The bright sunlight and mild weather favoured an outdoor trial run, and I had the ideal spot in mind: it had to be the dry dock at Briars Green. The description "dry dock" might suggest a harbour facility at a seaport, but Briars Green was way inland, and the nearest stretch of water was the local canal. This canal wound its way through the flat agricultural countryside, and its towpath was a favourite with walkers and fishermen alike. At Briars Green a spur of this canal ran northwards to the basin and sea locks at Tarlescough, and at this sleepy junction a dry dock was incorporated into the system to provide a facility for repairs and renovation to the large canal fleet of the last century. These days the commercial trade had dried up, and now the canal was primarily used for leisure purposes. Nevertheless, from an artistic viewpoint, the dry dock and adjoining stone cottages provided an ideal setting for brush and canvas; and this is where I set up for the afternoon trial.

It all went like a dream. My hand expertly sketched the view, the colours mixed perfectly, the brush covered the canvas effortlessly and the hours passed by in no time. However, as the painting progressed and the view began to take shape, I became aware of that peculiar (and I may say often annoying) feeling experienced by many outdoor painters who become engrossed in their work. Someone was standing behind me, observing my handiwork with a critical eye. On several occasions I turned to confront my audience, but each time I found

myself alone: yet this sense of critical observation persisted throughout the afternoon.

On the other hand the completed view of the dry dock could not,
as far as I was concerned, be faulted, even by my highly critical standards. In short the painting was a gem, my best work to date. I stood
up to pack away the easel, when a passer-by, out walking her dog,
stopped and emphasised the point.

"I say," she breathed in admiration, "that's really lovely."

"Mmm . . yes, I think it has turned out rather well," I answered,
trying not to sound too conceited by this flattering remark.

"Yes, it has indeed," she continued. "I'm very partial to figures in
a painting, and I particularly like yours — they're so lifelike."

"Figures . . ?" I blinked in astonishment. I didn't remember painting any figures. "Let me see . . ." I couldn't believe my eyes — but it
was perfectly true. Several figures had miraculously *appeared* in the
painting. An old lady stood at the door of one cottage chatting to a
workman while another woman leant out of an upstairs window, looking down at two children sitting on the ground in front of the stone
cottages — and I definitely hadn't painted them, that's for sure.

"Do you want to sell it?"

"No . . . I'm sorry, but I think I'll have to do some more work on
it," I replied, completely flustered by the whole business.

"Oh, I don't think you need do that," she cried. "The picture is
perfect. Please won't you reconsider — oh please . . ?"

I decided against parting with the painting there and then, but the
lady was so insistent (to the point that her pleas verged on the edge of
hysteria) that I took her name and address, and promised to let her
know if I changed my mind. I returned home in an extremely perplexed state of mind: it was further confounded by a singular development.

The figures in the painting had completely vanished.

* * *

The following day my neighbour saw me walking down the garden to my studio (my wife calls it the "National Gallery") and came over to the fence to ask about my painting trip

"How did you get on yesterday?"

"Fine," I replied. "It was just the sort of day for it."

"Did you try out the painting box? "Alec asked.

"Yes, it was great — ideal for outdoor work," I said. "I went to the canal dry dock at Tarlescough to try it out."

"Ah, yes," he nodded. "I know the place well. Let's have a look at the painting." I brought it from the studio and handed it to him. He whistled in astonishment.

"Wow," he declared. "This is really something. I didn't know you were this good at painting."

"Well, I've got to admit it surprised me too. It's my best one so far." Alec examined the painting, obviously enthralled with it.

"I must say it's absolutely marvellous how you've managed to capture the reflections in the water," he breathed, holding the painting at arms length. "Absolutely marvellous . . ."

'Reflections,' I thought to myself. 'I didn't paint any reflections in water — it was a dry dock.' I gaped, wide eyed, at my painting: another miraculous *appearance* confronted my startled gaze. The dry dock had filled with water, and the reflections of the cottage fell on the surface in perfect symmetry.

"I don't usually take much interest in Art," continued Alec, clearly besotted by the view, "but I do go for water and reflections. That's probably because I used to go fishing round there as a boy." He looked up at me. "How much do you want for it?"

"Well . . ." I mumbled. "It still needs a bit of work on it." I was in a bit of a quandary. I didn't want to part with it, and didn't want to hurt my next door neighbour's feelings: after all, he had given me the painting box. "And I did promise it to someone else yesterday at the dry dock." I saw the disappointment in his face.

"But I'll do another one for you, I promised, "— with more water and reflections next time." This promise went some way to mollifying his bitter disappointment.

"I suppose that'll have to do. It's a shame someone got there before me," sniffed Alec. "But be sure to let me know if the deal falls through." I left my glum neighbour and carried the canvas back to the studio. Once again I was confronted by a singular development.

The dock was dry. The water and reflections had vanished.

* * *

I sat in my garden studio contemplating the *masterpiece* propped up on the easel. The view was as I painted it the previous day. The dock was definitely dry, and there were no figures to be found on the canvas. 'I've heard of haunted houses,' I mused, 'castles, pubs— and even ghost trains. But this beats everything.' In my opinion the painting was in some way "haunted". 'Was it the place, the canvas — or was it the easel and paint?' However, the most unusual aspect of the situation was that the painting presented the viewer with his or her favourite quality, whether it be figures or reflections. This peculiar characteristic gave the painting another dimension — an mysterious ability to change the image and transfer ones likes onto canvas, thereby instilling a desire to buy it at any price.

'It's an artist's dream,' I thought. 'Whatever one painted could easily be sold for the highest price to any enraptured client.' I decided to put this theory (which to the reader must seem completely "half-baked") to the test. I collected a rose from the garden, a jam jar from the kitchen and set up this simple still life group on a table in the studio. Instead of using oils I decided to sketch the group in pencil. The first sketch was done sitting on a chair with a drawing board on my knee: I continually ran into difficulties. The pencil needed constant sharpening, the sketch needed several adjustments and the eraser made unsightly marks on the paper. The completed sketch was rather mediocre and I placed it to one side. I then set up the paint box easel and chair, and settled down for the second attempt.

I began to draw — and oh what a difference! Everything flowed effortlessly and the drawing quickly began to take shape: it had to be the influence of the easel. In the meantime a change in lighting and atmosphere gradually filled the studio: it became darker and cooler, and a musty (almost unpleasant) odour filled the confined space. And then, as on the previous occasion beside the dry dock, I became aware of someone standing behind me, observing my every pencil stroke, highly critical of my attempts. At the same time there was a subtle change in the ambience of the room: there was *another* present within the studio. Unlike my "critic" standing behind me, this presence pervaded the whole of the studio. It was a darker, more powerful being, malevolent in the extreme and menacing in intent. I wanted to beat a swift retreat, but somehow I held on and persevered: within minutes I had completed the sketch. The oppressive atmosphere immediately lightened — and I gazed at my second masterpiece in utter admiration. At that moment the studio door opened and Brenda, my wife, arrived to call me to lunch. She picked up the first sketch.

"Not a bad attempt, I suppose," she remarked, trying not to snigger. "It's a shame the jam jar is out shape and black smudges are all over the place (at this stage I must tell you that my wife is always highly critical of my endeavours) — otherwise it could go up with the rest of your National Gallery works of art."

'I bet it's one of her nagging ghostly ancestors who's been standing behind me,' I thought. I handed her the second attempt. Her expression changed — and she was totally dumbstruck for a change. Brenda looked at me, then at the sketch — then back at me, openmouthed, lost for words.

"Well . . ?"

"I can't believe it," she gasped. "Did *you* do this?"

"I certainly did," I replied, enjoying the moment (I had never seen her this way before) and savouring her astonishment.

"You actually drew this," she continued, almost in a whisper, "—

178

by yourself . . ?" I burst out laughing.

"What do you mean — "by myself". Of course I did it by myself," I cried. "Well, what do you think of it?" She slowly shook her head.

"I can't believe it," she murmured. "It's absolutely beautiful. I never knew you could draw so well. Those wings are absolutely sublime."

"Wings . . ?"

"The butterfly, darling," she smiled, "— and the fallen rose petals sparkling with dew. It's worthy of the real National Gallery. Absolutely wonderful . . .."

I took the sketch from her reluctant hand, and what greeted my eyes confirmed my half-baked theory about the home-made paint box. An exquisite butterfly, dew-soaked rose petals bathed in a sublime light and shade, and a crystal-like jam jar filled the paper.

My wife gazed at me in rapturous admiration, I gazed at the drawing in growing trepidation — and between us stood the "haunted" easel and chair.

Why, then, did I imagine my critic rubbing his hands in growing anticipation.

* * *

The proprietor of Jackson and Son [Framing, Restoration and Evaluation Our Speciality] pursed his lips: he was highly impressed.

"You say this is your own work," Mr. Jackson asked, holding the painting up to the light.

"That's right," I nodded, "— and the sketch. What do you think of them?"

"Remarkable," he replied after some deliberation, "— quite remarkable. Have you any other examples with you?"

"No, I'm sorry I haven't — just the canal scene and the sketch."

"A pity," he said in a disappointed tone. "If your other work is up to this standard I could certainly find buyers willing to pay handsomely for them — and I'm talking four figures here."

"Really," I blinked, taken aback by his assessment. "You think they are that good?" Mr. Jackson smiled.

"Let me tell you this," he said quietly. "I've been in this trade for many years, and if I hadn't recognised the canal at Tarlescough I would have said this was a fifteenth century Renaissance painting."

"Fifteenth century!" I exclaimed. "I can assure you it was painted last week."

"Quite so," he declared. "And the same thing applies to the pencil sketch. I have to say that it has all the qualities of Albert Dürer, the German artist, from the sixteenth century. This period is one of my specialities, and it's really amazing how you have managed to capture the Renaissance mood." Once again the haunted painting and sketch were exerting their spell on the mind of the viewer. "Up to now I have never believed in all that spiritualist nonsense about dead artists taking over the souls of the living painters — but after seeing your work . . ." I laughed at this weird observation.

"You can bet my wife would soon put a stop to that nonsense," I retorted. "She's very particular who she has in our house."

"I know it's easy to joke about these things," the pensive man shook his head seriously. "But there is something very strange about it all. Have you had any dreams — or any unusual occurrences?" I recalled my unseen critic: perhaps Mr. Jackson had a point after all.

"I suppose so — but not dreams," I replied, and told him of my experience on the canal bank with the unseen companion. His parting remark as I left the shop set me thinking.

"Well, in my opinion it's worth looking into," declared Mr. Jackson wisely. "From what you've told me there is something very odd about the whole business. On the other hand, they do say every cloud has a silver lining — so if you can produce work like this you could soon become famous and extremely rich."

'Famous and rich — perhaps money was the key to the whole business,' I pondered. 'Like the magic bottle and genie in those childhood tales the lucky owner has wealth and influence at his finger tips.'

180

In my case the "magic bottle" stood in my studio, and the unseen "genie" stood behind me when I used it. It would seem that I had let some powerful malevolent influence out, and may be it would be wise to cork it up again, recalling the down side of desirable wishes and the old proverb *"ye don't get summut for nowt."*

The easel held the key (or I should say *cork*).

* * *

Home-made was the starting point. The design of the easel, with its built in features, indicated an extremely clever mind at work, and it was to the construction of the paint box that I turned my attention. I began by dismantling the folding legs, and then the inner casing which held the sections for the paint tubes and other accessories: I came up with a blank. The flip-up easel top was next on the agenda, and it was here that I at last met with success. Imagine my growing excitement when I saw, on closer examination, that the wood grain on the outside of this top did not match that on the inside. The top was obviously made out of two thin pieces of wood, and with some careful working with a knife on the beading I managed to prise the pieces apart. Between these two pieces of wood I found some sheets of folded paper, long hidden from human sight, and secretly placed there when this peculiar device was first constructed.

With great care I patiently unfolded the paper sheets, laying them on the studio floor. I had expected some paintings or at least sketches of the original owner's work, but I was to be disappointed. Before me, spread out on the floor, were a set of tracings, or as they are known in artistic circles — "rubbings". I scrutinised each in turn, making rough sketches in my pad. The largest rubbings were of monumental brasses of a knight in armour and a man in mediaeval garments, fur trimmed with a purse slung round his waist. His hands were very indistinct, as if the "rubber" had run out of wax. The other sheets were smaller and consisted of rough tracings of what were probably wood carvings. I was, however, rather disappointed at not finding the signature of the brass rubber on any of the pieces.

I glanced at the wooden insert propped up by the window. As any artist will tell you, the marks of a lead pencil glint when light strikes them at a certain angle, and in this case the sunlight struck this wooden insert at this angle — and highlighted a pencil drawing on its surface. With growing excitement I reached for my sketch pad and within minutes had copied this drawing. It was a view of a church porch — and this too was unsigned by the artist. There was no indication as to the name of the church, or in what part of the country it stood. The crenellated outline of the building resembled that of the Tudor Perpendicular style, but the date could be from any century: however, the fittings and lock on the box did suggest the Victorian period.

"So your secret is out at last," I murmured with quiet satisfaction, contemplating the work of the unknown artist. "Now I wonder who you were?"

At that very moment the door burst open and a blast of cold air swept into the studio, lifting the rubbings from the floor and scattering them like confetti around the room. I sat there immobile, completely taken aback by this furious onslaught, and, as the papers slowly drifted down and settled around me, a shiver ran down my spine.

Someone was very angry indeed.

* * *

I made rough sketches of all the rubbings and tracings, before storing them in my art desk. I then turned to the sketch of the church porch: this was obviously the place to start. The porch was evidently very old, characterized by strong buttresses at each corner. It also had a room with a rectangular mullioned window situated above the carved four centred arch, topped by mock battlements and corner pinnacles. A figure stood in a niche set in the stonework, probably the patron saint of the church. The carving was that of a woman, which could help in narrowing down the search, and I kept my fingers crossed in the hope that it was a local church. At this point Lady Luck in the guise of the drinking habits of my next door neighbour played her hand.

"The Punch Bowl," Alec maintained vigorously, "— that doorway is next to the Punch Bowl in Altbank."

"Are you sure?"

"Of course I am," he declared. "I've knocked a few pints back in that pub, I can tell you. The church is just opposite, on the other side of the road."

And so it was just as Alec described it when I visited Altbank the following day. There could be no doubt about its identity, for the sketch matched the porch in every detail: this was the church I was looking for. It was open, and an illustrated guide book on the table behind the old door explained the origins and history of this picturesque building.

Briefly the church of St. Helen is the principal church of the twelve ancient parishes in the surrounding area, and is dedicated to Helen, supposedly the daughter of King Coilus (Old King Cole), sanctified after her discovery of the Sacred Cross in the Holy Land. The village itself goes back to Conquest times, and was selected by the Desmolines family as their 'estate of knight'. In the sixteenth century the original church was taken down and rebuilt in the Tudor perpendicular style, and the exterior of this peaceful building has remained unaltered to the present day, except for the addition of a Choir vestry at the time of the First World War. The interior contains some interesting items. Stone effigies and choir stalls, Caroline pulpit and ornately carved screen combine with the restored stained glass to imbue a sombre ambience of awe and reverence, which has spanned centuries of worship.

Everything was in its rightful place. Unfortunately this did not apply to the memorial brass in the tracing. Other brasses of Knights and their Ladies were set in the stonework of the Desmolines Chapel, and I had assumed, because of the sketch of the porch, that the tracings had come from this particular church. It seemed that I was mistaken – – there was no sign of the armoured knight from the paint box easel.

The tranquil setting and peaceful atmosphere induced a lethargic frame of mind, allaying to some extent my disappointment, and I sat down for a brief respite in one of the ancient pews. Contemplating the fine tracery work in the Nave and casually perusing the richness of carving I noticed a circular design in the screen: I referred to the guide.

> *The fine carving on the tester of the Chancel Screen de-*
> *picts the visitation of St. Helen, richly robed and crowned,*
> *by an angel in surplice and cassock. The True Cross, which*
> *she found in Jerusalem after a long search, lies uncov-*
> *ered upon the ground between the figures.*

My eye wandered along the line of pews down the north aisle, resting briefly on each bench end. And in an instant my mood of glum disappointment changed to one of growing exhilaration — I saw one of the unknown artist's tracings. The head and shoulders of a bearded man, dressed in banded tunic and wearing a plumed crown-like hat rising from two sheaves of wheat, had an almost pagan quality about it: but it was definitely one of the tracings in the easel. This had to be the right church, after all, and now the search was on for the other tracings; within minutes I had found them.

On one block of pews along the south side of the centre aisle I found the set of unusual alphabet carvings which matched certain letters in easel tracings, and on the opposite side I came across some unusual designs opening onto the **north** aisle. They were of a cross with hammer and pincers and a cross with nails respectively.

'I wonder why the artist chose these wood engravings in particular,' I mused. In my opinion there were other equally fine engravings on adjacent pews. 'The letters of the alphabet are a bit of a puzzle as well — almost like the ingredients for pagan spells.'

That left the two memorial brasses to find, but a thorough search once again failed to reveal them: I was out of luck. The declining rays of the sun filtered through the tracery and coloured glass to announce the lateness of the hour and the sonorous chimes of the church clock confirmed the fact. The afternoon had indeed passed quickly, but it was time to go and I reluctantly called off my search. Except for the missing brasses my visit had certainly been worthwhile, but I really needed to speak to someone who had a detailed knowledge of the church. I picked up a copy of the parish magazine and scanned the information on the rear page. There, sandwiched between Holy Communion and Choir Practice, I found the answer to my problem.

BRASS RUBBERS are welcome. Please contact Mr. Keith Thomas, our churchwarden, for permission and the issue of a licence.

I resolved there and then to attend the next Sunday service and make the acquaintance of the churchwarden. In my case it would seem that permission was unnecessary and a licence out of the question: I already had two brass rubbings authorised and paid for in another century. But, as I was later to discover, the price their creator paid for the privilege was more than a couple of Victorian shillings.

* * *

The Sunday morning service ended and the congregation rose and slowly filed out through the porch door: a sidesman pointed the churchwarden out to me.

"That's Mr. Thomas over there, standing next to the vicar," he said with a nod. "The one in the sports jacket."

I approached the gentleman in question and introduced myself. I showed him the sketches of the armoured knight and the mediaeval man, and briefly explained the reason for my visit and the nature of my problem. The sketch the man in the mediaeval garments received a cursory glance and a shake of the head: however, the armorial knight produced an immediate and enthusiastic response.

"Do you know, old chap, you're the first person to ask about this particular brass in years," Mr. Thomas answered, taking me to one side. "In fact — I have to admit that I've never seen it myself."

"So it isn't in this church after all," I replied. "That's a bit of a disappointment."

"Oh no — you've misunderstood me, old chap," he said with a smile. "It's definitely one of ours, I can assure you. It's been in there for centuries, but I haven't seen it and neither has any one else for over a hundred years." I stared at him in amazement.

"A hundred years . .?"

"That's right — come inside and I'll show you where it is."

I followed the churchwarden down the aisle to the old choir stalls at the east end of the church. There he stopped and pointed to the place where a row of stalls backed on to a side screen.

"That's where it is," Mr. Thomas indicated, "— underneath that lot. If you crouch down by that end stall you can see the edging of the brass on the floor." I did as he suggested: it was a tight squeeze, but I could just make out the metal line between the oak stall and the stone floor.

"Who was he?"

"Sir William Desmolines," he answered. "He died in the fifteen fifties. You can see his armorial shield up there on the screen — the one with the Cross Moline on it."

"How do you know it's him underneath the stalls, and not the other mediaeval fellow?"

"We've got a brass tracing of him," the churchwarden smiled, "— done in the late Victorian period, when part of this screen was lifted to renovate the organ — something to do with the pipes, I think."

186

"So you're definitely sure there isn't a brass of the other mediae-val man in the church?"

"No, I'm afraid not — it's not one of ours."

"And the tracing of Sir William," I asked, "— do you know who did it?"

"Yes, as a matter of fact I do," Mr. Thomas replied. "His name was Wainright — Joseph Wainright."

"Was he a painter — an artist?"

"That's right. We have one of his paintings in the Parvise — that's the room above the porch."

"Would it be possible to see it," I asked, endeavouring to restrain my excitement at this stroke of luck. 'So Joseph Wainright was the owner of the easel,' I surmised. At this point there was a subtle change in the churchwarden's manner.

"Well, I don't know if . . ." He paused, mulling over my request: he didn't seem to keen on the idea, and probably regretted mentioning Wainright's painting. Sensing his reluctance I wondered what the problem was.

"It's just that he's not that well known," I carried on, "— and I have one of his sketches on wood. I'd hate to miss an opportunity to see one of his paintings." The mention of the sketch tipped the balance.

"Well, I suppose so, since you've seen some of his work before," he answered somewhat reluctantly. "I've got a few things to do, so if you don't mind hanging about for a while in the porch, I'll be along in a minute."

I readily agreed, and didn't have long to wait. The churchwarden returned with bunch of keys, selected the largest, and unlocked a solid oak door set into the stone wall: we mounted the stairs to the Parvise and entered a musty rectangular room. Sunlight filtered through the small glass panes in a mullioned window, which overlooked the porch entrance below. Clerical vestments, old banners and notice boards adorned the walls and stacks of dusty hymnals, prayer books and church registers lay on shelves and in boxes along with assorted items left over from previous church bazaars and fêtes. There was no sign of a painting to be seen.

"They say this was a vestry for the chantry priest before the Reformation," Mr. Thomas explained, "but now, as you can see, we use it for storage."

"I can't see a painting anywhere," I queried, gazing round the room.

"No, you certainly can't," he agreed. "It has never been on public view. We keep it covered up — and you'll see why in a moment." He moved across the room to a large cupboard in the corner: it was heavily padlocked. Mr. Thomas unlocked it, opened the door and stepped back, his hand covering his nose and mouth.

"Phew," he gasped. "I don't understand why the cupboard always smells so bad." I could have ventured a reason for it. That horrible musty odour was very familiar to my nostrils — Wainright's easel had the same problem. Once again that unsettled feeling came upon me, and I sensed the familiar presence in the room, standing behind me, waiting . . . 'Had Wainright come to join us?' The churchwarden beckoned me over.

"Well, you wanted to see it," he muttered. "So here's your chance." He pulled a heavy black covering to one side, and I stepped forward to view the "Wainright". What I saw explained the churchwarden's reluctance (or I should say repugnance) at the viewing and the reason for it's internment in a padlocked cupboard.

The canvas was approximately three feet square, painted in oils and unframed: it was entitled *'The Visitation of St. Helen'*. And it is true to say that the overall composition of the work reflected that of the finely carved tester of St. Helen and the Angel on the Chancel Screen: but there the resemblance ended. The focus of the painting was on the word *visitation* — of the most horrifying sort. The painting depicted St. Helen in the act of saving, rather than discovering, the True Cross. Her crown had fallen to the ground, trampled into the soil, and her robes were ripped and torn by the long talons and claws of terrifying creatures as she desperately tried to prevent her merciless tormentors from dragging the cross into a fiery pit beneath the earth. These malevolent shapes were under the control of a guiding angel who had clearly come from below rather than above, and could be recognised by his cloven hooves and horns as that subject so often found in early religious works. This savage demonic figure was undoubtedly Satan himself. The gruesome scene was lit by the flames below, and the hellish light fell upon another figure, absent from the wood carving on the Screen.

This additional figure was dressed in a long black gown and held a palette and brushes in paint stained hands: it was undoubtedly a self portrait of the artist himself, Joseph Wainright (it was the practice of many artists in the past to include themselves in religious works of art). I gazed at his haunted features in awe. His bearded face was paralysed with fear and dread — and the reason for his dismay was plainly apparent. One taloned hand of the satanic figure was pointing at the demoralized artist and the other at the gaping hole in the ground. Demonic creatures, gathering behind the terrified artist, were poised to drag him into the fiery pit. Obviously something had gone wrong. The Saint had successfully overcome her antagonists and the Holy Cross was saved. Someone had to pay for the blunder and, judging by the look on the artist's face, he was all to aware who that person was: there was no escape. However, the subject matter apart, the quality and execution of the painting were magnificent. It was in every respect a religious masterpiece.

"You can see why it is kept securely locked away, can't you?" The painting clearly had an upsetting effect on Mr. Thomas, and he hurriedly re-covered the work of art. "It gives some people nightmares, you know — they don't want to come up here again, once they've seen it."

"I can believe it," I replied with a shudder. 'And not only nightmares,' I mused, thinking of my unseen companion and the menacing presence in the studio. I had Wainright's easel and his tracings — and his style. But after seeing his *masterpiece*, the last thing I wanted was his artistic *gift*. It was plain to see that he had acquired that from a painting master and a School of Art not of this earthly dimension. Keen as I was on improving my artistic endeavours, and having seen Joseph Wainright's graduation, I wasn't prepared to pay that entrance fee — and become his *apprentice*. I had been forewarned, but could a solution be found for my dire predicament in time?

"I wonder if you could do me a special favour," I asked the pensive churchwarden. His generous reply and my return, later that day, with a parcel securely wrapped and sealed in stout canvas solved my dilemma. Wainright's easel and tracings were ceremoniously padlocked in the old cupboard in the Parvise above the porch of St. Helen's Church, Altbank.

His tools were with his masterpiece at last.

* * *

Epilogue.

I received a letter from Mr. Thomas the other day: it contained two publications. The first is a Parish Magazine for the month of April, and the second (and most revealing) is the summer edition of the Friends' Newsletter. A certain passages in each booklet have been marked in red by the churchwarden.

The first passage is from the Parish Magazine.

> *Last Thursday the people of Altbank were stunned by the news of an act of vandalism to our beautiful church. During the previous night thieves struck and removed a section of the lead covering from the roof. Rain poured down onto the Choir Stalls and Nave floor, causing some water damage to the ancient screen and carved pews. However, the Rector is optimistic about the long term effect on these precious carvings, but signs of corrosion have appeared on the monumental brasses in the stone flooring and will*

have to be remedied as soon as possible.

The second passage refers to the restoration work.

All the monumental brasses have now been lifted for restoration, after being damaged by rain water in April. However, a great deal of excitement and speculation occurred when part of the Choir Stalls was removed for cleaning and the long hidden brass of Sir William Desmolines, who died in 1548, was uncovered. It had been uncovered once before, in 1887, during work on the organ, and a local artist, Joseph Wainright, had assisted in this work. He cleaned and reset the brass in the stonework, and his own tracing of Sir William can be seen at the Rectory.

The present excitement has been caused by the fact that when Sir William was prised from the stone floor it was discovered that his monumental brass was a palimpsest. This means, in lay man's terms, that it has been engraved on both sides. The figure of a man was found on the reverse, wearing the long fur-trimmed garments of the mediaeval period. He is clean shaven, and his thin hands are holding an palette and brushes. An inscription comprising his name and Latin text is engraved on the base, and we have discovered from records in the Guildhall, London, that he was an artist and goldsmith who worked for the Tudor Court. He originated from Germany and arrived here in 1540 to set up studio in Westcheap. He was expelled from the Guild in disgrace (there is a brief reference to souls and the Devil) but no record of his death exists. Therefore the brass was never used and returned to the London workshops.

Wainright, a reclusive and secretive man, died suddenly and mysteriously in 1889, and we do not know if he took

191

a tracing of this palimpsest before he reset the brass of Sir William in 1887, or the reason for its obscure position beneath the Choir Stalls. However the church brass rubbers have already made a tracing of this mysterious brass for the collection in the Rectory.

It would seem, thanks to vandals and inclement weather, that I've had a narrow escape. As an added precaution I've burned the pencil drawing and the painting of the dry dock (much to the disgust of my wife and next door neighbour) and taken up golf as a substitute for my previous hobby. Unfortunately, my peace of mind is continually afflicted by a disturbing thought.

'Did I leave any of my own brushes and tubes of paint in the easel, now securely padlocked in the ancient church in Altbank?'

I have a distinct feeling that the Victorian painter and his Satanic master don't play golf, and are loath to give up a budding apprentice. This feeling is reinforced by the latest article in the Friends' Newsletter.

NOLI AD MEUM SEPULCRUM STARE ET LACRIMAE
NON HIC SUM. NON DORMIS.
NOLI AD MEUM SEPULCRUM STARE ET PLANQERE
NON ILLIC SUM. NON MORTUUS SUM

There is much speculation over this Latin inscription from the reverse side of the palimpsest of Sir William Desmolines. The Rector tells me that it is an abbreviated form of an 8th Century Saxon prayer. He has kindly translated the inscription, and it reads

Do not stand at my grave and weep
I am not there. I do not sleep.
Do not stand at my grave and cry.
I am not there. I did not die.

AUGHTON

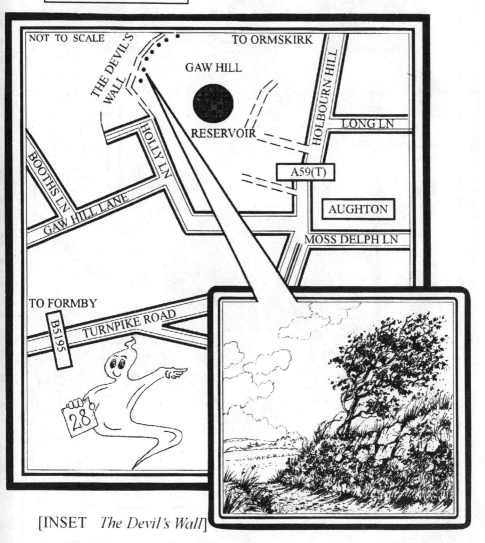

NOT TO SCALE

THE DEVIL'S WALL

TO ORMSKIRK

GAW HILL

HOLBOURN HILL

LONG LN

RESERVOIR

HOLLY LN

A59(T)

BOOTHS LN

AUGHTON

GAW HILL LANE

MOSS DELPH LN

TO FORMBY

B5195

TURNPIKE ROAD

28

[INSET   *The Devil's Wall*]

193

A WALL WITH A VIEW

The languid call of a solitary cuckoo floated from the distant wood, the repetitive notes of this seasonal visitor lingering on a gentle breeze, and Arthur Davenport, out for his customary afternoon stroll, idled in serene contemplation, drinking in the peace and quiet of the balmy summer's day.

This dreamlike trance was brutally shattered by the raucous clatter of a noisy diesel engine spluttering into life, and moments later a powerful farm tractor appeared round the bend in the dusty track and charged down on the dawdling rambler. Arthur Davenport leaped onto the grass verge in self preservation, pressing himself hard against the dry-stone wall to avoid the huge wheels of the machine as it thundered past in a cloud of dust. The ground trembled and shook under the weight of this man-made monster and the severe vibrations dislodged a stone boulder from the wall: it fell to the ground and rolled onto the track, coming to rest at the feet of the startled man.

"Damn nuisance!" Arthur Davenport spluttered as the tractor disappeared from view, and the fine dust began to settle. He stepped back onto the track, stooping down to pick up the weather-worn stone. "It's a wonder the wall is still standing," he muttered as he turned to replace the boulder in its original position. However, it seemed that the stone was not the only object to have been dislodged by the passing monster. Something lay in the cavity in the old wall — and it glinted in the sunlight.

'What have we got here?' mused Arthur, reaching in and pulling out this strange discovery. He sat on the wall and examined the object closely. It could be described as roughly oval in shape, and the size of a large egg. Gold-like veins ran through its core, and brightly coloured crystalline substances protruded at varying intervals from its irregular stonelike surface, sparkling and flashing in the sunlight.

"It looks like one of those geological specimens from a museum collection," he murmured thoughtfully, "— but it is very odd. I wonder what it's doing in the wall — and if there are any more like it?" He searched the cavity, scraping around the indentation where the object had rested, and came up with bits of rubble and sand. "This lot won't start a gold rush," sniffed Arthur, puzzled by it all. He replaced the stone block in the wall, the geological curiosity in his coat pocket, and continued on his ramble along the dusty farm track.

'Someone must have hidden it in the old wall,' he concluded thoughtfully, 'but for what reason — or for how many years I suppose that's anyone's guess.'

Arthur's subsequent experiences provided the answers to these simple questions. Unfortunately they were beyond belief.

* * *

Arthur Davenport climbed the style and followed the public footpath down the hill through sun-lit fields of ripened corn. The meandering track was edged at intervals by irregular clumps of bushes and broad-leafed trees, which cast long shadows over this undulating golden sea, a subtle warning to the leisurely traveller of the lateness of the hour. A light breeze stirred the calm and tranquil air, whispering through the leaves and rustling atop the seed laden corn in waves and eddies, a herald of departing day and approaching night.

Some forty minutes later, as the setting sun began its final decent and dipped below the far horizon, Arthur Davenport began his final ascent and reached the farm track and old weathered sandstone wall high on the hill. He paused for a moment, considering this ancient feature, and came to the conclusion (aided no doubt by the onset of weariness and the stiffness of joints), that it was a convenient and welcome place to rest awhile and recover his breath.

He sat on the wall, gazing out towards the horizon, contemplating the serenity of the fertile plain below. His eye wandered over the tranquil scene before him, resting now on woodland and farm, and then on distant spire and roof top. In the soft haze which rose from a swiftly cooling land the twinkling lights of house and cottage mirrored the emerging stars in the deep turquoise sky above, and Arthur Davenport wallowed in this vision of harmony and peace. Then his meditation was abruptly disturbed — something caught his attention.

It was the sudden appearance of a distant figure, possibly a fellow traveller, coming along the footpath in the fields below, heading towards the hill. Arthur was surprised and uncertain as to where the figure had come from, bearing in mind the fact that he had an uninterrupted field of view of the whole area, but it was clear where the figure was heading — towards him. There was something strange about it, in the way that it constantly looked back in terror as it hurried forward, that unsettled him. The reason for this was soon apparent.

Distant figures came into view through the haze, twisting and turning, casting here and there — as if searching. Then they found the path and his trail, and set out on the heels of their quarry. As the figure grew closer in the failing light Arthur had the distinct impression, before it passed into the clump of trees at the base of the hill, that, from the style of its dress, it was from another age. Knee breeches, stockings and frock coat could hardly be defined as modern attire. Arthur stood up, anticipating the arrival of this mysterious stranger, determined to move on. He waited, eye fixed on the path. The light began to fade and the minutes passed by — but there was no sign of the traveller. He did not emerge from the trees.

'Where is he? Had the stranger seen him and decided to wait there? Perhaps he was afraid?'

Arthur hesitated for a moment, eying the distant mob with growing apprehension, and then decided to investigate. He retraced his steps down the hill and followed the path into the trees. In the semi-darkness he searched the undergrowth, making his way through to the other side of the copse. To his astonishment he found that there was no one there — the traveller and his pursuers had vanished.

However, some one else had witnessed these strange events, for, as Arthur turned back along the path to the hill, he saw a figure sitting on the wall above, his dark shape outlined against the turquoise sky. Arthur (from his position some distance away at the base of the hill) had the impression that this stranger was wrapped in a long robe or cowl, and held a rod or staff — *which he pointed at Arthur in a most hostile manner.* The oppressive "watcher" sat motionless, gazing down upon the apprehensive rambler. Arthur halted, wondering whether he should carry on and meet this unfriendly looking stranger, or retreat down the hill.

He decided to go on and by the time he reached the track beside the wall, he found, to his great relief, that the mysterious figure also had vanished into the night.

* * *

Now in his seventieth year and all alone in the world, Arthur Davenport had recently moved into Sycamore House, a select retirement home on the other side of the hill. A long illness (relating to an afflic-tion of the mind rather than to the body) had precipitated matters and a milder climate, fresh air and regular exercise were prescribed. He had finally taken the advice of his doctor, sold his large house in the chilly north east of the country, and moved to Ormsley, a small mar-ket town situated in a pleasant and temperate area in the county of Lancashire. He now occupied a furnished self-contained unit under the watchful eye of Mrs. Jones, the resident warden.

"You'll be late for supper, Arthur," the vigilant warden greeted him in the entrance hall. "Where on earth have you been 'till now? It's almost dark."

"Sorry, Mrs. Jones," Arthur apologised. "I'm afraid I got held up on my way back — stopped by that old wall on the hill — saw something very peculiar." He went on to recount the strange occurrence and the warden listened

"It doesn't surprise me, walking up there at this time of night," answered Mrs. Jones with a nod. "You do know what they call that place round here, don't you?"

"No, I don't think so . . ."

"Well, you wouldn't, being a newcomer to the area," she said gravely. "They call it the Devil's Dyke."

"Devil's Dyke? That's an odd name," replied Arthur, somewhat sceptically. "What has it got to do with the Devil?"

"Well, the Devil is supposed to have built the wall, so the tale goes," answered Mrs. Jones, "but nobody knows why. Anyway, some of the older folks round here say the place is haunted, and won't go near it at night."

"Well, I can assure you it wasn't the Devil I saw being chased tonight," Arthur informed her, "but I'm sure there's some logical reason for it all."

"May be there is — but you won't catch me up there after dark," shivered Mrs. Jones. "Anyway, you'd better get a move on, or you'll miss your supper."

Reviewing the warden's fanciful tale and his own unsettling experience on the hill, Arthur came to the conclusion that he needed something stronger than cocoa and biscuits. What better than stiff tumbler of whisky (aptly named the 'demon drink') to prevent an resurgence of his old nervous affliction.

Unfortunately, as events unfolded, Arthur found a tumbler was totally insufficient for the purpose. The remedy (although he didn't know it at the time) lay in the right hand pocket of the coat in his bedroom wardrobe.

* * *

On closer examination Arthur Davenport came to the conclusion that the was something very odd about the old dry-stone wall, or the "Devil's Dyke" as Mrs. Jones mysteriously described it. It was approximately eighty yards long (he estimated by pacing its length) and five feet high, and ran beside the farm track. However, for most of its length it was hidden from view by overgrown vegetation, brambles and the like, but here and there the rough stone facing was clearly visible, especially in the central section were Arthur had rested the previous evening.

'Yes,' he thought, climbing up and surveying its length with a puzzled frown, 'there's definitely something odd about it.' Then he realised what it was. 'There's no reason, as far as I can see, for the wall to be here in the first place. It doesn't begin or end anywhere in particular — it doesn't keep anything in or out, as a wall should.'

It seemed the obvious conclusion, for the wall enclosed neither field or garden, or formed any sort of boundary. It was as if someone had set out to build a length of wall in the middle of nowhere — for no apparent reason.

"I'm sure that's something the Devil wouldn't dream of doing," murmured Arthur, contemplating the panoramic landscape from the top of the wall, "— unless a soul or two were involved in the proceedings."

At that moment his attention was drawn to a figure moving quickly along the tree-lined road some distance away. The speed at which the figure travelled surprised him, until it broke from the cover of the trees and Arthur saw it was on a horse. Arthur was even more astonished by the rider's clothes, for (although the horseman was some fair distance away) Arthur could see he was not wearing normal riding gear: furthermore, the purposeful way in which the rider spurred the horse on, head and body arched forward over the mane, left Arthur with a distinct and disturbing impression.

"He's like one of those old highwaymen," he blinked, as the strange horseman galloped into a stand of trees — out of sight. He did not reappear — but to Arthur's amazement something else did. A coach and four, as if plucked from one of those chocolate box Christmas cards came into view, travelling slowly towards the trees. "I bet the fellow is hiding there," gasped Arthur, "— waiting." He wanted to shout out, to warn the oncoming coach of the danger, but the distance was too great and moments later the coach had reached the trees — and the waiting rider. Arthur stood on the Devil's Wall, full of apprehension and awe, waiting for the tragic events to unfold, for the shots and cries — and the horseman's escape from the scene of his crime. Arthur waited in vain.

As time went on there was still no sign of movement on the distant road and Arthur grew impatient: he could wait no longer. Visibility was beginning to deteriorate with a sudden change in the weather, as the sun disappeared behind storm clouds and a band of rain swept in from the west. Clambering down from the wall he hurried along the farm track to seek a different vantage point, hoping to catch a glimpse of the coach and the horseman — and that's when he received the second shock of the day. Gazing across the fields below he found, to his astonishment, that the panorama had subtly changed. Just before low cloud and rain blotted out the view he saw that buildings now stood on the site of the wooded copse, modern light standards had replaced the trees on the highway, and the muffled sound of rush hour traffic reached his ears.

Arthur looked back towards the Devil's Dyke, somewhat perturbed by this strange development. He was surprised to see two figures sitting on the wall, gazing out over the plain below. He hadn't seen them on the footpath leading to the wall, but no doubt they were walkers taking advantage of the convenient resting place. Pulling the hood of his anorak over his head as the first drops of rain began to fall, he set off at a brisk pace, retracing his steps along the farm track.

"That's rather odd," mused Arthur, as he approached the motionless figures sitting in the driving rain. "They don't seem to be bothered about getting wet, and they're certainly not wearing the right sort of gear for this weather. Unless they get a move on they'll catch their death of . . ." He stopped short. A sudden flurry of driving rain temporarily blinded him, and when he cleared his eyes he saw the space on the wall was empty. The mysterious figures had vanished. Arthur hurried on, thoroughly unnerved by this third shock of the day. He recalled his conversation with Mrs. Jones. "Anyway, some of the older folks round here say the place is haunted, and won't go near it at night." Perhaps she had a point.

'I suppose there might be something in it,' he thought, judging from his recent experiences. 'That view of the horseman and coach could be described as "haunting" — and those vanishing figures . . ?'

He arrived back at Sycamore House, soaked through despite his anorak. Mrs. Jones greeted him at the door.

"You must get out of those wet clothes straight away, before you catch pneumonia," she said to the dripping resident. "You all must be mad going out in this weather at your age."

"All . . .?"

"Yes — those other two as well!" snorted Mrs. Jones.

"Other two . . .?" Arthur paled. "What other two?"

"The two that followed you back along the footpath," replied Mrs. Jones smartly. "I saw them from the upstairs window — and they looked a sorry pair indeed — in clothes totally unsuitable for this weather."

Arthur stared at her open mouthed. It would seem, if Mrs. Jones was correct, that his travelling companions from Devil's Dyke had followed him home — and now knew where he lived. Unfortunately the trouble with ghosts is the random way in which they pop up every so often, and the detrimental effect it can have one's the mind — not to mention the lack of medication to treat it. Once again Arthur Davenport resorted to that age old remedy, "demon drink", for temporary relief. It was to be short-lived.

* * *

"You ought to know the rules by now, Arthur," the resident warden admonished him at breakfast.

"The rules, Mrs. Jones . . .?" Arthur answered, somewhat mystified by her tone of voice.

"Yes — about guests. You know we have to sign them in — fire regulations."

"Guests — fire regulations . . .?" Arthur looked blankly at Mrs. Jones.

"Your guests last night," she retorted impatiently, "— the two ramblers."

"The ramblers . . .? I'm afraid I don't understand you, Mrs. Jones."

"You know the rule. If you invite guests into Sycamore House, you have to sign them in first."

"I didn't invite anyone, I can assure you," replied the puzzled man.

"Well, I can assure you that I saw them come in — and follow you up to your flat," she declared. This stark observation rendered Arthur speechless: his mouth dropped and he went as pale as a ghost. "So in future, if they visit you again, please sign them in."

Talking of ghosts, this would seem an appropriate time to reveal one or two details concerning Arthur's recent nervous illness. In general terms it could be termed Melancholia, a condition where there is profound emotional depression, and in Arthur's case this was accompanied by delusions and periods of insomnia. Psycho-analysis uncovered a tragic incident from his past, long buried in his subconscious, an incident which returned to haunt him. This "haunting" (or delusion) became frequent in later years and his doctor eventually prescribed a course of psychotherapy. The treatment proved successful and the nature of the haunting was finally revealed under hypnosis. The following extract from the psychiatrist's report summarised this delusion.

'The patient, Arthur Davenport, was referred to me as suffering from bouts of depression, involving whispering

voices and vivid nightmares associated with feelings of persecution. The patient was placed in an hypnotic trance and prepared for regressive suggestion. Details of his earlier life began to emerge and when he regressed to his fifteenth birthday the probable cause of his melancholia was revealed. During this period of his life a family tragedy occurred. His mother and younger sister were drowned in a boating accident. The circumstances of this tragedy are simple enough. The birthday party on the small boat hired especially for the occasion, the excitement of the day and the patient's boyish high spirits combined in a fatal instant to overturn the heavily laden craft in the weed infested lake. The mother and sister were unable to swim, and, despite the patient's efforts to save them, were unfortunately drowned. Although it was deemed an accident by the authorities at the time, the patient blamed himself for the tragedy, and this, in my opinion, is the basic cause of the patient's delusion regarding his mother and sister, "his whispering companions from the other side". Treatment for the condition can now begin and therapeutic results are expected from suitable counselling sessions.

The treatment worked: Arthur eventually recovered and moved to Ormsley, to spend his twilight years in happy retirement in Sycamore House — that is until Mrs. Jones' reference to his "visitors".

That night, for the first time since his illness, he heard "his whisperings" again, but in this instance the "whisperings" were more like moans and groans, and the "companions" were definitely not of the female sex, judging by the heavy footfalls outside his flat door. On previous occasions the "sounds" had always been inside his head — but not any longer. They came from the corridor outside his door, and he came to the conclusion that they were the uninvited ramblers. He grew weary of the noise and decided to confront them, whoever they were. He threw open the door and prepared to give *them* a piece of his mind — but, to his astonishment, he found the corridor empty — and silent as the grave. A suffocating odour of mildew and decay, tinged with a hint of damp heather, hung in the air, and clammy fingers of mist eddied over the floor to swirl and curl round his bare legs.

The visitors had departed, unknown and unsigned.

* * *

"This is very interesting," murmured the distinguished gentleman. He picked up the stone from the library reading room table, and examined it under the light. From his scholarly bearing Arthur deduced the man was an academic, and a heavy academic tome, tucked under his arm, served to confirm this opinion. He looked at Arthur with a curious expression. "Can you tell me were you found it?"

"In a dry-stone wall on the hill the other side of Ormsley — behind Sycamore House," replied Arthur. The answer had an immediate impact on the scholar, and he blinked, almost dropping the stone in surprise.

"You actually found it in this area? That is unusual."

"Is it? I don't really know much about this sort of thing," replied Arthur, "— so I thought I might find something about stones in the reference library. Do you think it is some sort of fossil or geological specimen?"

"It's a specimen, right enough," the man returned, "— but it isn't your usual geological specimen."

"How do you mean?"

"What I said," replied the man in a rather pompous manner. "You can take my word for it. Charles Benson's the name, and, before I retired, I was head of a Geology Department for a number of years. This sort of thing was my speciality — so I know what I'm talking about. This specimen is not geological — it is man-made."

"Man-made . . .?" It was Arthur's turn to blink. "You mean some one made it."

"That's right — and I haven't come across anything like it before. Most interesting . . ." Charles Benson, the retired geologist, sat down beside Arthur and, after contemplating the sparkling crystals and shining gold veins in the stone for some moments, proceeded to give an expert opinion on the specimen.

"It is definitely a fusion of various materials," he began. "The most unusual feature of the stone is its composition. It is, as far as I can judge without the benefit of laboratory tests, a mixture of minerals — metals, crystals, bones and rock samples fused together into a solid mass. However, each of these materials has a different fusion temperature or melting point, so that theoretically it should be impossible to manufacture such a specimen."

"You mean some of the ingredients would burn away when a certain temperature was reached?"

"That's correct — these crystals would either disintegrate, the rock content crumble, or the metals burn away in the high temperatures involved." Charles Benson handed the stone back to Arthur. "Yes, I must say it is a very strange find indeed — the hill near Sycamore House, you say . . .?"

"Yes, that's right. The locals call it the Devil's Dyke."

"Really . . ." he mused. "Well, I'd like to have a wander round the place myself, sometime — and perhaps you could show me that dry-stone wall and the exact spot were you found your stone, if you wouldn't mind?"

"Not at all," declared Arthur. "It would be a pleasure — and you never know . . . we could find something else of interest, as well."

"Of interest . . . perhaps," the retired geologist nodded. "On the other hand, with a name like Devil's Dyke, may be "disturbing" would be a more apt choice of word."

It was. Later that night, as Arthur closed the curtains before retiring to bed, he casually glanced out of the window of his bedroom. The window overlooked the style and footpath which skirted the field and disappeared into the distant wood before winding its way up the hill towards Devil's Dyke. At that moment a full moon broke through a band of cloud, bathing the landscape in a soft light, and Arthur's attention was drawn to the edge of this distant wood. Two figures emerged from the trees, moving slowly along the footpath towards Sycamore House. Every now and again they disappeared from view as clouds obscured the moon, plunging the footpath in darkness, but their progress was relentless and they eventually reached the style as the moon broke cover, lighting the scene below his window. The sinister *visitors* from Devil's Dyke had come to call, and Arthur was totally shocked by their dreadful appearance.

It was painfully obvious they did not belong to the "living", for their attempts to climb the style were pitiable in the extreme and distressing to watch. Arthur's first impression was that the visitors were both blind drunk and incapable. However, after several attempts to climb the style the first man eventually managed to straddle the top step, wavering unsteadily backwards and forwards. He turned and reached down to help his companion over the wooden barrier, and Arthur, to his horror, now saw the reason for this excruciating behaviour. The man's head flopped about uncontrollably, wobbling from side to side, his eyes bulged from their sockets and his tongue protruded from his gaping mouth — and then Arthur saw the vivid red scar around his throat. *The man's neck had been stretched and broken.*

The second man was in even worse condition. He was shaven-headed and sightless, his clothes in shreds — and the jagged wounds and bruises on his body suggested some form of extreme torture before he died. The ghostly pair literally fell over the style into a sprawling heap on the ground, and lay there for some time in the moonlight. But then, to Arthur's dismay, the figures began to stir. Somehow they managed to clamber to their feet and continue their journey, staggering along the path to disappear from view round the corner of the building. After what he had just seen, Arthur had no intention of confronting his '*visitors*' in the corridor — face to face — at close quarters. He spent a sleepless night under the covers of his bed, while they, in turn, spent the night outside his door, eternally restless, patiently waiting for a new companion to come out and join them on Devil's Dyke.

Charles Benson's observation was right — "*disturbing*" was indeed a more apt choice of word.

* * *

"Do you remember the conversation we had the other week, Mrs. Jones — about the footpath that runs beside Devil's Dyke?"

"Yes, I think I do, Arthur," replied Mrs. Jones, nodding her head.

"Didn't you tell me that some people say the place is haunted?"

"Yes, that's right — and I do too. You wouldn't catch me walking around there at night, I can tell you!"

"So — have you ever seen any . . . ghosts?"

"No, I haven't — and I wouldn't want to, either," returned the warden with a shudder. "But believe me, some folk have seen them."

"Them . . .?" Arthur pressed on. "You actually know people who have seen ghosts up there?"

"Yes — my mother-in-law for one," Mrs. Jones declared, "when she was a young girl. She saw the ghost of the priest who was buried at Lythiall Abbey. He was caught up on the hill, near Devil's Dyke, trying to escape from the priest hunters."

The description was vividly clear to Arthur. He had seen the event himself, albeit centuries later. He had also seen the bloody end to the story.

"And then there was one of our residents who passed away the year before last," Mrs. Jones continued. "Now he told me that he definitely saw a ghost one night, when he was taking a short cut along the top path. He told me it was the ghost of a highway man who was hanged up on the hill years ago."

She paused, recollecting the old resident's description of the apparition. "He said the ghost looked horrible," she went on, "— with its head lolling about on its shoulders, eyes bulging and tongue hanging out. It fair shook him up, he told me." Arthur knew the feeling only too well. "Anyway," continued Mrs. Jones, quickly changing the subject, "I expect you'll be going to the opening, Arthur?"

"Opening . . .?"

"Yes, the grand opening," Mrs. Jones replied. "Didn't you get a leaflet with your morning paper?"

"A leaflet . . .?" Arthur frowned. "No, I don't think so — anyway I haven't read the paper yet."

"Well, I'm sure it will interest you, considering you spend most of your time walking on the hill," observed Mrs. Jones. "They're opening a nature reserve beside the reservoir, and all residents in the area have been invited to go along to the ceremony."

"Oh, now I come to think of it I did see workmen over that way a few weeks ago — but I thought it was something to do with the reservoir since the water company was privatised."

"It is. The new water company has put up the money for it," declared Mrs. Jones, "but as far as I'm concerned it's all a publicity stunt before they put up our water bills as well." With this caustic comment on the economic pitfalls of privatisation she departed and Arthur went in search of his morning newspaper. He found the leaflet.

GORE HILL NATURE RESERVE
SPONSORED BY NORTHERN WATER
GRAND OPENING TODAY AT 2 pm
EVERYONE WELCOME

Arthur decided to take up the offer and set out for the ceremony immediately after lunch, arriving at the reservoir just in time for the official opening by the Mayor of Ormsley. To his surprise he saw Charles

Benson in the crowd and made his way through the cheering assembly to join him.

"I didn't expect to see you here today," he said to the equally surprised geologist. "Are you interested in this sort of thing?"

"Not as such," replied Charles Benson. "It's the actual reservoir that interests me — sedimentary rocks, artesian bores and pumping methods, you know." Arthur didn't know.

"It sound a bit too technical for me," he laughed. "I'll have to take your word for it."

"It explains it in layman's terms in here," sniffed Charles, handing him the official programme of events, "— and it has one or two highly fanciful details about the place as well. No doubt they'll interest you more than facts about pumping equipment." They certainly did.

'Over the hill, to the north of the reserve, an interesting archeological feature can be found beside the footpath to the old turnpike road. It is a dry-stone wall which dates back to earlier times, possibly before the origins of Ormsley, and is known locally as the "Devil's Wall" or "Devil's Dyke". Its origins are steeped in folklore and legend and have been attributed to various colourful sources. One ascribes the building of the wall to the Norse God Odin, who is reputed to have built many bridges in the county, and dropped some of the boulders for this work on Gore Hill, when his apron strings broke. Another such tale involves an Ormsley tailor who made a pact with the Devil. The demon had to build the wall in the space of one winter's night to gain the tailor's soul. It would seem the Ormsley Demon succeeded, and the wall gained a sinister reputation over the years.'

"Far-fetched, don't you **think**," commented Charles Benson, observing the serious expression on Arthur's face. He, in turn, wasn't so

210

sure when he read on.

> *'There have been several instances of ghostly sightings in the vicinity of the Devil's Wall. The ghost of a Jesuit priest has been seen on the footpath. The unfortunate cleric was captured by priest hunters during his flight from Lythiall Old Hall, where he had been in hiding for several months, during that time of religious persecution in the seventeenth century. He was tried and executed at Lancaster. Another apparition is said to be that of Ormsley Jack, the highwayman who robbed travellers on the turnpike road. It was said that he used the hill as a vantage point to spot the approaching coaches and would hide in the trees in wait. He was caught and hanged on a gallows erected especially for that purpose on the hill above the wall, overlooking his hunting ground.'*

"Norse Gods and Devils, indeed," Charles Benson went on. "All superstitious nonsense from a geologist's point of view. While we're here let's have a look at the wall — and see if there's a rational explanation for it all."

"Good idea," agreed Arthur. "It's this way."

The pair set off in the direction of Devil's Dyke, wending their way around the hill and along the path above Sycamore house until they reached the track beside the wall some half an hour or so later. Charles Benson was immediately impressed by the unobstructed views across the plain below.

"This is an ideal place to build a fortification, you know," he declared. He contemplated the dry-stone wall for some moments. "It could be that the wall is a relic of some past occupation — an outer defensive curtain wall, perhaps?"

"It's not very high for something like that," observed Arthur, joining the speculation. "I could easily get over it!"

"That's right," agreed the geologist, "— and it's not a field boundary, either, as far as I can see. Can you show me where you found that specimen of yours?"

"Over there, in the middle section of the wall." The geologist followed Arthur along the track to the spot where the stone had been displaced by the farm tractor. He bent down and quietly studied the wall.

"Now this is interesting," he murmured, "— very unusual. Can you see it?"

"See what . . .?" replied Arthur, totally mystified. The wall looked exactly as he had last seen it.

"The position and shape of the stones, old chap. Stand back and concentrate on the whole surface of the wall." Arthur followed his instructions, stepping back and squinting at the wall. "Have you spotted it yet?"

"Not really," replied Arthur, shaking his head slowly. To his untutored eye they just looked like different shaped boulders to him.

"Well, let me mark the stones and see if that will help." Charles Benson picked up a piece of loose sandstone from the track and proceeded to scratch the surface of various stones in the wall's surface. To Arthur's astonishment, a pattern began to appear.

"It looks like a geometrical design," he declared in amazement.

"That's right," the geologist replied. "You can see where the builder has used the ends of the boulders to form the pattern — like a set of dots in a children's puzzle book — not immediately apparent to the untrained eye."

"It's certainly a puzzle to me. And what's more," Arthur suddenly realised, "— this stone in the centre of the design is the one that was dislodged." He gripped the stone and carefully prised it out of the wall. "This is where I found my specimen."

The geologist bent down and peered into the cavity, tracing his fingers round the entrance and sifting through the rubble and sand.

"There's nothing out of the ordinary, as far as I can see," he remarked, and Arthur replaced the stone. However, Charles Benson did notice something out of the ordinary when he straightened up. He pointed to the top of the wall.

"Now here's another unusual feature. Have you noticed how the capstone above the wall pattern is slightly lower and longer than the others — a sort of natural seat?"

"Yes — now you mention it," Arthur replied. "That's where I normally take a breather when I use this footpath. It's the best place to sit and take in the scenery as well."

"Yes, I see what you mean," declared the geologist, perching himself on this natural seat. "From this position you could easily see anyone coming or going." Arthur couldn't agree more. He had seen more than he'd bargained for. "I'll bet this is where the highwayman sat on the lookout for unwary travellers," Charles Benson continued humorously, "— and, if you believe those "old wives tales", perhaps the Devil himself sat here — waiting for lost souls."

He frivolous comment wasn't short of the mark.

* * *

Arthur greeted Charles Benson in the library, and they sat down in a corner of the reading room.

"Mrs. Jones gave me your message," he said, "It sounded rather serious."

"I wouldn't go so far as that," Charles Benson laughed. "Not yet, anyway. I've been meaning to get in touch with you since the Open Day and our visit to Devil's Dyke, but I've been away for a few days at my daughter's home in the Midlands. Now — about that unusual discovery of yours — have you brought the stone with you?" Arthur nodded, and the geologist's next comment added to the mystery. "Something has been puzzling me while I've been away — been thinking about it since our last meeting." He produced a magnifying glass and examined the stone again. "If I didn't know better, I could swear that the gold content was the product of this stone — as if a chemist had actually managed to create that precious metal from common or garden geological ingredients."

"You mean the person who made this stone discovered a way to manufacture gold?" Arthur was clearly amazed by the thought.

"Well, it does sound a bit far fetched, I know," Charles Benson nodded with a hint of a smile. "And then there's the stone pattern in the wall. I'm sure it's a pentagon design — used in magic circles . . ." He paused for a moment. "Do you know what I think you have stumbled on — what this stone is?"

Arthur shook his head. He had no idea.

"The Philosopher's Stone."

Judging by his blank expression, this disclosure obviously meant nothing to Arthur. He had no idea what a "Philosopher's Stone" was. "Is it worth anything?" he asked hopefully.

"Worth anything . . .?" the geologist laughed aloud. "I'll say it is." He stood up. "Hold on a moment while I check the reference section." Some moments later he returned with an old dilapidated volume. He ran his finger down the index and then quickly thumbed through the pages. "Just read this."

Arthur read the caption and the accompanying article.

The Philosopher's Stone.
Throughout the centuries alchemists have sought to discover the secret of the transmutation of base metals into that most precious commodity desired by Man — gold. The resulting matter of this chemical process was known as the Philosopher's Stone (although its existence is debatable) but to the alchemist it was a divine and perfect substance. In other words the Stone was both eternal and immortal. However, its possession, as in most things potent, had certain side effects which, on first appraisal, would seem highly beneficial to the holder of this myste-

214

rious and magical stone. The elderly were rejuvenated, the impotent became virile and those in despair regained their happiness. It had the power to cure all illness and restore perfect health. Unfortunately, the Stone was double-edged and these highly beneficial attributes had to be weighed against a side effect which one should avoid at all costs, since, by its very nature, it could classed as highly undesirable for one's general well-being and injurious to a balanced state of mind. The Stone resurrected the Dead. Therefore, the holder of this magical object, whilst having an infinite future, could never escape the chains of the past, and those poor souls in torment, once resurrected, were ever present, ever yearning.

"It makes you sit back and think, doesn't it?" Charles Benson reflected. "On the surface it's a totally unsupportable inference to make — and yet . . ."

From Arthur's point of view it wasn't. His recent experiences definitely supported this far-fetched and implausible idea. The thought of those tormented souls, the *ramblers* from the hill, as constant companions filled him with dread. Arthur related, as best he could, the events in question, and Charles Benson considered them in silence. He pushed the stone back across the table to Arthur.

"Well — it all sounds horrendous to me — and I particularly don't like your description of that "watcher" fellow. My guess is that you've pinched his "stone". If I were in your shoes," advised the geologist grimly, clearly shaken by his friend's account, "I would be inclined to get rid of it — as soon as possible. If you don't . . ."

He paused, giving Arthur a moment to let his advice sink in. "If you don't, Arthur — as time goes on there'll be more unwelcome guests, that's for sure."

* * *

Arthur Davenport, deeply troubled by his friend's alarming disclosure, and in a quandary as to the remedy for its speedy resolution, decided that he must get rid of the stone, the cause of his torment, as soon as possible. With this decision uppermost in his mind he returned to Sycamore House by way of the road which skirted the hill: he had no intention of using the footpath ever again. He looked with grave misgivings over the fields towards Devil's Dyke basking in the hot summer sun — and saw something which greatly disturbed him. In the far distance, he glimpsed four figures, hazy in outline and indistinct in dress, perched on the dry-stone wall — resting — watching. However, he was almost certain that they were now three adults and a child. Mrs. Jones confirmed it, when he arrived at Sycamore House.

"Don't forget to sign the four of them in, Arthur," she said to the astonished man. "The way you're going on — making all these new friends — we'll have to put a limit on your visitors." As an afterthought, she added "and you do seem to make friends with such troubled people. I must say the lady and her little girl looked ever so sad and lonely."

Arthur was speechless. He dashed up to his flat. There were no visitors. It was empty. He leant against the door, his ear to the wooden panel — and heard the first whisper.

"Arthur . . . Oh, Arthur . . ."

It was a woman's voice, soft and gentle, beyond the door. Another faint whisper, child-like and plaintive, reached his ear — and he remembered it from that time so long ago.

"Arfer . . . Arfer. . ."

It was the voice of a small child — of his long departed sister, Emily.

"Oh, Arthur . . . it has been such a long time . . . we have been waiting for you to join us, my dear . . . can we come in . . .?"

Arthur was unable to answer his mother. His nervous affliction had suddenly returned — and, as a trickle of brackish water and tendrils of dank pond weed seeped beneath the door and gathered in a pool around his feet, he slumped to the floor, staring silently into space.

* * *

Epilogue.

Charles Benson came across this ancient rhyme in "Annals of a Market Town, 1765", a dusty volume concerning a short history of Ormsley, which he purchased at a church bazaar.

> *'From Devil's Dyke there is a view*
> *Of times long gone, of terrors past*
> *Some say 'tis false, some say 'tis true*
> *'Till Doctor Mancel came at last*
>
> *Upon those ancient stones to make*
> *A place to sit and there to meet*
> *The Ormsley Demon. For our sake*
> *From God's elements, and fiery heat*
>
> *He conjured forth a stone so rare*
> *And so Owd Nick he did expel*
> *To that dark place ye all know where*
> *Be warn'd, seek not that view of Hell.*

This ancient rhyme, it seems, is the only reference to Doctor Mancel, an obscure alchemist and "watcher on the wall", and to the awesome properties of his "unique stone" (Charles Benson is now positive about its effects, judging by his friend's present condition). So far, the geologist's painstaking research into the matter has been fruitless, and the fate and resting place of the strange Doctor Mancel remains shrouded in mystery.

Arthur Davenport, on the other hand, remains permanently confined. The only cause for concern (if one can call it that, considering the lengths that medical science go to achieve it) is that he doesn't seem to grow a day older. In fact, one specialist is of the opinion that Arthur Davenport is actually growing younger.

The exact location of his *stone* is firmly locked away in his mind and is, to date, unknown.

INCE BLUNDELL

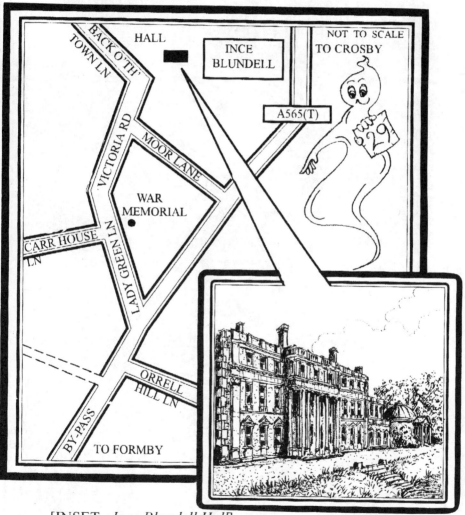

Plain Ghost Trail   29

HALL

INCE
BLUNDELL

NOT TO SCALE
TO CROSBY

BACK O'TH'
TOWN LN

VICTORIA RD

MOOR LANE

A565(T)

WAR
MEMORIAL

LADY GREEN LN

CARR HOUSE
LN

ORRELL
HILL LN

BY-PASS

TO FORMBY

[INSET   *Ince Blundell Hall*]

RITES AND CEREMONIES

I clearly recall my first meeting with the tall Australian sporting a wide-brimmed bush hat. His name was Bill Dunscomb and he was staying with a friend of mine, and one of the reasons for his visit to this country (touring aside) was rather unusual: he had come to trace his ancestors, or I should say one of his ancestors. That, in itself, is not unusual, because one often hears of the brash American returning to this part of the world to trace his Scottish or Irish ancestry (the subject, I may say, of book and film). But in Bill's case, however, the unusual aspect of the case was that one of his ancestors had been transported to Australia in the eighteen forties; and, it seems, his original home (or so Bill thought) was in Lancashire.

Here, in this flat coastal area, open to the gales that sweep off the Irish Sea and backed by the bare moorlands of the Pennine Chain, were the "roots of the family tree". So his inquiries focused on early Victorian times and embraced an interest in anything to do with that period : churches and chapels (and more especially their attendant graveyards) were of special interest, when it came to searching for his ancestor's family name. In the course of conversation, and with this in mind, he inquired about the older buildings in the area, and I was able to point him in the right direction. I accompanied him on several occasions, but we were unable to find anything which could throw any light on his quest: however, in the course of these visits a friendship developed, helped no doubt by the similar interests and attitudes to life in general. It was on one of these expeditions that I recalled an invitation I received some years ago, and it was prompted by the words OPEN DAY AND GARDEN PARTY on the notice board of a local church.

221

"That reminds me of an interesting Hall," I commented, pointing out the notice to Bill. "I'd forgotten about the place until now."

"Hall . . .?"

"Yes. Ince-Blandwall Hall — not far from here."

"I think that's sounds a bit up-market for my family," Bill sniffed. "I bet my double Great Grand Father was transported for stealing silver — not owning it!"

"I thought it was gold bullion," I returned, bursting out with laughter.

"What ever it was, he still got transported," he replied. "Anyway, we've had no luck with churches so far — so if you think it's worth a visit?"

"Oh, I forgot to mention that the Hall has a small church, or I should say, family chapel. So it's worth a visit on that score." Bill warmed to the idea. "Mind you," I continued, "you'll have to keep your hands off the altar plate."

His reply, as you probably have guessed, would be rather unsuitable for inclusion in this narrative.

* * *

Ince-Blandwall Hall was completed for the Blandwall family in 1750 and followed the classical design so popular with the landed gentry during the eighteenth century. Set in landscaped gardens, on an estate surrounded by a high wall, it was the quintessential country gentleman's residence. The main structure was built in red brick with a facade which included a columned portico in sandstone, quoins and parapet marked with balustrades and attendant decorations. An imposing monumental arch and intricate wrought iron gates, flanked by reclining carved lions, marked the principal entrance to the hall, and the long tree-lined avenue eventually divided at a miniature lake and fountain to form a circular drive ending at the front door.

A latin inscription on the front of a delightful Garden Temple in the grounds of the Hall reflected the sentiments of the time.

Hic ver assiduus atque alienis menibus awstas
Here is always spring and even in other months summer

This imposing Hall replaced the original building, which was deemed unfashionable for those times and had out-lived its usefulness. Over the years it had fallen into a state of disrepair, and was now used for storage and livestock: it lay some distance away from its younger neighbour, hidden from view by surrounding woodland. However, there were two features which made Ince-Blandwall Hall somewhat unique in its architectural pedigree. The first was a splendid family chapel which had been added to the rear of the Hall in 1858 (to replace the secret chapel situated on the first floor) and was unusual in that it adjoined the stabling and workers' quarters, and merged with the rest of the buildings to be almost imperceptible as a chapel to the casual observer.

The second was a more unusual feature (probably the only one in England) which, unlike the first example, immediately struck the casual observer by its incongruity. Some would say that it was totally out of keeping with the overall architectural style. It was a replica of the Parthenon, modelled from the original church in Rome. It had been added to the Hall by Alfred Wold, who inherited the estate from his cousin, to house his collection of rare sculptures (often referred to as "Roman marbles") acquired on his travels in the Mediterranean at the end of the eighteenth century.

And it was here, in (or I should say "on") this antique addition to the Hall, that Bill literally stumbled on the name he had travelled around the world to look for. A sharp gust of wind had whipped his bush hat from his head, rolling this fine example of antipodean head wear across the shale path into the long grass beside the Parthenon wall.

"Damn it!" Bill snorted, tearing after it, much to the merriment of the Hall gardener, who had just rounded the corner pushing his wheel barrow.

"Your mate can't half shift," he chuckled, taking this opportunity to mop his brow and take a breather.

"He certainly can," I laughed. "He's an Australian — and that's how he rounds up his stock."

"Well, I hope my boss doesn't meet him," he sniffed. "He'd hire him straight off as a beater for the toff's pheasant shoot to save money — and do all of us estate lads out of a nice little earner."

In the meantime Bill was rummaging in the grass for his hat. He suddenly let out a yell, and straightened up.

"Crikey, come over here, mate!" he exclaimed. "Just take a look at this!"

I hastened over to the excited man, who by this time was on his knees, pulling the foliage from the stone base of the wall, showering the path with blades of long grass.

"If my boss sees him doing that," the gardener called out, "he's likely to sell the lawn mower and do me out of a job as well."

By this time Bill had cleared a patch of ground and was pointing at the stonework.

"Down here," exclaimed Bill, rubbing the mellowed surface of the old stone. "There — can you see it?"

I got down beside him, and immediately saw the reason for his excitement. The words engraved in the stone were worn, but still legible.

A. DUNSCOMB

An perfectly incised hand, forefinger pointing to the name, completed the engraving on the stone facing.

"Can you believe it — a Dunscomb in this place?"

"Well, it is a bit of a turn up, I must say," I replied.

The gardener came over, his curiosity aroused, no doubt, at the sight of two grown men on their knees to all intents and purposes in the act of worshipping this classical addition to Ince-Blandwall Hall.

"Ah — I see you've found one of the mason's marks," he observed. "He left his hands over there — on one of the window sills."

'A loss of hands would be a great disadvantage to a stone mason's trade," I mused, rather puzzled by this intriguing comment. And then I saw "them", and chuckled to myself. Two finely sculpted hands, set at opposing ends of the sill, were beautifully carved into the sandstone, as if carrying the stone block. It would seem that *hands* were Dunscomb's trademark.

"Left his hands," exclaimed Bill, also puzzled by this strange remark. "I'll have you know that's probably one of my ancestors you're talking about." I nudged Bill and nodded towards the "hands" on the sill: he quickly saw the point.

"Well if he was," returned the gardener, "he was responsible for putting this oddment up." I gathered from this remark that the gardener wasn't too enraptured with this architectural masterpiece, and his next comment explained the criticism.

"My missus has got to clean it, and it takes some doin'."

The outcome of this conversation, the explanation for our visit and Bill's enthusiasm over his discovery resulted in an invitation to view the interior of the Hall.

"They're away at the moment, and my boss is out for the day," the friendly gardener said, "— so you can have a look round the place if you like."

We took up his offer like shot, and soon found that he was remarkably well informed about the Hall, which, considering his family had worked there for generations, was a definite bonus when it came to the history the Ince-Blandwalls. His stories about their quirks and eccentricities, an entertaining mixture of anecdote and historical detail, also revealed a family link with Tasmania, which I have abridged for sake of space.

It seems that Frederick Joseph, the third son, was sent off to New Zealand at the time of the expanding colonies. He became a sheep farmer, and then moved to South Victoria, Australia. Family connections and influence possibly helped in his rise to the position of Governor of this state, followed by the Governorship of Tasmania. Our guided tour of the house and chapel failed to reveal any further mention of A. Dunscomb. However, the gardener pointed the way forward.

"You'll probably find he went to work on their estate in the south of England," he suggested, as we prepared to leave, "— Cookham Manor, it was, in Sussex."

Then, once again, the bush hat exercised its influence on the proceedings: Bill, during the grand tour, had unfortunately misplaced it.

"I think I put it down on the table by the chapel door," he said. "I'll only be a minute." He turned and hurried back into the house.

* * *

Bill entered the lobby and paused to get his bearings. 'Was the chapel to the right or left?' At that moment he saw a figure some distance down the dimly lit passage to the right. As far as he could judge it was the figure of an old man in a long cloak, and in the way he moved, with one hand pressed against the passage wall for support and the slow stumbling motion of his gait, it was obvious the man was in severe pain.

"Excuse me, mate," Bill called out. "Is this the way to the chapel?"

There was no reply. The man continued on his painful way, and Bill felt reluctant to enquire further. 'But perhaps the old gentleman needed some help?' Bill followed this strange figure and, on reaching the end of this dark passage, he saw the man was already part way up a flight of narrow stairs, moving unsteadily, his hoarse breath and shaking limbs creating a spectacle of severe pain and exhaustion. Bill called out again.

"Need any help, mate?"

This time the shaking figure halted and slowly turned to face "his good samaritan". Bill gasped with shock. He was confronted with an inflamed face, distorted and swollen, a vivid reddish mass of burning flesh. Eyes glared from behind this horrid countenance, and a mouth, now barely visible because of the swelling of this awful infirmity, opened painfully.

"I need no help, my friend," croaked the shivering figure, "but I thank you, all the same. I am come, at last, to administer the Last Rites." And with that obscure remark the mysterious figure turned and went on his painful way up into the dark recesses of the Hall.

Bill stood for a moment, dumbfounded.

'It must be the whacky owner of the place,' he thought. 'And, by the look of him, he's going to need the last rites himself any time now.'

Then a sound, a sort of muffled gasp of astonishment followed by a rising crescendo of panic-stricken cries, echoed from high within the house: the noisy commotion ended abruptly with a scuffle. Bill stared up into the gloom, and the next instant the old man came bowling down the stairs, rolling and bouncing until he hit the floor with a tremendous thump, sprawling at Bill's feet.

But it wasn't the same man.

The upturned face that stared up at him was very old, but it was also devoid of that disfiguring illness. However, it was transfixed with a horrible frozen expression of absolute terror, as equally disfiguring as that of the "wacky" owner. A clerical collar and cassock indicated the unfortunate man's profession — and his crumpled attitude indicated he was dead.

* * *

"Thanks for the tour of the Hall — I'm sure it has made Bill's day," I said, thanking the gardener for his kindness and hospitality. Some moments later we were both startled by a muffled yell, followed by an ashen-faced Bill dashing out of the Hall.

"Come quick," he gasped. "There's been an accident — I think

227

he's dead!"

"Accident . . .? Someone's dead?" The gardener looked mystified. "You must be mistaken. There's no one in the Hall — they're all away."

"But I tell you there's someone in there — at the bottom of the stairs!"

We hurried into the house, Bill leading the way: he turned down a narrow passage.

"He's going the wrong way," the gardener muttered. "This doesn't lead to the chapel." Bill turned the corner and stopped in his tracks: he was obviously baffled.

"I don't understand," he cried, staring at the empty floor at the bottom of a narrow flight of stairs. "He was definitely here — and I'm sure he was dead."

"Well he ain't here now," the gardener sniffed. "You've imagined it." Bill's expression suggested otherwise.

"There's the other fellow upstairs — he must have seen the body."

"Believe me, mate," the gardener replied. "There's no one here."

"But I saw them," Bill answered vehemently. "I definitely saw them both!"

"What did they look like?" I asked.

"The dead one was a clergyman, and the other one looked as if he would be joining him shortly," Bill replied. "I thought he was the owner of the place."

"Well I can assure you he wasn't — the owner's a lady and she's away 'till next week," the gardener asserted. "And the other one definitely wasn't my boss. The only church he goes to is the Red Lion in the village."

The troublesome bush hat was retrieved from the chapel, and we left Ince-Blandwall Hall, Bill, for his part, severely shaken (even for an Aussie) by his experience, and myself intensely curious about the whole affair.

* * *

Cookham Manor, Sussex, can be found in the Doomsday Book, and its beginnings mirrors that of similar estates throughout our English countryside. To judge from early pictorial views of this ancient manor it has managed to survive the ups and downs of political parties and divisive governments, adapting to the many social changes during the intervening centuries with hardly any alteration to structure or situation. Thanks to the National Trust Association, it would remain so for the foreseeable future. And we arrived to "lift the curtain" and peer into its "historical recesses" in our search for his ancestor, A. Dunscomb. I say "we", because Bill had asked me to accompany him on this second stage of his journey.

"I don't fancy another experience like that,' he confided to me, "and if you could spare the time I'd be glad of your company, mate." By now I had to admit my curiosity was aroused to such an extent that I was hooked on finding an answer to Bill's quest and the explanation for his mysterious encounter, and so I had no hesitation in accepting his invitation. And as it turned out it was my suggestion which had an invaluable influence on our search: we took out membership of the National Trust, and in so doing opened the door to the next discovery. Our arrival coincided with a guided tour of the property by the Cookham Vale Antiquarian Society, and the secretary of this band of "historical diggers" was only too delighted (when I told her that we had a real live Australian "digger" in our midst) to extend a warm invitation to us.

"By all means, please join us," exclaimed the studious lady. "I'm sure you'll find the tour most interesting." And so it was. Links with Ince-Blandwall Hall were apparent in many features of the manor, and the tour guide certainly knew his stuff. Unfortunately the interior of the house revealed no link with A. Dunscomb, much to Bill's disappointment.

"Well, Mr. Dunscomb," asked the secretary, at the end of the tour, "— did you enjoy your visit?" Bill was about to reply when the guide, who had overheard this question, intervened.

"Did you say Dunscomb?" The guide was evidently excited.

"Yes, that's right," I replied, and proceeded to introduce my friend and give a brief account of his stay in England. The reason for his visit, however, had a marked effect on the interested guide.

"Well, I'll be blowed," he replied, and beckoned us to follow him. "Come with me — there's something I'd like you to see." We followed the man out of the front entrance, skirting the gravel drive, to the stables and workers quarters at the rear of the manor. He stopped by the corner of the gatehouse and pointed to a cornerstone set low in the wall.

"Take a look at this."

We bent down — and Bill let out a gasp. The name A. Dunscomb and '42 were clearly visible in the sandstone surface. Once again the mason's mark contained an additional item, inserted between the name and the date: the superb carving of a hand with the forefinger pointed towards the name.

"That's a stroke of luck," I cried, turning to Bill.

"It is," he gasped in astonishment, turning to the guide. "Do you know anything about him?" The guide nodded.

"Yes, as a matter of fact I do," he replied. "His story is rather unusual, to say the least. He was a skilled mason, and was employed by Sir Alfred Wold, an eccentric member of the Wold family on the construction of a replica of the Parthenon at his Ince-Blandwall estate in Lancashire. The mason was highly thought of by Sir Alfred, who also employed him on the restoration of Cookham Manor, his other estate, at the turn of the nineteenth century: you can see his mark here."

We contemplated the familiar "signature" of Bill's ancestor.

"He certainly had a talent with a masonry chisel," I commented, admiring the carved hand. "He must have been sought after as a mason."

"He was — but not as stone mason."

"Oh, really," said Bill. "Was he gifted in other ways?"

"Well — the Bow Street Runners thought so," the guide chuckled.

"Bow Street Runners . . ?" Bill was puzzled.

"The police, mate," I said. "The police were after him."

The guide laughed.

"That's right, I'm afraid," he replied. "Unfortunately his talents extended to stealing, or to be more exact, breaking in with intent to steal."

"He was a burglar?"

"Not exactly. He was charged with entering Cookham Parish Church with intent to steal, and his sentence was transportation."

"Transported — for that. I don't believe it!" Bill was utterly shocked at this stark disclosure. He had expected to learn that his ancestor had been transported to Australia for a really serious offence; but not for something so trivial.

For my part the sentence seemed totally ridiculous.

"Transported for entering a church," I snorted. "I can't believe that."

"I have to agree," nodded the guide. "The church was unlocked and nothing was taken. But unfortunately it seems that certain evidence was laid against him by a friend of the Wolds, and he was shipped off to Tasmania, or Van Dieman's Land as it was then known, to serve his sentence."

Bill was stunned and mortified. "Trust British justice to go over the top," he muttered.

"Well, you could always check the church records," the guide advised. "Miss. Horrocks, the Antiquarian Society secretary, could help you with that."

He called to the studious lady, and, after a brief discussion, the matter was settled. And so later that afternoon, with the permission of the vicar and some industrious help from the antiquarian secretary, a despondent Bill was presented with evidence which confounded his worst fears about the dismal sentence.

Andrew Dunscomb
Second son of Joseph Dunscomb (native of Little Ince,
Lancashire) and Mary Appleby (of this parish)
Willow Cottage - Lower Comb
Occupation - stone mason

A faded cutting was attached to this entry.

Whereas
at this present Quarter Session of the Peace Andrew Dunscomb late of Cookham in the County of Sussex is and stands (upon the evidence of Charles Croxley) convicted of entering the Church of St. John, Cookham with intent to commit a felony, insomuch as to steal such valuable plate to the detriment of the above Parish
It is thereupon Ordered and adjudged by this court, that the above named Convict be Transported beyond the Seas to such a place as Her Majesty by the advice of Her Privy Council shall think fit to direct and appoint, for the term of ten years.
By the Court
Deputy Clerks of the Peace.
Destination - Port Arthur - Van Diemen's Land
For the attention of Commandant Symonds

The evening was drawing to a close when the secretary and I left the silent church. Bill remained to contemplate the day's events and the desolate circumstances of the stone mason's life: it was indeed a sad end to his visit to the mother country. And as he sat there, in melancholy state, pondering the awful predicament of his forebear, he gradually became aware of a figure standing in the shadows beside the vestry door. He recognised the bearing and distorted features of the old man at once. He *last saw him on the stairs of Ince-Blandwall*

Hall.

The figure moved painfully into the dark vestry, and Bill immediately followed, just in time to see the outer door, which led out into the graveyard, closing. Opening this door he stepped onto the gravel path, scanning the gravestones, and spotted the old man some distance away, moving through the ancient graves. Bill again followed and saw the figure pause beside an imposing crypt, enclosed within rusted ornate iron railings, and slowly fade away in the evening ground mist. The name of the incumbent family was carved on the lintel above the entrance, partly covered by moss. Bill stepped over this rusty guardian into the long grass and moved up to this edifice. Scraping away the moss covering he revealed the family name.

Sacred to the memory of the Cowper family of Cookham and Bath
Per limen mortis transgressus, in pace iaceo
Depono quod onus tollere iussus eram
Iam tollendum aliis terrestri pondere dignis
Ne fidem fallas, haec mea vota manent

However, he also revealed something else, tucked away beneath the stone lintel. A name, now familiar to him, and a perfectly carved hand with forefinger pointing, lay before his eyes.

 A. DUNSCOMB '44

Bill Dunscomb gazed with some disquiet at this mason's mark. Why, at this solemn moment, did he think of the Last Rites? With this thought uppermost in his mind he hurried from the tomb and reached the lÿch gate with a sense of relief. It was short-lived, for, in the gathering darkness he saw a figure slowly rise up and painfully make its way through the mist-shrouded graves — in his direction. Bill decided not to wait.

* * *

Bill returned to Tasmania, and I must say I was sorry to see him go. However, he asked me to keep in touch with him, and I promised (after he had told me of his experience in the grave yard of Cookham Church) to send him any information that I could find on the Cowper family. And, as it turned out when I paid a visit to Cookham Vale some months later, I did come across an unusual story, related to me by the secretary of the Antiquarians.

"Yes, I have done a little research on it," she remarked, when I asked her about the Cowper family vault. "There is a rather intriguing legend about the Cowpers which might interest you." She rummaged through sheaves of paper.

"Ah, here it is," she continued, handing me a sheet of handwritten notes. "I came across it years ago amongst some old church papers." I perused the neat copperplate handwriting.

'Sir Jeaves Cowper, a devout catholic and staunch sup-
porter of the Royalist cause was entrusted with a secret
mission during the Civil War. The Parliamentary army,
as a matter of course, were reducing the castles and strong
points of opposing forces, wherever they were victorious,
but certain puritan iconoclasts went a step further and
vandalised churches. Sir Jeaves received information that
the church at Battle Abbey, founded by William 1 (the
Conqueror) after the Battle of Hastings (the altar stands
on the spot where King Harold fell), was selected for such
treatment, and was given the task of saving the renowned
stained glass window of that church. The fourteenth century window, depicting the story of John the Baptist, had
acquired during the reign of the Plantagenet Kings the
reputation of a talisman which, while it rested there, prevented an invasion of our southern shores, and should it
ever be removed would lay the nation defenceless against

invasion. This window was carefully removed and secretly hidden away (along with certain valuable items of church plate) and the Cowper family became the custodians and fervent guardians of this precious piece of English heritage. It was buried, so the legend says, in the vault of this family and remained there for two hundred years, the obligation of stewardship and guardianship passing to each successive member of the family. The Latin inscription on the tomb roughly translates as

*Beyond death's portal I lie at peace
My earthly burden I now release
To others worthy of this task
Break not the oath, 'tis all I ask.*

However, when the tomb was opened in the nineteenth century (around 1850) there was no trace of this window. Like the tomb of the Pharaohs there were signs that the tomb had been expertly opened and the window (if it was ever there in the first place) removed. Clarence Cowper, the steward at that time, came under suspicion by the family, and left the country in disgrace, never to return. The whereabouts of the window is unknown.'

The secretary handed me another sheet of notes. The handwriting in this case was more of a scrawl, and rather difficult to read.

"The reference to Clarence Cowper interested me," she said, "so I made a few notes at the time."

*'Clarence Cowper - only son of Thomas Cowper, Esq., of Bath.
Went to Cambridge and trained in medicine to become a physician and surgeon.*

235

Distantly related to the Wolds of Cookham Manor and Ince-Blandwall Hall, Lancashire. Acquainted with Charles Croxley* (met at Cambridge) who helped Alfred Wold on his Parthenon at Ince-Blandwall Hall, and persuaded him (Clarence) to remodel the family vault at Cookham.
Employed a local stone mason (gifted carver) on this work (subsequently transported for suspected burglary on evidence of Croxley) in 1844.
*Charles Croxley

A general description - cold and austere. An avid historian and fanatical antiquarian - advised Alfred Wold on the presentation of his Roman antiquities collected for Ince-Blandwall Hall - had a passion for legend (possibly found out about the buried treasure of Battle Abbey from Clarence Cowper).

Career
Brilliant academic stay at Cambridge and recruited into the clergy for service in Tasmania - rose quickly to position of Diocese Commissary for Tasmania under the presiding Bishop of the time. Eventually returned to England because of severe mental problems and an extreme nervous disorder associated with delusions of persecution (he often saw visions). He stayed with Sir Alfred Wold (a Cambridge acquaintance) to recuperate, but his mind gave way and he died suddenly in mysterious circumstances at Ince-Blandwall Hall, Lancashire.'

I communicated my findings to Bill without delay, and some weeks later his reply arrived with an invitation to visit his country. He had often invited me in the past, but time and commitments had prevented me taking up his offer. However, a short sentence in this letter changed all that.

"I've found that window."

* * *

I stood on a dusty track in the hot sun, the light breeze raising flurries of red dust which eddied around my feet before swirling off across the parched ground. Blackland Church lay before me, surrounded by trees and enclosed within a stone wall, a setting perfectly familiar in an English countryside. In this case, however, this perfect setting was in the southern hemisphere, or to be exact, the municipality of Glamorgan and Spring Bay in Tasmania, and within this isolated colonial place of worship the missing window of Battle Abbey looked out over wild bush and mountain landscape. In a country where a primitive, childlike aboriginal people had wandered for thousands of years, only to be swept away by white invaders in less than fifty years, gums and eucalyptus replaced oak and cedar, and parched grassland replaced lush meadow and hedgerow.

Bill waved from the porch door, and I entered the cool atmosphere of the building, glad to escape the heat of the blazing sun. I looked down the length of the nave to the altar and up at the mediaeval window. It blazed with colour, casting a variety of hues over wall and pew.

"I heard about this place from a mate of mine," he said. "I told him about my visit to England and that I was interested in churches, and when he mentioned he'd seen an old stained glass window in the outback, I thought I'd follow it up." Bill handed me a booklet from a stall beside the door.

"It tells you all about the window in here," he said. "It's a shame that Cookham Sheila couldn't be here to see it."

"You've absolutely right," I laughed, but his reference to the studious secretary of the Antiquarian Society only served to highlight the incongruity of the situation. An English fourteenth century stained glass window, secretly buried for over two hundred years, now stood marooned at the other end of the earth in a virtual replica of Cookham Vale church: it was a real turn-up for the book. I turned to the passage describing this mediaeval masterpiece.

The Window of St. John the Baptist.

The east window, from the Church of Mary the Virgin at Battle, near Hastings, consists of two main parts, the central panel and upper panel. These depict our Lord and His connection with John the Baptist which include the Baptism and eventual end, the prize demanded by Salome. Soon after the church was consecrated, certain quarries (individual panes of glass) were wilfully damaged and the breakage remained unrepaired for some time: this was duly reported in the press. The situation was remedied by a local tradesman (whose name is not on record) who replaced the missing quarries with 19th century glass. However, the actual figures are, undoubtedly, genuine 14th century work. Mystery surrounds this window and the circumstances of its acquisition are somewhat obscure. The first Rector of Blackland, the Reverend Charles Croxley, a secretive man, brought this window from England, and maintained a strict silence with regard to it, as well as other valuable religious gifts which he donated to this church.

"Well . . ." Bill asked. "What do you think?"

"Cowper's window, without a doubt," I answered. "That crafty blighter, Croxley, got it out of England — no wonder he wouldn't talk about it."

"Especially if Andrew Dunscomb helped him steal it from the Cowper vault and ended up in chains in Port Arthur for his trouble." It was a sobering thought. I turned the page and was confronted by a paragraph which added a further dimension to the chilling saga.

> *Blackland Church was originally built, at the request of the Rev. Croxley, for the Convict Probation Station and District Civilian Administrative Centre of Bushy Plains. Some 200 convicts and a regiment of Foot were stationed here, and convict labour, which included skilled stone masons, built the church, an exact replica of one in Sussex, England. All Rites and Ceremonies conducted in this area are recorded in the Register.*

"Can you believe it," I gasped in astonishment. "Convicts built this place." Bill stared at me in astonishment.

"Are you thinking what I'm thinking?"

"Yes," I nodded, and we began to search for that familiar mason's mark. We split up. I took the inside and Bill went off to search the outside of the church. It wasn't long before I heard an excited yell, and dashed out to find Bill by the east window.

"Look!" His finger traced that name and hand, so familiar to us, hidden beneath the stone sill.

A. DUNSCOMB

"So he helped to install the very window that condemned him to a life of misery," I cried.

"And all for that b.... Croxley, as well," cursed Bill. "I bet Dunscomb broke the window when the church was finished."

We left the church, well satisfied with our visit. As we were driving past the gate I noticed another visitor in the doorway. He wore a long black cloak, which was extremely unusual considering the extreme heat, and he looked decidedly infirm.

"I don't remember anyone else in the church," I observed. "Did you see that old chap, Bill?"

Bill glanced in his driving mirror, turned pale and screeched to a halt. I nearly went through the windscreen.

However, the strange cloaked figure had mysteriously vanished.

* * *

Swansea lies on the sandy shores of Great Oyster Bay, sheltered by the rocky cliffs and bleak granite mountains of the Freycinet Peninsula. Originally known as Great Swanport, the town became the administrative centre for the county of Glamorgan, Australia's oldest rural municipality, founded in 1860. This area on the East Coast of Van Dieman's Land (later changed to Tasmania in an effort to expunge the dreadful image created by the inhuman brutality in the penal institutions and the barbaric extinction of the native aborigine population) was selected for development, and the first settlers sailed from Hobart Town to take up their land grants in 1821. They were assigned convict labour (a virtual form of slavery) to build their houses and clear the land, and a small regiment of soldiers was stationed in a barracks, sited on a promontory at the edge of the town named Waterloo Point after the famous battle, to guard the convicts and the settlement. And here, in this quiet seaside town, lived a descendant of Andrew Dunscomb.

While I had been busy in England chasing up the Cowper family, Bill had delved into his family's past, tracing and contacting relations, following up any leads however slim. His persistent enquiries paid off, and led us to an old colonial residence on the edge of the town. This quaint stone dwelling belonged to an aunt, and she, as it turned out, was a direct descendant of Bill's ancestor. This house also revealed a secret, concealed for over a century. In the attic we found an old battered trunk, filled with an assortment of family memorabilia. In amongst these items was a leather-bound bible, with the faded blue details *No: 28 (Port Arthur) Property of Her Majesty's Commissioners* stamped on its fly leaf. Marginal pencilled notes, scattered throughout this volume, left us in no doubt that it was the convict bible of Andrew Dunscomb. A brief examination was enough to confirm our suspicions of his dealings with the Rev. Charles Croxley and his arrest and transportation to Van Dieman's Land.

The cool evening was so refreshing after the heat of the day that we decided to take a stroll into the town: this took us along the deserted esplanade which ran beside the sandy beach. The view across the bay, to the mountains and islands lit by the dying sun, was at its best at this time of day, and the gentle swish of the surf on the white sand accompanied our steps as we headed for Waterloo Point. But someone else was ahead of us, out for a stroll, taking the evening air. However, the distant figure moved slowly and painfully and, from my companion's startled gasp, I knew Bill had already made his acquaintance — on other occasions. We hurried forward in the fading light and saw the figure turn inland, up a narrow lane and through a gate in a weathered stone wall. We followed and found ourselves in an isolated pioneer graveyard where the early settlers were interred (this seems to be the fashion in Tasmania whereby the church is separated from its graves. In this case it was situated behind the town).

"Look, he's standing over there," Bill whispered, pointing to a section of headstones in the long grass, partly hidden by trees: here the figure had paused to rest.

"Yes, I see him," I returned quietly. The figure turned, and I saw his face for the first time. "My God — you were right about the Last Rites — he's about done for." The figure swayed for a moment, and then collapsed to the ground, and by the time we reached this spot he had vanished. We searched around the graves and in the long grass, but found no trace of the apparition.

"Damn it all — he's followed me all the way from England," Bill moaned, leaning back against a headstone. "I can't seem to get rid of him. If it goes on like this I'll be getting the Last Rites." I was about to reply, when, to my utter astonishment, I saw the hand — *the Dunscomb hand.*

"Well, you're in the right place for the ceremony," I gasped in astonishment.

"What do you mean," he replied, observing my startled expression, "— the right place?"

"Just look at the headstone you're leaning on!" He stepped back, and gazed at the stone.

Sacred
to the memory
Clarence Cowper
Physician - only son of Thomas Cowper, Esq.
Cookham and Bath, England.
Died Aug. 12, 18—
Aged 43 years.

Above this inscription was carved a hand we both knew so well — but in this case it was pointing across to a crucifix, as if to say "I accuse . . !"

We stood in silence, sadly gazing down upon the overgrown grave of a disgraced English gentleman, now resting far from his native land. We left the pioneer graveyard as darkness fell over Waterloo Point.

* * *

Returning to the house we found Bill's aunt rummaging through the memorabilia in the trunk.

"Fancy that," we heard her say. "I've not seen this since I was a little girl." She undid a pouch, and tipped the contents onto the table. "I used to play with them when I was a child." *Them* lay on the table, sparkling in the lamp light — and we immediately knew what they were. Several pieces of coloured glass lay before us — stained glass quarries, broken from the ancient window in Blackland Church all those years ago.

The next day we examined the jumbled scrawls in the margins of Andrew Dunscomb's bible in more detail, and I set before you the relevant notes in a proper sequence of events.

'Croxley was on good terms with my employer Mr. Wold and he sought me out to do a job for a gentleman friend of his from Cambridge. Cowper was his name and he came from a very old family and he was in some way related to the Wold family I do not know how.

Croxley advised him to replace some of the sandstone facings on his family vault and hired me to do the work.

One night Cowper came full of drink and Crafty Croxley as I was wont to call him found out some secret thing that was hidden in the tomb for hundreds of years.

He told me it was treasure and fool that I was did believe him. We broke in and opened the tomb but never found treasure only pieces of old coloured glass and old plate.

Old Crafty was fair excited and gathered the glass and plate up and off and away but I was sore ashamed and stayed to finish the sealing.

But I was caught in the churchyard and given up by Croxley and sent for transportation and ten years of Hell to Port Arthur.

But the commandant had wont of skilled men and I was took to Blackland to build a church there.

And God punished me yet again for I saw Crafty Croxley there and the coloured glass that was a church window which I broke in secret to spite him.

I made ticket of leave and then pardon and wandered abroad 'till I came to Great Swanport. T'was many years there I saw Cowper sore ill - he had come to take me but relented when he saw my words of shame in my probation bible.

I carved his stone and writing from his family tomb in Cookham and placed "the blame the pointing finger speaks" and he went on to search him out to give him the Last Rites.

I wait in fear that he will come for me again God save my soul.'

I travelled to Hobart and called in at the Tasmanian Archives Office (in the spirit of the Cookham Antiquarian Society) to research the dilapidated grave in the Swansea pioneer cemetery: my visit was fruitful and I came away with a photocopy of a cutting from the 'Tasmanian Mail' and the death certificate of Clarence Cowper.

Obituaries
C. Cowper, late surgeon to our colonial forces in New Zealand
Tasmanian Mail 18th August, 18—

Register of Deaths in the district of Glamorgan 18—
No: 51 on 12 Aug. 18— Clarence Cowper - Male 43 years - Physician and Surgeon
Cause of death - erysipelas (synon. St. Anthony's Fire)

It remains a mystery why Clarence Cowper came from New Zealand to die of St. Anthony's Fire, a painful and extremely disfiguring disease, in Swansea of all places. Perhaps he had come to spend a holiday in Tasmania, and was taking the east coast scenic route through Blackland, staying at the coaching inn. One could imagine his consternation and horror when, on visiting the distant church, he saw his family legacy, the fourteenth century window of St. John the Baptist, and discovered (as we had done) the mark of the convict mason who had worked on his family vault in Cookham. Then he found the name of the man, his erstwhile friend and trickster, who had donated the window. It wouldn't take long to realise what had happened; the deception and theft from the vault under the guise of renovation.

Clarence Cowper became ill, and wanted revenge. He could have traced Andrew Dunscomb through the his Ticket of Leave, and arrived in Swansea to administer the Last Rites to one of the men responsible for his disgrace and exile. Perhaps Andrew Dunscomb's years of suffering in Port Arthur, and his contrition in the bible gave him grace, and he was spared. In any event the convict mason carved the dead physician's headstone, and indicated with a carved hand the true culprit in the affair. A century later Bill saw the outcome of the ceremony on the stairs of Ince-Blandwall Hall.

* * *

We had a ceremony of our own to perform. The stained glass quarries were divided equally, and shared between Bill and myself. Bill's share was placed in a plain wooden casket, and secretly buried in the overgrown grave of the unfortunate physician, and I, when I returned home to England, secretly placed my quarries in Cookham churchyard and Ince-Blandwall Hall respectively.

I'm afraid I cannot divulge their exact resting places for fear of a visit similar to that of a nervous cleric in the last century. I am not quite ready for St. Anthony's Fire and the Last Rites yet.

FORMBY

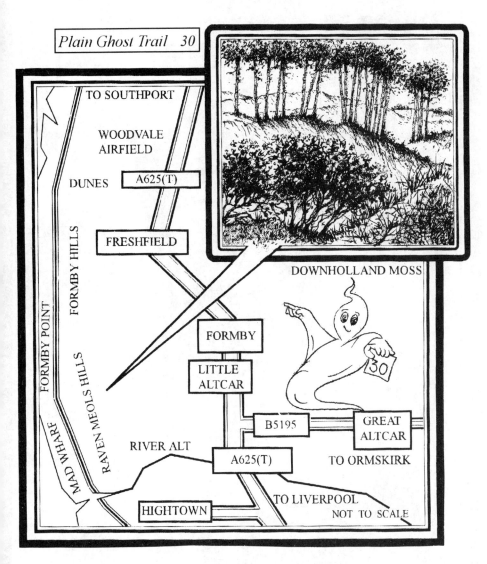

Plain Ghost Trail 30

TO SOUTHPORT

WOODVALE
AIRFIELD

DUNES   A625(T)

FORMBY HILLS

FRESHFIELD

FORMBY POINT

RAVEN MEOLS HILLS

MAD WHARF

DOWNHOLLAND MOSS

FORMBY

LITTLE
ALTCAR

B5195

GREAT
ALTCAR

RIVER ALT

A625(T)

TO ORMSKIRK

TO LIVERPOOL

NOT TO SCALE

HIGHTOWN

30

[INSET   *The Raven Meols Hills, Formby*]

PATH
CLOSED

A FAMILY VISIT

The south of England bore the brunt of the tempest, suffering massive destruction in the process. This onslaught came from the tail end of "Hurricane Gloria", the ferocious storm of 19 . . which had ravaged the eastern seaboard of the United States in late September of that year. As the storm turned and continued its progress, sweeping across the grey mass of the North Atlantic Ocean, weather forecasters predicted a gradual decline in its strength and severity, declaring a general gale warning for the Bay of Biscay and the Channel. They got it wrong. Contrary to informed opinion, "Hurricane Gloria", when it reached our southern shores in early October, seemed, for some reason, to redouble it's strength and fury, and, to the mortification of the Insurance Companies and the desperation of the Emergency Services, it proceeded to cut a swathe of damage and disruption throughout the counties bordering the English Channel. Huge tides battered the coast and breached sea defences, torrential rain burst river banks and caused widespread flooding, all this adding to the misery of the inhabitants of that region.

However, the rest of the country was not to be spared the attentions of this fierce reminder of the power of Nature's wrath. To the consternation of the forecasters and authorities alike, the hurricane suddenly veered, as if guided by an unseen hand, and began to travel in a northerly direction, swiftly heading inland. Property and vegetation suffered accordingly as the hurricane raced northwards. Displaced slates and tiles, toppled chimney stacks, dislodged bricks and shattered glass littered the towns and villages of Southern England in the wake of the demonic wind, while uprooted trees, broken fences and flattened crops bore testament to "Hurricane Gloria's" inexorable progress over the countryside.

It is true to say that during past centuries such storms of this magnitude rarely visited our shores: however, historical records reveal that when they did strike they altered the shape of our coasts in the process. There was no heavenly or earthly protection against the fury of their terrible onslaught, and coastal towns and villages either disappeared beneath the sea or were marooned miles inland. It would seem that it was now the turn of the twentieth century to receive such a visit from mother nature — under the totally inappropriate name of "Gloria".

* * *

Mary Rymmer contemplated the rough notice fastened to the stile. It was clear enough to her, but not to her dog, Barney.

FORNBEY NATURE RESERVE
FISHERMAN'S PATH CLOSED
SECTIONS UNDER REPAIR DUE TO EROSION

"Sorry, Barney," she said with a shrug, "— no walk today, I'm afraid." Barney gazed up at her and wagged his tail. He couldn't read, and was unwilling to forego his early morning jaunt, erosion or otherwise. In a flash he squeezed under the step, and shot off down the sandy path. His mistress called him back: Barney paused momentarily and looked back.

"Here, boy — come . . .!" Mary yelled. He responded with a sharp bark and a wag of his tail, and then continued on his way into the trees. His furious mistress climbed over the style and set off along the path in hot pursuit, hoping the nature reserve warden wasn't nearby to reprimand her. She soon came across the reason for the closure. A bank of windblown sand blocked the path, and further on a debris of broken branches, splintery boughs and drifts of leaves from a fallen pine tree displaced by subsidence totally blocked the path. It hadn't deterred Barney though, and a distant barking in the dense forest confirmed it.

"Barney . . . here boy, here!" The barking continued, and dog failed to appear. Mary grew impatient and came to a decision. "Just wait until I get my hands on you," she muttered in annoyance. Clambering over the mound of loose sand she skirted the tangled branches and pine roots and made her way into the undergrowth. From the direction of the sound she quickly realised that her dog had strayed well away from the path, and was deep into the pine forest. His strident yapping disturbed the early morning tranquillity, swamping the light breeze which rustled and whispered through the tall pines, and overpowering the sound of a gentle sea which surged and broke on the distant shore. Mary struggled and fought her way through the tangled mass of vegetation, trying to pinpoint the barking with great difficulty. Gradually the sound grew louder, and Mary eventually burst from the thicket into an open area of sand dunes topped with marram grass: the barking came from somewhere within this solitary expanse.

However, she now didn't have to rely on sound alone, for, to her relief, she saw a line of canine footprints stretching ahead of her in the sand. She set off, following the trail though the dunes, and, as the barking grew louder, she saw flurries of sand flying into the air: they came from the other side of a large dune. She climbed the sand hill, and peered through the rough grass. At some recent period, probably during the winter storms, part of the dune had collapsed, no doubt undermined by the constant burrowing of the rabbit population and subsequent erosion by the elements, leaving a sheer face of sand below. From a cavity in its surface the tip of Barney's tail wagged furiously, accompanied by excited barks and showers of sand. He had obviously found something.

"What is it?" cried Mary, scrambling down and pulling her excited dog away. "What have you found, you little rascal . . . rabbits, no doubt?" It was immediately apparent that the tattered remnants of cloth clamped firmly between the dogs teeth, which he shook furiously from side to side, had nothing to do with rabbits, or any other species of the nature reserve's wild life for that matter. For a brief moment Mary had the terrible suspicion that her inquisitive and wayward dog had uncovered the remains of a body. Her suspicions were somewhat allayed when she saw a sand-encrusted shape, uncovered by her canine digging machine, protruding from the bottom of the hole. It wasn't a body, but a block of stone.

"What's this you've found?" cried Mary, brushing away the sand. "It certainly isn't a rabbit burrow." She uncovered another block next to it, embedded in the sand. This stone differed from its companion, in that it had several shapes engraved on its surface. These markings had the general appearance of letters, and gave the impression of a religious significance, but Mary wasn't clear what they were.

"I wonder what they mean," she mused, "and what are these stones doing here? May be they are foundations of some old building — although I can't understand what it is doing out here in this isolated part of the coast." She came to the conclusion, religious signs aside, that it was probably the remains of a fisherman's cottage, long buried in the sand from earlier times. Barney responded with a wag of his tail and a sharp bark. He picked up the tattered cloth remnant and shook it.

"Now, you rascal, let's see what else you've found."

She finished the work begun by her dog, tracing the strands of cloth back into the sand and some minutes later her patience was rewarded. She came across a small cavity set in the stone foundation, and within this secret space she found a bundle concealed there. She reached in and withdrew this mysterious discovery, which had probably lain hidden beneath the sand for goodness knows how long. The rotten cloth fell away to reveal a casket, metal edged and discoloured. The hasp and hinges had long since corroded into a solid mass, sealing the box for the time being. The mistress and her dog gazed silently at the strange object lying on the white sand.

'It could be buried treasure, I suppose,' Mary thought, visualising jewels and gold coins.

Barney, possibly thinking of dog biscuits, approached and cautiously sniffed this old casket — and immediately gave his opinion on the subject. He bared his teeth and gave a low growl, backing away from his mysterious find, his tail between his legs. Something about it greatly disturbed him — made him uneasy.

"What's the matter, boy?" Mary asked, stroking her dog. "Don't you like it?" Barney growled again and pulled away, as if to say "*put it back — leave it were it was*". Perhaps her original suspicions were correct after all, and this strange discovery was, in some way, linked with something gruesome and macabre.

In the event she should have taken more notice of her dog.

* * *

The metal-bound casket, cleansed of its mantle of encrusted grime, lay on the kitchen table. It was in remarkably good condition, considering the time it had been in the ground, its state of preservation aided, no doubt, by the dry sandy nature of the area. Here again, on the metal edging, she discovered faint incisions in the corroded surface, signs similar to those on the foundation stones beneath the sand dunes. The wooden shell had fared better than its metal counterparts, which were so badly corroded in places, aided, no doubt, by the salt content of the sand, that the ancient metal flaked off at the touch of Mary's duster. David, her live-in partner (for want of a better description), was charged with the task of reversing the ravages of salt and sand, taking great care with the hinges and hasp, which had seized into a solid mass. With patient scraping and light oiling he was able to loosen the hinge pins sufficiently to break nature's corrosive seal. The casket could now be opened.

"This is it, David," Mary breathed in a fever of anticipation. "We're going to be rich — have lots of lovely money."

253

"I'm keeping my fingers crossed too, love," her partner replied. "I can pack the job in, if you're right about this." (It has to be said at this point that David's high powered executive "job", although well paid, had an irksome disadvantage: he often had to spend weeks away from the pleasures of home and the hallowed greens of the local golf club). "Go on, then — let's see what in it."

The grating hinges noisily opposed this unwarranted intrusion, as Mary slowly prised the lid open, releasing an unpleasant odour into the kitchen.

"Phew . . . it's nearly as bad as your aftershave," she snorted, wrinkling her nose in disgust at the pungent, musty smell.

The couple gazed at the contents of the casket and Mary uttered a disappointed gasp. The sight which caused her disillusionment could hardly be described as "buried treasure". Instead of the anticipated "gold and jewels" Mary saw a rough bowl-shaped object. Its rim was uneven and jagged, and the cracks and indentations on it's yellowed surface indicated extreme age and some very rough usage during it's lifetime.

"Well, one thing's for sure," declared Mary thoughtfully, "— it certainly wasn't designed for soup or corn flakes."

Her disappointed partner picked it up and examined it closely.

"I don't know what it was designed for either — or even the sort of pottery it is. I'd like to see where you found it. There must be a reason why someone buried it out there in the first place — very strange indeed — a real mystery." He looked down at the dog. "On the other hand, it might come in handy as a bowl for your dog biscuits, Barney," he sniffed. This idea was totally rejected by Mary's faithful canine companion. Barney uttered a low growl of disapproval and slunk away to his dog basket in the corner of the kitchen.

"I'm afraid this isn't going to do much for our bank balance, after all," observed Mary disconsolately.

"Not to say my golf handicap," replied her partner, placing the odd-shaped bowl back in the casket and closing the lid.

However, the current state of Mary's bank balance was not in question. The balance of her mind, in the days to come, was to be an entirely different matter.

* * *

Mary was sure — they were definitely out there, lurking in the pine woods — waiting. *But for what*?

It had begun a week or so earlier, shortly after the discovery of the casket, while David was on a business trip to his parent company in Germany — and it was the behaviour of Barney which first alerted her to the fact that something was wrong. The dog, usually so enthusiastic about his customary exercise in the nature reserve, was now reluctant to leave the house. It seemed that Barney had developed a extreme aversion to that part of his daily routine. To put it simply, the dog was afraid of the pine woods and sand dunes.

The house, Shore-side Cottage, nestled at the edge of these sand dunes and pine forest which stretched for miles along this part of the coast, separating Fornbey from the sea. The isolated house (the nearest other dwelling was some two miles distant) stood at the end of a rough track on what was once the old coast line, before windblown sand settled on the underlying marshes, creating the sand dunes along this stretch of coast. It has been said that they were of comparatively recent origin, since no dunes existed there before 1600, and it was also said that they arose from sand blowing from a huge sandbank that had closed the mouth of the River Fornbey, changing its course. Before then (according to old maps of the area), the river had flowed out into sea by Shore-side Cottage. This isolated spot had not affected Mary unduly — until now. She rarely saw anyone, except for the occasional walker and tradesman, and only during the day. And then, one evening, as day gave way to night, she caught her first glimpse of the *visitors*.

Peering through the kitchen window in the fading light she saw two children, a boy and girl, emerge from the dark wood. Their sudden appearance took Mary by surprise, for in all the years that she had lived there, she had never seen visitors in that part of the wood before. In the dim light Mary guessed that the boy was about ten years of age and the girl slightly younger, possibly around six or seven. She was further surprised by the state of the children's clothes. Rags would be nearer the mark, for they were in tatters, and hung from their youthful frames, barely covering the children's pale, emaciated bodies. She was also shocked to see that the children were barefoot. They stood motionless for some moments at the edge of the wood, staring at the house — *as if waiting.*

'What were they doing here? Were they lost? Did they need help?'

These questions ran through Mary's head as she recovered her composure: she opened the kitchen door and went to call to them. There was no one there. The children had vanished, and Mary was left to ponder her mysterious visitors as the dying rays of the sun were extinguished by approaching night, and a light sea mist spilled gently out of the pine wood and rolled across the garden to her feet.

* * *

Mary inquired about her youthful visitors in the village.

"Two young children — a family living near you — in the wood?" The postman pondered for a moment. "No . . . I don't think so. The nearest house is 'Pine View', and I know for sure that they haven't any children staying there."

Enquiries at the Police Station proved fruitless as well. "Definitely no children reported missing, Miss. Rymmer," the constable declared. "It's the end of the holiday season, and most of the holiday homes are empty. I haven't heard of any newcomers in that part of Fornbey either. The school might be able to help, I suppose. In the meantime, I'll have a look around the place. Let me know if you see any suspicious characters hanging about — don't hesitate to ring in."

The policeman gave her the station number, and Mary thanked him for his offer. She left the police station, reassured by the knowledge that, in the absence of David, she now had the weight and majesty of the Law for support. Unfortunately, Mary was to find that this support, considering the nature of the problem, would prove to be virtually useless, when, on the following night, she had cause to take up the policeman's offer.

* * *

Mary, alarmed by the loud snarls and growls from the kitchen, sprang to her feet, spilling her tea on sitting room carpet in the process. She ran into the kitchen and saw the dog, tense and trembling in his baskets, glaring at the back door.

"What is it, Barney!" cried his startled mistress, bending down to calm him. "Is there some one out there . . .?" The dog looked up at her and whined. "Is it those children again . . . have they come back?" Hackles raised, he bared his teeth in reply.

"It's all right, boy," said Mary in a soothing tone of voice. "I'm sure they're harmless — they're only little children, you know." She went over to the window and drew the curtain. What she beheld was neither childish nor harmless.

In the half-light she saw that her previous youthful visitors had returned and were again standing motionless at the edge of the wood, staring at the house. However, on this occasion they were accompanied by two adults, probably their parents — and their appearance sent a shiver down Mary's spine. The sight of the mother, emaciated and pale as death, was enough to cause a shudder of dismay. This frightening creature was dressed in a long black gown, once fine and opulent, but now tattered and in ribbons which fluttered and flapped in the night wind. Torn remnants of what was once a shawl barely covered her shoulders. Wisps of hair straggled from beneath an old fashioned bonnet, partially covering her face, which was fixed with an expression of terror. Her companion was even more horrible to behold. A high collar, red braided tunic and buckled sword belt disclosed the fact that he was a military man from another age and the uniform was in an equally advanced state of dilapidation. Its frayed condition gave the distinct impression that this soldier had just come through a battle — and had lost. A huge gash rent his forehead and blood ran down the side of his powder-blackened face. Furthermore, his battle-scarred appearance was compounded by singular gruesome detail — the absence of his left forearm, shot or cut away in the heat of battle. All that remained of this limb was a bloody stump which dangled limply by his side.

The other arm, however, was healthy enough, for the mortally wounded man raised and shook it aggressively at the house, fist clenched in a gesture of rage and menace. The tormented mother gathered the children to her — and the spectral family slowly began to move from the pine trees, advancing across the lawn in a most hostile fashion. It was clear to Mary that this visit was not of a friendly nature, and she shrank from the window in dread. Barney, sensing the impending confrontation, let out a mournful howl and ran from the kitchen in panic, squeezing under a convenient armchair in the sitting room for safety.

It was time to call for support. Moments later Shore-side Cottage resounded to the onslaught of the unwelcome visitors as they battered and pounded the kitchen door. Mary rang the police station before leaping into her car to escape from the embattled house.

She met the constable at the end of the track, and, after a brief hysterical plea, he returned with her to the cottage to investigate. They found Shore-side Cottage silent, the garden empty, and no sign or evidence of the enraged family. The constable was puzzled by the it all, and Mary didn't know what to say — or how to explain it. In any case, she reasoned, the "long arm of the Law" would have absolutely no power or influence on her recent visitors. All indications showed that they could not be reached, for the simple reason that they were under some other jurisdiction — *from beyond the grave.*

* * *

"We haven't had any trouble up to now," David remarked, when Mary told him about her visitors. "As far as I'm concerned this funny business only began after you found your so called "buried treasure". Mary had to agree. They had lived in Shore-side Cottage for over three years, and it had been peaceful and completely uneventful.

"Perhaps you're right — it could have been the casket, I suppose."

"I'd like to see where you found it," David continued. "Can you remember where the place was?"

"I think so," Mary replied. "It was in the middle of the pine woods in the nature reserve."

"Well, there's no time like the present," he declared, reaching for his coat. "Let's go." Barney refused to move from his basket, and they set off without him.

Some twenty minutes later they arrived at the stile at the entrance to Fornbey Nature reserve. The closure notice had gone — and so had the sand barrier and fallen tree. The path to the sea shore had been cleared, and this immediately caused a problem: Mary had great difficulty in remembering the place where she had made the detour into the forest.

"I'm sure it was somewhere around here," she muttered, casting around for a familiar landmark. "Yes, there it is — through there . . . where the tree fell." The evidence was plain to the eye. A jagged gap in the undergrowth showed the exact spot where the tree trunk had crashed to the ground.

They set off through the tangled vegetation, here and there coming across broken branches and trampled earth, clear signs of Mary's original journey. Following this trail with great difficulty they eventually burst out of the oppressive undergrowth and arrived, more by luck than design, at the open area of sand dunes.

"Here it is," declared Mary with relief. "I found Barney digging in the sand — somewhere in the middle of that lot." She set off into the dunes, her partner close at her heels. It didn't take long for her to realise that, as in the case of the fisherman's path, the dunes had changed. Much to her annoyance and frustration, she couldn't find the exact spot.

"The side of one of these dunes had collapsed, and Barney dug down and found something buried in the sand," Mary explained. David looked at her with a puzzled air.

"Well, if you say so," he replied. "The hole must be here." They searched the area, and came up with a blank. The hole in the sand dune couldn't be found.

"You know what the trouble is?" David observed. "These sand hills look the same — you can't tell one from another. All it needs is a sharp breeze and the sand gets blown about all over the place. Unfortunately your spot has been well covered up by now."

"I'll bet Barney could find it again," declared Mary, as the disappointed pair turned to retrace their steps. "We should have brought him along."

"Good idea," said David with a nod. Unfortunately, a meeting at his company's German headquarters the next day precluded another search for the time being. "We'll try again when I get back. In the meantime, see if you can find out a bit more about Fornbey's past. Perhaps you can dig up something else besides an old box."

"Right — I will," Mary decided eagerly.

What she subsequently unearthed required a considerable amount of digging — literally.

* * *

Mary discovered her first clue at the Altker and District Flower Show, an annual event held in the church hall in Little Crumsby. During a conversation with the chief steward she brought up the subject of local history. Her tentative inquiry about origin of the area was met with an enthusiastic response.

"Ancient history," the steward said warmly, "— you're within a stone's throw of ancient history. Come along and I'll show you." She followed him out of the hall, along a shaded path to the village church, and then through the graveyard and long grass to a rough perimeter wall.

"There's your ancient history," declared the perspiring man, pointing to the base of the wall. "You can't get more ancient than that." Mary gazed at the wall. It was approximately four feet high, constructed with irregular sandstone blocks, and partially covered with moss and creeping ivy. She could see that it was old, but she wouldn't go so far as to describe it as ancient. She looked at the steward with a perplexed expression.

"I . . . I'm afraid I don't understand," she began. "I know this wall looks old, but . . ."

"Not the wall, my dear," laughed the steward. "That stone down there — with the markings on it." Mary bent down — and came upon her first clue. This stone, which was slightly larger than its counterparts, had rude cross incised on its surface: it was accompanied by faint markings — and Mary instantly recognised some of them. She had last seen them on the surface of the stone in the sand and on the metal edging of the casket in Shore-side Cottage.

"This stone goes back to the time before Christianity reached these shores," the steward explained to the surprised 'historian'. "They say it is an old pagan stone from a burial ground near here, and those are supposed to be Druid signs on its surface. Others say it could be an primitive Viking grave marker or early Christian church foundation stone, when the cross was later added to those ancient symbols."

"What do they mean?"

"Nobody knows for sure. Some long forgotten language, I presume," answered the steward. "If you're really interested in this sort of stuff, you should come along to the talk in the church hall tomorrow night."

"Talk . . ?"

"Yes — by Mr. Granston. He's in the Antiquarian Society and is supposed to be the expert on this area. He's giving a talk on the history of Ansdall, Fornbey and Altker — so I'm sure he'll be able to tell you more about this stone."

After she heard Mr. Granston's lecture the following evening, Mary was delighted to find the steward's assumption was spot on. The knowledgeable expert from the Antiquarian Society was able to tell Mary more about the ancient stone — and other related matters. These related matters, on the other hand, transformed Mary's initial delight — into one of panic.

* * *

Mr. Granston's talk about the origins of the area, and the historical aspects of its development was very informative and wide ranging, (and it was also very long). So, for purpose of brevity, I set out below the parts of the lecture which had a bearing on Mary Rymmer's search.

> *"Ptolemy's map (the earliest known map of this area) has caused some speculation over the ages. It shows one estuary serving an interior which was predominately made up of huge lakes and small islands, and a densely afforested coastline which has long disappeared beneath the sea. Traces of this forest can still be seen today near the mouth of the River Fornbey. There is some evidence to show that ancient Britons had a settlement near this river, and an example of their sign language can be found on an ancient stone in the wall of the church. Although the meaning is now lost, it is probable that the signs refer to their pagan religion, Druidism. Invading Celtic tribes dis-*

placed this culture, followed by the Romans, Saxons and Vikings. We think the Vikings, on their conversion to Christianity, used this stone in their burial ground, carving a cross on its surface, intermixing Pagan and Christian religious influences. A primitive chapel, dedicated to Saint Wulfstrad, is known to have existed near the old river estuary at Fornbey, and relics of their settlement and burial ground were found near the shore, after a storm in 1886 eroded the coastal dunes. Both Nature and Man have played a significant part in the shape and development of the area. Violent storms, sea-quakes and tidal waves caused by geological changes in the sea bed, have periodically altered the coastline, destroying three towns and threatening the reclamation of the land behind the coastal barrier in the process. Windblown sand also played its part, obliterating small settlements, such as the port of Hargarmells. This settlement once stood at the mouth of the River Fornbey, before the river changed its course, and lies somewhere under the present nature reserve. Every now and then we stumble across long buried secrets, uncovered by the elements, which illuminate the hidden past on which our present culture is based."

Mary, on hearing this reference to buried secrets, realised she had stumbled on something of that nature, and possibly the site of the early Viking chapel mentioned earlier in the lecture. At the end of the evening she approached the expert antiquarian.

"I did enjoy your talk, Mr. Granston," she began, "— especially the part about the lost settlement and the chapel."

"I'm glad you found it interesting," he replied.

"You mentioned that the chapel was dedicated to a Saint . . .?" Mary paused. She couldn't recall the name.

"Saint Wulfstrad — one of the first Viking bishops," he answered.

"He was an interesting character, by what little we know of him. He was a fierce, warlike 'run of the mill' Norseman, a pagan chief of the first order, until his conversion to Christianity. As often happens with these 'larger than life' characters, their folklore tells of his powers to control the elements, and so protect homes and harvests from the ravages of the weather. When he died his remains were venerated and used as talismans for protection against the wind and rain."

"If they believed that . . . well, they sound a right superstitious bunch to me," declared Mary. "We can't even control our weather today."

"Superstition or not," chuckled Mr. Granston, "the legend goes on to say they kept a relic of his body in their chapel at Hargarmells, and an ancient pagan stone, which I told you about in the lecture, marked his temporary resting place in the burial ground."

"Yes, I've seen it — and the funny marks?"

"They're from the "old language", my dear," he said. "The stone was probably from a Druid altar, and the signs — a prayer to Nature or pact with their Gods, no doubt — are still a mystery."

"And the relic . . .?"

"Ah . . . Wulfstrad's head," replied Mr. Granston thoughtfully, "– – part of his skull, so I believe."

Mary paled at this disclosure. The sight of the jagged bowl-shaped object, lying in the casket in a cupboard in her kitchen, flashed through her mind. 'It surely couldn't be the skull of an early Viking bishop,' she thought with growing apprehension.

"You look startled, Mrs. . . .?"

"Miss. . . . Miss. Rymmer."

"Rymmer," Mr. Granston blinked, "— with a 'y' . . .?"

"Yes — that's right." For some reason her name clearly fascinated him.

"Rymmer . . ." He repeated. "Now that is interesting."

"Oh, really . . .?"

"Yes, it is, my dear," he continued. "Your name has long been associated with this district, and can be traced back to those early times. In fact your ancestors were probably those original Norsemen who settled in this area so long ago."

"Oh, yes . . . I have been told about it on several occasions," answered Mary, somewhat perplexed. It didn't seem all that interesting, since many other local names could be traced back to the same period.

"It's not just the name, Miss. Rymmer — but your family custodianship." He noticed her puzzled expression.

'Family custodianship . . .?' thought Mary. "What the devil is he going on about?'

"We were discussing the legend of Saint Wulfstrad," he continued, "— and it so happens that a Rymmer held the position of custodian of his relic. His job, like the high priests of ancient times, was to guard it, and this task was passed from one generation to another, down through the centuries. On several occasions, however, things went disastrously wrong. The legend goes on to say that, when the relic was removed, some form of catastrophe struck the area. As I mentioned earlier, in my talk, towns were destroyed, flood gates were breached and the land ruined by sea water, or windblown sand changed the coastline — and the legend says this happened whenever this holy relic was disturbed."

"I don't believe that," scoffed Mary. "You can't blame a Rymmer for that sort of thing."

"Quite right," Mr. Granston agreed with a wry smile. "All superstitious nonsense, of course — but it helps to add spice to dusty historical fact. For instance, I sometimes tell the story of Old Nick Rymmer, who used the holy relic for necromancy, and the port of Hargarmells was obliterated by sand as a consequence. Then there's the unfortunate Rymmer family which, some say, haunts Fornbey shore. One of these Rymmers, so the tale goes, was pressed into the army against his will, and when he lost his life in battle, his destitute wife, with two small children to support, supposedly went mad. She uncovered the Saint's relic — and used it as a sugar bowl. A terrible storm arose and the coastal flood gates were breached, causing widespread damage and loss of life."

Mary gaped, wide-eyed, in astonishment.

"I know what you're thinking, my dear," he continued. "Pure speculation and old wives tales. I've heard of some novel ways of weather forecasting — but a ghostly family haunting the sea shore — well, I ask you . . .?"

He didn't need to ask — Mary got the picture. Only, in her case, it certainly wasn't pure speculation. She'd recently had a *family visit* — and the ghostly family in question was very angry indeed, as any custodian would be in the present circumstances.

"As a matter of interest," she spoke hesitantly, "— what if you discovered this relic — what would you do?"

"There's no danger of that, Miss. Rymmer," laughed Mr. Granston with a shake of his head. "I'm sure it doesn't exist."

"But if it did — and you found it?"

"I think I'd be inclined to leave it where it was. We antiquarians try to approach the subject scientifically, you know . . ." He paused for a moment, pondering the question. "But in my experience," he went on seriously, "there are just some things which we can't explain scientifically — and that could be one of them."

By this time Mary had the scientific answer to her problem — it required a dog, a shovel and some vigorous digging.

* * *

Mary didn't sleep that night. The Rymmer family had returned. Under a calm and cloudless sky they stood motionless at the edge of the wood, bathed in the light of a full moon.

They were not alone. They were accompanied by other ghostly companions, who remained in the shadows — *watching and waiting*.

On this occasion, however, Mary deemed it unnecessary to call for support from the local constabulary. She knew why they had come, but the visitors would have to be patient for the time being. Judging by their wild appearance and outlandish attire, Mary came to the conclusion that many of them were very distant relations, possibly the contemporaries of Saint Wulfstrad himself.

The dawn sky heralded the departure of night and the ghostly figures faded from the scene. Now Mary could get on with the task of righting her unfortunate blunder. Being a Rymmer, and a direct descendant of that spectral family from beyond the grave, she was no longer afraid or apprehensive. The adage "blood is thicker than water" passed through her mind, as she prepared for her return to the sand dunes. Barney, too, seemed more at ease, as if he was aware of the situation, and need not feel so afraid.

As a matter of interest, and with those previous weather catastrophes in mind, Mary checked the forecast before she set for the nature reserve later that day. It was settled for the north of England, but with gales and a severe weather imminent for the Bay of Biscay and the Channel. She estimated she had plenty of time to complete her task. Unfortunately, she hadn't reckoned on the difficult and time consuming business of finding the remains of Saint Wulfstrad's chapel beneath the ever shifting dunes — and the caprice of "Hurricane Gloria".

* * *

Darkness was falling and Mary, her hands blistered and muscles aching with pain, was worn out and in despair. Things just hadn't gone according to plan. For a start, Barney's nose failed to live up to expectations and he had been unable to pinpoint the exact spot of his earlier discovery. In fact he took no interest in the proceedings whatsoever, and just mooched dejectedly around the dunes, which were, by now, riddled with numerous holes and mounds of sand. So far the search for the ancient chapel had been fruitless. The sound of rustling leaves and swaying branches in the distant pine trees changed all that. It announced the first whispers of "Hurricane Gloria's" visit to Fornbey.

The marram grass atop the dunes began to bend and wave as the approaching breeze increased in strength, and eddies of fine sand rippled and hissed in and out of the dunes, adding to the growing crescendo. This noise was suddenly augmented by another — that of Barney — barking excitedly. Mary quickly found him: he was shaking and pulling at something buried in the side of the dune — a piece of tattered cloth, a remnant of his previous visit. The dog had at last found the holy place.

Mary began to dig furiously, and from that point on the wind began to grow in intensity, whipping up stinging clouds of sand which choked and blinded her. She was buffeted and pummelled by the raging element, as she strove to keep her balance in the ever shifting sand, and such was the violence of the attacks that, time and again, she was sent sprawling down the side of the dune. "Gloria" howled and shrieked around her, determined, it seemed, to prevent the return of the holy relic to its rightful place. In the fast-fading light Mary persevered in her crucial task with a grim determination, willed on by the presence of vague, insubstantial shapes which swirled and hovered around her in the clouds of sand. Her *family*, mindful of the catastrophic penalty if she failed, had arrived to lend their spiritual support. Then, just as the exhausted digger was on the verge of collapse, her shovel struck a hard object, the sound ringing, bell-like, through the dunes. It was a stone.

Battling on against the demonic force of the malevolent wind she gathered her strength and continued to excavate the pit — and within seconds she uncovered the other stones. The fierce wind roared in frustration — Barney whined in terror — and Mary cried out with relief as she placed the holy casket in its original resting place in the foundations of the ancient chapel, and swiftly covered it with sand.

From that very moment the power of the wind began to abate. Denied a ruinous catastrophe, foiled by the relic of a Viking Saint, "Hurricane Gloria" dwindled to a blustery, spiteful squall, which moaned and groaned around the dunes of that desolate place. The spectral shapes departed with sighs of contentment, and Mary, her momentous task completed, and with her faithful companion by her side, trudged wearily home.

Later that night she had another visit, not from her new found family — but from the village constable. He was accompanied by a female colleague.

"Can we come in, Miss. Rymmer?" the policeman began. There was a hint of sadness in his voice. "I'm afraid we have some rather bad news . . ."

* * *

Mary bumped into Mr. Granston as she was leaving the doctor's surgery.

"I was very sorry to hear about your . . ." he began, and then paused, at a loss for the right word.

"David . . . my partner," Mary replied sadly. "Yes, it was a shock. He was travelling home in that dreadful storm, you know — when he had the accident — a tree in the road . . ."

"Yes, I read about it in the local paper, my dear. You could say that "Hurricane Gloria" was one of those weather catastrophes that crop up every now and then. It did an awful lot of damage and many people lost their lives," observed Mr. Granston thoughtfully. "Considering the amount of destruction it caused around the country we escaped relatively unscathed in this part of the world. I've heard people around here say it was a minor miracle, and I recalled our little conversation — you remember — the lecture in Little Crumsby." Mary nodded. She remembered it all too well.

"I couldn't help but wonder," he continued, "— if Saint Wulfstrad's relic really does exist somewhere out there in the sand — under the watchful eye of a Rymmer, of course." He turned to go. "By the way," he added, "— did I mention that the custodian of the relic was always of the male line of the family? "

Mary shook her head.

"Well, it would mean, if the legend of the relic is true," chuckled the antiquarian, "that you can't apply for that worthy position, my dear."

Mary smiled.

In her case it was no longer a problem. She carried a legacy of her relationship with David — and the doctor had just informed her that it was to be a boy.

APPENDIX

A note as to the inspirational sources from which the stories in '*Tales, Weird And Whimsical*' and '*Encounters With Plain Ghosts*' (the first two books in the series) are derived.

An obscure name on a map, an intriguing half-hidden sign on a lonely country lane, or perhaps an unusual building glimpsed through a gap in a hedgerow — these everyday aspects are the inspiration for series. An ancient bell hanging speechless without its clapper, a ghostly typist driving a vintage Austin 'Seven', or a vague grey shape standing in the shadows of a disused chapel, these are the prime ingredients served up for the whimsical imagination. Add some chimes at midnight, a figure at a darkened window, or the moss-covered name on an ancient tombstone, and you have the recipe for a macabre feast — but be prepared for a severe bout of earthly indigestion.

ABOUT THE AUTHOR

T.M.Lally was educated at Hutton Grammar School, near Preston, and, on leaving school, worked in the Borough Treasurer's Department in Southport. He spent his National Service with the 9th Lancers in Germany and then went on to study at Didsbury Training College. He has taught in Tarleton, Formby, and Southport, the area in which the haunting stories are set. His interests include camping and caravanning, musical composition, painting and drawing, and he plays several musical instruments, possessing a wide musical experience ranging from jazz to orchestral and brass band work.